AN (UN) ROMANTIC COMEDY

PHOEBE MACLEOD

Boldwood

First published in Great Britain in 2023 by Boldwood Books Ltd.

Copyright © Phoebe MacLeod, 2023

Cover Design by Head Design Ltd

Cover Photography: Shutterstock

A CIP catalogue record for this book is available from the British Library.

Paperback ISBN 978-1-80426-282-5

Large Print ISBN 978-1-80426-283-2

Hardback ISBN 978-1-80426-281-8

Ebook ISBN 978-1-80426-284-9

Kindle ISBN 978-1-80426-285-6

Audio CD ISBN 978-1-80426-276-4

MP3 CD ISBN 978-1-80426-277-1

Digital audio download ISBN 978-1-80426-280-1

Boldwood Books Ltd
23 Bowerdean Street
London SW6 3TN
www.boldwoodbooks.com

To my mother, Margaret, with whom I've always been able to talk about anything.

1

'OK, Chris. I think it's safe to say that Tina isn't a fan of your gift. Talk us through it.'

I can't say I blame Tina. The vibrator sitting on the table between Chris and his wife is most politely described as 'challenging'. 'Enormous' would be another suitable word, along with 'what the bloody hell?', which I accept is a phrase rather than a word.

In my time as a sex and relationship therapist, plenty of vibrators have come and gone through my treatment room. I'm generally fairly positive about them; when I think they will be beneficial I recommend them, but they can be controversial and, when I think they might make things worse, I steer well clear. However, the object that Chris has brought in to therapy today is quite unlike any of the vibrators that I have ever recommended. During the brief demonstration that he gave, it wriggled, buzzed and thrusted in a most alarming manner. It also lit up with a selection of flashing lights, which completely confused me. What on earth would they be illuminating? If none of that, or the sheer size of the damned thing, were enough to put you off, the noise would. It's difficult to describe, but if you think of angry hornet meets asthmatic road drill, you wouldn't be far away. As a modern-day object of torture, I could see it faring pretty well; I have no doubt that you could disembowel someone pretty successfully with it. As a sex toy? Dear God, no.

'I thought it would spice things up, do you know what I mean, Poppy? And,' he looks at me lasciviously, 'I thought it might be something she'd like to use while I watched.'

Tina looks revolted and I can't say I blame her. This is their fourth session and, frustratingly, I don't seem to have managed to get through to Chris at all so far. Their presenting issue is not particularly uncommon – a mismatch in libido that's causing friction in their marriage – but so far Chris has resolutely refused to acknowledge that the problem is anything to do with him. In his mind, Tina just needs to stop being so uptight and everything will be hunky-dory. What he has failed to see is that the constant pressure he's putting her under to do more exotic stuff in the bedroom is making things very difficult for her.

I know where it's come from; I wouldn't be much good at my job if I didn't. Chris is patently a heavy porn user, even though he swore blind he wasn't when I gently challenged him about it in our first session. But, when we talked about his fantasies, it was like a one, two, three checklist from the porn industry. I glance at the clock: fifteen minutes left in today's session and then I'm not seeing them for two weeks, so it would be really good if we could get a breakthrough today.

'Why do you think Tina isn't wild about the vibrator, Chris?'

'I dunno. It's the top-of-the-range, and it literally does everything! It cost a pretty penny, let me tell you.'

I seriously doubt that. The control panel looks like it was assembled by someone doing a home electronics project and the rest of it isn't much better.

'OK, let's go back a step. Do you remember when we talked about the four Ps and the four Cs?'

'Erm, yeah.'

'Talk me through them.'

'So, you said that a lot of men think about sex as the Ps. Position, performance and penis size.'

'Great. Do you remember the fourth one we talked about, which specifically relates to pornography?'

'Umm, power.'

'That's right, there's a power imbalance portrayed in porn, which would be unhealthy in a real-world relationship. Now, what about real-world sex – what did we talk about there?'

'The Cs.'

'Can you remember what they are?'

'Sorry, not exactly. I remember consent, but I'm not sure about the others.'

'That's one of them, yes. You've also got communication, connection and compromise. So, if we look at your present to Tina here, do you think it falls more into the Ps or the Cs?'

I think we may be starting, finally, to make a bit of progress, as he blushes slightly and averts his eyes.

'I don't know.'

'Let's walk it through. Have you and Tina ever talked together about using a vibrator?'

'Umm, we did a bit.'

'What does that mean?'

'I'll tell you what it means,' Tina interrupts. 'It means he mentioned it to me once and I told him there was no way and I thought it was incredibly tacky.'

'Chris?' I prompt him.

'Well, yeah. She did say that, but I thought she'd change her mind once she saw it.'

'I see, and what prompted you to go for this one, rather than something smaller and more discreet, such as a bullet?'

'Bigger is better, isn't it? I don't see how those little ones could be satisfying; you'd barely feel them.'

'I'm not going to let us get drawn into a discussion about different types of vibrators and their uses, as I don't think that's going to help us here. Let's go back to the Ps and Cs. We've established that Tina made it clear that she wasn't interested in vibrators on the whole, but you felt that you could change her mind with this. Is that a fair reflection of your thinking?'

'Yes, I thought if she just tried it once...'

'Even though she made it clear she didn't want to? How do you think that made her feel? Was that an example of good communication, of you making a connection together and compromising, or were you trying to use your power to coerce her into doing something that she'd already said she wasn't comfortable with?'

'No, I wasn't trying to coerce her. I was just trying to open her mind up to new possibilities, that's all.'

'I just don't get what's wrong with what we have now. Why does it need to be spiced up?' Tina chips in.

'Would you like to elaborate?' I ask her.

'I know he says it's boring, but I like the missionary position. I've tried some of the things that he's asked for, but they're either uncomfortable or downright degrading. There was a position he wanted to try the other week that reminded me of going for a smear test. How is that supposed to make me feel sexy?'

'How does it make you feel? Tell Chris.'

She turns to him. 'It makes me not want to have sex with you at all, Chris, because I worry you're going to start asking for weird stuff, so I push you away by telling you I'm not in the mood, or whatever.'

'And you find this frustrating, I expect,' I say to Chris.

'Of course I do. Sex is important to me. When she says no, it makes me feel like she doesn't want me, that she doesn't love me.'

'Rejection is never easy to deal with, I agree, particularly in a marriage. Do you understand what she's saying, though?'

'I want to, it's just that there's so much out there that we haven't tried, and I wonder if we're missing out? The only way to find out is to try it, and I've never asked her to repeat anything she hasn't liked.'

'So you're worried that everyone else is having a better time than you, because they're all doing things you aren't? Let me put your mind at rest there. Very few people, a tiny minority, in fact, get a thrill from extreme sex acts. Many of the positions that you'll see if you look online aren't used because they're satisfying for the participants. In fact, most of them are deeply unsatisfying, but they provide a good view of what's going on for the camera. You say you find the missionary position boring, but do you know how many animal species mate face to face?'

'No.'

'Pretty much just us and bonobos, which are apes similar to chimpanzees. The same for recreational sex. For most animals, mating is purely an act of procreation. What a privilege to be able to do it just for fun, and to look into each other's eyes while we're doing it! That's why the missionary position is so popular, because it provides not only a physical connection, but an emotional one as well. I'm not saying you shouldn't try other things, but only if you're both comfortable with them. This is where communication and compromise come in. If you can learn to talk openly about this stuff, and explain to Tina why you want to try something, it'll be easier for her to understand and you may find she's more willing. Does that make sense?'

'I don't like dirty talk. It makes me feel cheap,' Tina objects.

'I'm not suggesting dirty talk, Tina,' I explain. That's something that works for some people, but by no means all. I'm talking about open and honest communication. Right, homework time. I'm going to impose a sex ban until I see you next, in two weeks' time.'

Chris looks absolutely crestfallen and Tina looks delighted.

'I want you to talk instead. So, what you're going to do is this. You're going to tell each other what you like about sex. Each sentence must begin with either "I like it when you...", "I would like it if you..." or, "I think this could be improved if we..." Do you think you can do that?'

Tina's not looking quite so pleased now, but Chris has perked up a bit.

'The important thing here is that you both do it; it won't work if one of you pushes out a long shopping list and the other says nothing, OK? What we're doing here is learning to communicate about sex openly and without shame. It might feel awkward to begin with, but trust me and stick with it. If you can learn to talk about it, the positions and all the other stuff won't matter, because you'll be connecting better, learning to compromise where there are differences and, above all, building trust. I'd like you to do this at least three times before we meet next. The first time should be in a totally non-sexual location, fully clothed in your sitting room, for example. Depending on how you get on, you can up the ante a little bit each time; maybe move to the bedroom for the second one, but stay fully clothed. You can be naked the third time if you're both comfortable with that, and you can also touch each other, but you must not have sex. All clear?'

They both nod.

'Great. Are there any questions?'

'What shall I do with this?' Chris asks, indicating the vibrator.

'I have no idea. There isn't exactly a second-hand market for these things, I'm afraid.'

'It's unused though.'

'I'm sorry Chris. I think you're best off putting it in the bin and chalking it up to experience.'

'I don't suppose you'd like it? Professionally, I mean.' He blushes as he realises what he said.

I consider it for a moment. I do have a drawer of various sex toys in my desk, purely for illustrative purposes, but it's so big, I doubt whether it will fit in there, and I can't think what I'd use it to illustrate, apart from how not to do it. I know my colleague, Rachel, would like to see it, though; I'll never be able to describe it adequately to her.

'If you're happy to leave it, I wouldn't mind showing it to my colleague. Purely for professional interest. After that, we will dispose of it. Is that OK?'

'Fine with me. Thanks, Doc.'

Tina walks out into the reception area, buttoning up her coat, so I take advantage of having Chris on his own.

'There's just one more thing, Chris, while I remember.'

'Yes?'

'Give the websites a rest for the next couple of weeks, will you? Concentrate on Tina, OK?'

He blushes furiously, but nods. I don't like having to be so direct with clients, as it can put them off and break what is often a very fragile connection, but I think we've made real progress here, so a little more pressure might just do the trick. I watch them leave together before going back into my office to write up my notes and pack up for the day. I leave the door open so I can hear when Rachel's last clients leave. We normally head to the pub for a quick drink after work on a Friday, but I have a little surprise in store for her first.

2

'Hands up! Don't move and don't turn around!'

As soon as I heard Rachel's clients leave, I stole over to her office door and waited until her back was turned. I managed to creep in unobserved, and I'm now pressing the vibrator into the small of her back.

'Shit, Poppy! You made me jump, you cow. What the bloody hell is that?' she asks, as she turns around and claps eyes on it for the first time.

'A little gift from ChrisTina,' I tell her. We don't normally give clients nicknames, but their two names run together so perfectly it was impossible not to. 'He bought it for her to spice things up, and unsurprisingly she wasn't keen. What do you think?'

'It's obscene. Where on earth did he get it from?'

'I don't know, I haven't seen anything like it before. eBay?'

'Maybe. And why have you got it?'

'I managed to convince him that it wasn't appropriate. He was going to throw it away, but he gave it to me so I could show it to you. Look, it has lights and everything!' I turn it on to show her, and her eyes widen as it begins gyrating and flashing.

'What on earth do you need lights on a sex toy for?'

'I don't know. It might be helpful if you were using it in the dark, I guess, so you could see where you were going?' I turn off the light in her office and close the door so we can appreciate the vibrator in all its illuminated glory.

'I don't know about you, Poppy, but if all I could see was that coming towards me, making that horrible noise, my first instinct would be to run,' she observes.

'It is a bit of a mood killer,' I agree as I turn the lights back on and switch off the vibrator. 'I'm not surprised Tina didn't like it – are you?'

She takes it off me and examines it carefully. 'Is it waterproof?'

'I doubt it. Would it work as a massager, do you think?'

She fires it up again and places it between my shoulder blades. 'Any good?'

'It's tickling more than anything. Try pressing a little harder.'

She complies but, after a few moments, it starts making a horrible grinding sound, as if the parts inside are ripping themselves to pieces, and then there's a loud crack and it stops moving completely.

'Aw, you've broken it,' I say. 'No Secret Santa for you this year if you're just going to break the gifts I bring you.' I take it off her and throw it in the bin.

'You can't put it in there!' she exclaims. 'You'll traumatise the cleaners, especially if it comes back to life unexpectedly and starts buzzing or moving. They might think it's a snake or something and call the RSPCA. That would really land us in hot water.'

'What am I supposed to do with it, then?'

'I don't know. Take it home and put it in your own rubbish.'

'There's no way that thing will fit in my bag, and my rubbish is frequently attacked by foxes. Can you imagine the stories my neighbours will construct about me if they see that outside my house?

Isn't there something we can put it in so the cleaners won't know what it is?'

We search our offices and eventually wrap the vibrator in a polythene shopping bag, which we seal up with copious amounts of Sellotape. We've taken extra care to remove the batteries, to prevent it from being turned on accidentally. Once we're happy that it looks innocuous, we lock up and head to the pub.

'Are you looking forward to your week off?' she asks me, once we're settled with a couple of glasses of wine.

'Honestly? Not really,' I tell her.

'But your baby sister is getting married! That should be exciting, no?'

'No.'

'Why not? Don't you get on with her?'

'It's a week with my mother, and she'll be bringing the usual truckload of disapproval. She thinks what we do is dirty, smutty and shameful, remember?'

'You're right, I'd forgotten.' She puts on a pompous voice. 'You are a disgrace with your desire to help people. Why do they feel the need to air their dirty linen in public, anyway? Much better to repress everything and simply not talk about it.'

I can't help but laugh. 'The problem is, Rach, you'd be funnier if you weren't so close to the mark. That's exactly how she is.'

'Oh, for goodness' sake. This is the twenty-first century, not the nineteenth. It's a shitshow of people struggling to cope and make sense of their lives. If we're not there to help them, who will be?'

'I agree with you, of course I do, but that's not how my mother thinks.' I put on a similar pompous voice. 'Problems are not there to be addressed, brought out into the open and resolved. Problems are there to be shoved firmly under the carpet and not talked about, especially problems to do with, well, you know what.'

'You mean s-e-x?'

'Don't say it so openly, you brazen hussy!'

'Poor you.' Her eyes are full of pity. To be fair, I know Rachel's parents well, and they're furiously proud of the work their daughter does and the massive amount of training we both had to go through to get to where we are. They are literally the polar opposites of my family and, to my shame, I have had the odd fantasy where they've adopted me. But then her parents are in similar work; her mother is a psychologist and her father a psychiatrist. There's a certain amount of friendly competition between them, and I always remember with a smile one of Rachel's mother's remarks to me: *James thinks he's God, because all psychiatrists do. In reality the only difference between him and me is that he writes prescriptions.*

Rachel is still looking at me with concern in her eyes. 'Doesn't she understand any of it?'

'Nope. Basically, to her, I'm some sort of pervert who gets off on listening to other people talk about their sex lives. I think she genuinely believes that what I do is morally wrong, and she's passed that attitude on to Rose and Lily.'

'Rose is the next one up from you, isn't she?'

'Yes. Andrew's the oldest. He's married to Zoe and they have two teenage children. They're fine. Zoe's a nurse, so she gets what I do. Next comes Rose, married to Steve. They have two daughters aged eight and ten. Rose and I have never really got on. I was the youngest until Lily arrived, so she had this hang-up about me being my parents' little princess, and we were too set in our ways to change when Lily was born.'

'Remind me how much younger than you Lily is?'

'Ten years. I'm not sure she was planned, but you don't like to ask these things, and Mum would never admit it anyway.'

'And you're stuck with them for the whole of your week off?'

'Yup. Lily and her fiancé, Dan, are driving down to Cornwall today, as are Mum and Dad. The rest of us are following tomorrow. Every day between tomorrow and the wedding has a theme, I believe, although I have to confess I haven't read the emails in depth. I guess I'd better read through them all before I go, in case there's some sort of dress code.'

'And the wedding itself?'

'Next Saturday, at the church in Newquay that Dan's parents go to, followed by a reception at a local hotel. All the other guests are staying there, from what I understand. The bridesmaids and ushers are coming down on Wednesday, with the stag and hen dos on the Thursday so everyone has time to get over their hangovers, if there are any, in time for the wedding. It's all been planned with military precision.'

'It sounds like it. I'm guessing there won't be any penis-shaped accessories at the hen do or strip clubs for the boys?'

'Absolutely not! She's the family Christian, ever since she found God at secondary school.'

Rachel sniggers. 'You make it sound like God was hiding in a classroom or something. It does sound like a bit of a chore. Why Cornwall?'

'Good question. The church she and Dan go to normally is plenty big enough for all the guests they wanted to invite, but it's also hideous and there's nowhere suitable nearby for people to stay. Dan's parents live in Newquay, and they're really involved with the church there. His dad is a churchwarden and his mum sings in the choir, if I remember right. He grew up there and used to go with them, so that means they can marry there. There was a bit of a kerfuffle because Lily and Dan wanted their own vicar to come and do the service, but Dan's mum said it was disrespectful to the vicar down there, who's also known Dan since he was a boy.'

'Bloody hell. Talk about overcomplicating things!' Rachel exclaims.

'I know. Don't get me wrong, I wish them every happiness in their marriage, but I do vaguely resent having to take a whole week out of my life for it. I could be lying on a beach in the Mediterranean instead, being served delicious cocktails by a tanned, handsome barman.'

'You never know, there might be some interesting single men when the ushers come down.'

'I think it's unlikely. Dan's a nice enough guy, but... Well, let me put it this way: they're a good match.'

'What do you mean?'

'He's never going to set the world on fire. Worthy, but a little dull. Plus, I'm not really looking for anyone at the moment.'

That's not strictly true. I'd love to meet someone, fall in love and get married like Lily is, but that's another downside of the job. I meet someone I like and we get chatting, but the subject of work always comes up fairly early. I tell them I'm a sex and relationship therapist, but somehow they hear, 'I'm a sex expert.' From that point forward they're either intimidated by me, worried that I'll be scoring their performance somehow, or they come over all competitive. None of these approaches are conducive to a successful relationship, so I've been single for the last four years and I haven't even dated anyone for the last twelve months. It's a cruel irony that I spend my life helping other people with their relationships when it seems I'm unable to form one myself.

Rachel has been a bit luckier. She's blissfully happy with Sarah, a teacher she met through a dating app five years ago. They've been together ever since and moved in after their first anniversary. It wouldn't surprise me if there were wedding bells there before long.

'Is there any downtime? If the weather's nice you could escape to the beach with a book and pretend you were in the Med,' Rachel continues, searching for any positives we can pull out of it.

'God, I hope so. If I don't get time off from them, I might end up drowning myself!'

'Please don't do that. I need you.'

'Aw, Rach. Are you going to miss me while I'm gone?'

'No, I just don't want your client list on top of mine, that's all.'

'You're such a softie. I can feel my heart melting.'

I know she's going to miss me, the same way I miss her when she has time off. I first met her when, newly qualified, she joined the same NHS practice as me. I was a year ahead of her but we soon became friends and we decided to set up our own private practice two years ago. Some people said it was a crazy move, but Rachel was right when she said it's a shitshow out there, and our books soon filled up. As our reputation grew, so did the waiting list, and we're currently trying to decide whether to bring another therapist on board. The financial plus is obvious, but we're both worried about the effect of a third person on our office dynamic. Rachel and I work very well as equal partners, and we don't necessarily want to put that at risk. We talk about it every so often, and then end up kicking the can down the road.

After an hour or so, we head off in our separate directions. I'm in luck tonight. When I reach Tonbridge, there is a free parking space right opposite my tiny, terraced house, and I quickly reverse the car into it.

The cat has obviously heard my key in the lock because she's waiting for me in the hallway and immediately starts wrapping herself around my ankles, purring loudly. I bend down to pick her up, and the purring is so deep and loud that I can feel it resonating through my shoulder.

'Hello, you,' I say as I stroke her soft fur. 'Have you missed me?'

The purring intensifies, and there's a slight chirrup in it now.

'You're not going to be so happy tomorrow,' I tell her, as I carry her towards the kitchen to get her dinner. 'It's a week in the cattery for you, I'm afraid.'

She's completely unperturbed by the news and resumes circling my feet and chirruping while I empty a sachet of her current favourite food into her bowl. I learned early on not to buy cat food in bulk; as soon as I did, she would turn up her nose and refuse to have anything to do with it. Hopefully the current favourite will last for the week she's away in the cattery.

Once the cat is dealt with, I pour myself a glass of wine and wander through to the sitting room. The answerphone is blinking to tell me that I have a new message. I hit the button to play it, and almost immediately wish that I hadn't.

'Poppy, it's your mother. We're just about to leave, but I needed to remind you that there will be children in the house this week, and they don't need to be stumbling across any of your smutty literature. You might like to do us all a favour and leave all that stuff behind. See you tomorrow, don't be late. We'll be eating at six because Lily has organised some icebreaker games to help us get to know Dan's family a bit better. She's told them that you're a marriage guidance counsellor, so please keep to that story. We want them to think that we're a normal family.'

I sigh. Several years ago, not long after I'd moved into my house, a teenaged Lily sneaked up into my bedroom and found a biographical book I was reading that Rachel had recommended. It was called *Nice Girls Don't... But They Really Ought To*, and told the story of a young woman's journey to sexual empowerment. Out of curiosity, she'd picked it up and flicked through it. To be fair, it did have some pretty explicit passages in it, but nothing that you wouldn't expect a teenager to know about. Unfortunately, instead of putting it back on the bedside table and leaving it there, she brought it down to the living room and showed it to my mother, who took one look at the first chapter and hauled me off to my kitchen for a dressing-down. I've never been allowed to forget the incident, even though it was in my house and Lily had no business being in my bedroom.

I'm not even in Cornwall yet, and my mother is already irritating me. I shove the cottage pie that I've defrosted into the oven and head upstairs to read Lily's emails and pack for the week ahead.

3

Hi everyone,

I'm super excited that Dan and I are finally tying the knot, and thank you for being part of this hugely special occasion for both of us!! Please find the itinerary below:

Friday – Bridal Party (yay!!) travel to Mawgan Porth to prepare the house and allocate bedrooms.

Saturday – Family arrival day. You can arrive any time after 12 p.m. Before that there may not be anyone here to welcome you as we'll be food shopping, etc. We will be eating at 6 p.m. sharp – please make sure you're on time as we have some icebreaker games after dinner so we can all get to know one another!

Sunday – Dan and I will be going to church in Newquay, and you're welcome to join us! As you know, our faith is really important to us, and we're really looking forward to saying our vows in the church where Dan grew up, but the vicar has also promised that he will say some prayers of blessing for us on Sunday! There will be a roast dinner at the house in the evening, cooked by Dan's parents (thank you so much – love you guys!).

Monday (weather permitting) – FIRST BEACH DAY! We'll be topping up our tans so we look our best for the big day. Don't forget the sunscreen – we don't want anyone getting burned!

I can't bear it any more. Apart from the huge over use of exclamation marks, the enforced jollity of it all is making me feel nauseous. I scan the rest of the email looking for dress clues, making sure there isn't a fancy dress party I haven't spotted, but it's all pretty anodyne stuff. There's quite a lot of time on the beach, a water-sports day and a shopping day so we can pick up various knick-knacks and anything we might have forgotten (a not-so-subtle wedding present reminder, I reckon). I move on to the next email, which is directed purely at me.

Poppy,

Thanks for agreeing to be a bridesmaid and coming to all the fittings. I've got your dress and will take it down to Cornwall with me. Please don't forget the 20 denier black tights and the shoes – it's so important that you all match. Also, please no talking about your job – I don't want Dan's parents to get upset.

Love,
Lily

That one hasn't cheered me up either. Morosely, I start chucking clothes into my case. The cat, who has finished her dinner and followed me upstairs, thinks this is a tremendous game, and is currently engaged in quite the tussle with a pair of my socks. Thankfully, the all-important tights are still in their box and of no interest to her, otherwise I'm sure she'd have taken great pleasure in ripping holes in them. The dark-blue satin shoes that I will be wearing under my bridesmaid's dress also make it into the case unmolested. More in hope than expectation, I pack a couple of swimsuits and bikinis. I have got a selection of work-related books to read, but they're all on my Kindle, so I shouldn't risk offending anyone. I'm briefly tempted to drive back to the office, pick up a load of sex toys and hide them under everyone's pillows, but I realise that's probably childish and, as my mother would say, 'needlessly provocative.' I don't know what it is about my family; I'm a fully functioning adult, but they somehow reduce me to a rebellious adolescent every time I see them. Even Lily manages to patronise me and get my hackles up, despite being so much younger.

After a while, I'm fairly certain I've got everything I need. There are a few things, like toiletries and make-up, that will have to go in tomorrow, and I'll double-check it before I go, but I've gone as far as I can tonight. The alarm on the oven sounds to let me know that my cottage pie is ready, so I wander downstairs, throw together a quick salad to go with it, top up my wine, and settle down to eat. Normally, I'm excited the night before going away for a break, but this time I just feel resigned and a bit sad. The cat, emotionally articulate creature that she is, has decided that I'm no longer of any interest now that I'm neither feeding her nor giving her things to play with, so she's curled up on the sofa, fast asleep.

There's nothing on the TV I want to watch, so I make a start on my holiday reading after I've eaten and cleared up. As well as the work-related books, I've also downloaded some light fiction, and I select one of those in the hope that it will improve my mood. The story is undemanding and funny, which is just what I need, so it keeps me happily entertained until bedtime.

* * *

I'm up early the next morning to take the cat to the cattery. As anyone who owns a cat knows, getting said animal into the cat carrier is a task only slightly less fraught with danger than trying to give a cat a bath or a pill. I try to lull her into a false sense of security with an extended love-in after she's had her breakfast, but I can tell she's spotted the carrier in the corner of the room and is wary. I've watched countless online videos that show how to load a cat into a carrier, but none of the cats in them seem to transform into thrashing wild animals in the way that mine does when I want her to do something she doesn't like. I have a suspicion that the cats in the videos are sedated. Sure enough, the usual tussle ensues and, by the time I've managed to get her body and all of her limbs inside and closed the door, she's a hissing ball of rage and I'm nursing a couple of livid scratch marks on my forearms. Ignoring her yowls of displeasure, I pack a bag with her bedding, a couple of her favourite toys, and her food.

The journey isn't much better. I turn up the radio to try to drown out the furious yowling coming from the back of the car. She has a habit of wetting herself whenever I drive her anywhere, so I bought myself a rubber boot liner some time ago, which I can just wipe clean when I need to. When we get there, I'm not at all surprised to see the usual puddle. I've got tissues and wet wipes, so I'll deal with that after I've dropped her off. Despite the friendly greetings from the staff, she's still in a foul temper when I leave her. I do feel guilty, but the cattery is very nice and I know she settles in fine, because they send regular video updates.

By the time I've cleared out the mess in the boot, driven home and loaded my luggage, it's nearly eleven o'clock. My satnav is predicting just under five hours to Mawgan Porth, but I'll need a couple of toilet stops and a lunch break, so I suspect it will be nearer six hours in total, which gives me an hour's leeway before I fall foul of the deadline. Let's just hope there aren't any accidents or other traffic problems. Mum and Lily will never let me hear the end of it if I'm late.

One of the reasons I try not to spend too much time with my family is that it forces me to confront where it all went wrong. I was close to my mum when I was growing up, and I got on reasonably well with my older brother, Andrew, even if Rose and I fought most of the time. When Lily was born, I genuinely wasn't jealous of her. Yes, it meant that I wasn't the youngest any more, and I had to share Mum with yet another sibling, but there was still plenty of love and laughter to go around.

Where does my dad fit into all this? He doesn't, not really. He was always at work in the week, tired in the evenings, and his weekends were filled with tasks like mowing the lawn and washing the car. He pretty much left the parenting to my mother and, on the rare occasions when she demanded he intervene, he'd always say something like, 'Do what your mother tells you,' and that would be the end of it. He's best described as benign but detached.

Things first started to deteriorate when I hit puberty. Suddenly, my body was changing in all sorts of ways, and I was fascinated by it. As the hormones kicked in, I began to understand what it meant to be a sexual human being. We'd been taught the basics of how reproduction happened at school, and I'd been as certain as all the other girls in the class that there was no way we would ever let a boy do *that* to us. It all sounded absolutely appalling when I was eleven. At fourteen, though, it didn't sound appalling at all; it sounded like it might be fun. I wasn't ready to try it myself, but I wanted to know everything about it. Whenever I was on the family computer and nobody was around, I searched online for all the information I could find about sex. I learned very quickly to steer well clear of the videos, but I devoured any articles I could find. You know the type – ten ways to improve your orgasm, twenty positions to try this summer, that sort of thing. If they were particularly good, I'd print them off and hide them under my mattress in the bunk bed I shared with Rose, so I could read them over when I was alone.

Naturally, it was only a matter of time before I was found out. Dad was looking through the search history for the website of a plumbing supplier he'd visited a few days before, and all the sites I'd been browsing also came up. Rose and I were watching TV in the living room when it had all kicked off – prime seats for the family drama, as it turned out. I remember the conversation as if it happened yesterday.

'Hazel, can I borrow you for a moment?' he'd begun, innocently enough. 'There's something on the computer I don't understand.'

'You know I hate that thing,' Mum had countered from the kitchen. 'Ask one of the children.'

'Umm, I think I'd like you to see it first.'

'Oh, for goodness' sake!' she'd exclaimed, marching into the sitting room in her apron. 'What is it? I'm in the middle of getting dinner ready.'

'It seems someone has been using the computer to look at,' and here he'd lowered his voice to a stage whisper, 'sex stuff.'

There was an agonising pause while she looked through the list, before she'd screeched up the stairs, 'Andrew, come down here *at once!*'

'What?' he'd asked a few moments later.

'Don't "what" me.' Mum's face was almost puce with rage. 'You've been looking at filth, haven't you?'

'No!'

'Don't lie. The computer has the evidence.'

'That wasn't me!' he'd insisted, before peering more closely at the screen. 'Why would I be interested in that?'

To this day, I don't know which link he'd selected, but it was obviously something relating purely to female pleasure, because Mum's fury was immediately diverted onto Rose and me.

'Which one of you girls is it?' she'd hissed.

'Poppy,' Rose had answered immediately. 'She's got a whole load of dirty stuff under her mattress. I can show you.'

A quick search of our bedroom was enough to convict me and, after taking away all my pieces of paper, Mum subjected me to a long lecture which was supposed to leave me in no doubt that sex was dirty, shameful, and should only ever happen within a marriage.

Unfortunately for her, it had completely the opposite effect. My natural curiosity couldn't stop picking over the contradiction between what I'd read and what she had said. They couldn't both be right, could they? There was only one way to find out.

I started going out with Findlay when I was fifteen. He was everything I thought I wanted in a boy – he was good-looking and muscly – and I couldn't wait to try sex for real with him. When we eventually got the opportunity at his parents' house after school one day, I was trembling with excitement and nerves. But the sex was wildly disappointing. It wasn't anything like what I'd read about, and I cried afterwards, thinking that Mum must have been right after all, and the internet was just one big lie. We tried again, several times, and it did get a bit better, but it was still nowhere near what I'd been led to expect.

I wondered whether it was something wrong with Findlay, so I dated a few other boys in the school after we split up, but the spark never happened and I developed a bit of an unfortunate reputation in the process. Once again, Rose dobbed me in to Mum after she'd heard some of the boys joking about me, and I was subjected to another long lecture about 'girls with loose morals', grounded for a month, and dragged to the doctor for a check-up. It wasn't until I left school and started going out with Jack, a twenty-five-year-old guy I met at my gap year job, that it finally clicked. He was the first man who took the time to find out what worked for me, and I loved him for it. I still look back on the few months we were together before I left to go to university as one of the happiest times of my life.

My interest in therapy started while I was at university. I was in a tight-knit group of girls on my psychology course, and they talked openly and freely about their sex lives. I quickly learned that most of them weren't having great sex either, and that they felt it was something they had to do to keep their boyfriends happy rather than something they actively enjoyed. Armed with my years of research and my experiences with Jack, I counselled them and felt a rush of pleasure when they told me what a difference I'd made.

Needless to say, both my parents were horrified when I told them that I intended to train as a counsellor and then specialise in sex and relationships. My mother banned me from even mentioning it in the house, in case I corrupted Lily with my filth. I moved out of the family home in Paddock Wood into a shared flat as soon as I was able, saved like mad to raise the deposit for my little house in Tonbridge, and I haven't looked back. Since then, my interactions with my family have been as short as I could make them. I see them for birthdays, Christmas and life events like weddings and christenings, and that's about as much as I can tolerate.

The rest of them are all still as close as ever, which makes the unfairness of it all even more acute. Andrew and Rose both drop in to see my parents with their families on a regular basis, and Lily is only leaving home now that she's getting married. I can't help thinking that she's rushing into it at twenty-three, but I've been told firmly to mind my own business whenever I've tried to raise it. To be fair, with the exception of me, my family have all married young.

One thing is certain. This is going to be an exceptionally trying week, and I'm going to have to bite my tongue most of the way through it.

4

It's five to six when I pull up outside the house my parents have rented in Mawgan Porth. The driveway is nearly full, but I just about manage to squeeze in. The front door flies open as I'm grabbing my cases out of the boot.

'Poppy, where have you *been*?' my mother scolds. 'We're just about to dish up! Come on, you'll have to take your cases up later.'

I'd love to tell her that I've *been* on the road for seven hours, that I was caught in stationary traffic for nearly an hour on the M5 after an accident blocked all the lanes, that I've been *doing my bloody best to get here on time*, but I can see she's already decided that I'm late on purpose, just to annoy her. Instead, I say nothing and follow her meekly into the enormous open-plan kitchen and dining room at one end of the house.

If the rest of the house is anywhere near as nice as this room, I'm in for a treat. The kitchen is huge, with one of those range cookers that have a gazillion hotplates and a griddle on the end. There's a big, American-style fridge with built-in dispensers for water and ice, and a separate wine fridge next to it, which I'm happy to see is well stocked. My family may be sexually repressed, but they do enjoy a drink. The white kitchen units sit under a granite worktop that must have cost a fortune, and there is certainly no shortage of space or cupboards. The dining area beyond has a glass roof and bifold doors looking out into the garden. The table is already fully occupied; as well as my parents and Lily and Dan, Rose is there with her husband Steve and her two little girls, Olivia and Evie. Zoe and Andrew are sitting opposite with their teenaged children, Freddie and Sarah, next to them. At the far end of the table are three people I don't recognise, who must be Dan's parents and his brother, from the look of them.

Mum is ushering me towards the table, and I can see that I've been placed between the woman I assume is Dan's mother, and Freddie. I like Freddie, but he's like every sixteen-year-old boy I've met, communicating mainly through grunts and spending most of his time glued to his phone, as he is now.

'Anita, this is Poppy, my second youngest,' Mum announces to the woman next to me as she practically shoves me into my seat. 'Poppy, this is Mrs Williams, Dan's mother.'

'Please, call me Anita,' she says with a warm smile. 'Mrs Williams makes me feel a hundred years old. Lovely to meet you, Poppy. Did you have a good journey?'

I don't get any time to answer, because Lily stands up and claps her hands.

'Now that everyone is finally here,' she begins, with a pointed look at me, 'I'd just like to say how excited Dan and I are about this week. We're going to have so much fun, and I get to marry the love of my life at the end of it! Before we say grace, I'd like to say a big thank you to my mum and dad, who have not only rented this amazing house for us to stay in, but also cooked tonight's dinner. Please raise your glasses in a toast to my mum and dad!'

OK, this is awkward. Everyone has a glass of something, except me. They haven't even filled my water glass.

'Here you go, put a quick splash of this in,' Anita says, handing me a bottle of white wine. I smile gratefully at her and pour some into the glass just in time to join in with the toast.

Mum bustles off into the kitchen, followed by Lily and Rose.

'Would you like a hand?' I ask, taking a quick swig of wine in case they say yes.

'Read the rota.' Lily replies in annoyance. 'Rose and I are serving tonight, and you're on washing-up.'

There's a *rota*?

'Was it in one of the emails?' I ask. 'I'm pretty sure I checked them all.'

'No. It's here,' Lily points out a piece of paper fixed to the wall in the kitchen. 'If you'd have got here on time, you would have heard me explain it. We've divided the jobs up so everyone takes their fair share.'

I guess things could be worse; at least Mum is a fairly tidy cook and tends to wash up as she goes along so, even though there are a lot of people here, the washing-up shouldn't be a mammoth task. I'll study the rota after dinner and check that I'm not washing-up on Lily's night to cook. I swear she'd use every pot and pan in the kitchen even if she were only boiling an egg.

'I think we're having chicken. Are you happy with white, or would you prefer red?' Anita asks, and I turn my attention back to her. She's managed to get hold of a red wine bottle as well, and she's smiling softly at me. At least someone seems pleased that I'm here.

'White is perfect, thank you,' I reply, and she tops up my glass from the bottle. The plates are starting to arrive from the kitchen and Anita is one of the first to be served. The chicken casserole smells amazing. I normally eat later than this, but I realise I'm actually quite hungry. I'm obviously out of favour for being late, because I'm the last of the adults to get a plate, even though Mum is normally a stickler for serving the women before the men. I notice that Sarah, Zoe and Andrew's fourteen-year-old daughter, gets a different plate from everyone else, and raise my eyebrows questioningly at Zoe.

'She's a vegetarian, as of two months ago when they watched a film at school about farming,' she explains.

'It was horrific,' Sarah adds. 'I don't know how anyone could eat meat after seeing those poor animals going to the abattoir.'

'I'm sure they don't suffer,' Mum tells her as she takes her place. 'They stun them first, so it's completely painless.'

'Not if it's halal,' Dad chips in, earning an irritated look from my mother. 'Isn't it against their religion for Muslims to stun animals before slaughtering them?'

'I think they can stun them, but the animals mustn't die from the stunning itself,' Zoe offers.

'Thank you, Bill and Zoe. I'm sure we all feel much better for those little nuggets of information,' she replies tersely. 'Who's saying grace then, Lily?'

Dan gets to his feet, and I try to look suitably respectful while he thanks God for the food, the week ahead, and pretty much everything else he can think of. I can see Mum starting to twitch out of the corner of my eye; she won't be pleased if the food she's worked so hard to produce goes cold while Dan drones on. When he finally wraps up, we all say, 'Amen' and start eating.

'Hello, Freddie. How are you?' I ask my nephew, after a couple of mouthfuls.

'Yeah, OK,' he replies, without looking up. I'm quite impressed by the dexterity he's showing; he's holding his phone in one hand, banging out a message with his thumb, and shovelling food into his mouth with the other.

'Freddie! Answer Poppy properly and put your phone down. How many times have I told you not to bring that thing to the dinner table?' Zoe scolds him. Out of the corner of my eye, I spot

Sarah lower her phone and place it face down on the table before her mother notices that she's just as guilty.

'Let me just finish sending this,' he replies, as his thumb continues to dance over the screen.

'I'm so sorry,' Zoe says to me. 'I swear he's addicted to that thing. We've had to set up a rule that their mobile phones go on charge in the kitchen before they go to bed, otherwise I'm sure they'd both be up all night chatting to their friends. God only knows what they find to talk about.'

'Don't worry about it,' I reassure her. 'We were all his age once, and I'm sure we were just as bad.'

My brother Andrew decides to join in the conversation at this point. 'We didn't have smartphones back then, though, did we? We had to wait our turn to use MSN Messenger on the family computer. Do you remember that, Poppy? The fights you and Rose used to have over whose turn it was and how long you'd been using it for. The phone was just as bad. How anyone ever got through to us in the evenings, I'll never know. One of you was always on it, gassing away.'

'Oh, and you never used it at all, I suppose?' Rose challenges him, surprisingly aggressively. 'I seem to remember Mum and Dad having to give us set times for a while, because you were always on there gibbering sweet nothings at Zoe when you came home from uni.'

I glance up at Rose and notice that her eyes are slightly glazed and her cheeks are flushed. She's obviously had a few glasses of wine before dinner, which always makes her feisty. Her husband, Steve, has also picked up on it because he places his hand over hers and gives it a squeeze. There's a slightly awkward atmosphere following her outburst, and I'm aware of Freddie taking advantage of it to pick his phone back up and continue his conversation.

'This is a delicious casserole, Hazel. You must give me the

recipe,' Anita says to my mother, in an obvious attempt to defuse the sudden tension in the room. It works to the extent that Rose stops glaring at my brother and resumes eating. Slowly, the conversation starts to flow again.

'Are you staying here as well?' I ask Anita between mouthfuls. I know they live fairly close by, but this house looks big enough to sleep half of Cornwall.

'No,' she replies. 'We're not far away so, although we're going to be here quite a lot, we thought it would be easier all round if we went home in the evenings. Dan's also staying with us, so it will give us some time as a family before the wedding.'

'Oh, I thought he'd be staying here with Lily.'

'No. They decided on separate beds until they've officially tied the knot. I know it's not the modern way, but I admire their strength of character, don't you?'

'I do, but it's a lot of change all at once, isn't it? At least if a couple have lived together first, they know each other's foibles in advance. Dan and Lily have no idea what they're letting themselves in for.'

'Is that a personal or a professional view?' she asks. 'Your mother told me you work as a marriage guidance counsellor.'

'It's a bit of both, I suppose. Marriage is a big step, and combining it with moving in together for the first time is really ramping up the pressure.'

'But then you could also argue that it makes the journey of discovery all the more exciting, because there's so much still to learn. It makes buying wedding presents more fun as well, because they don't already have a home set up with everything they need in it. My friend Janice's daughter got married a few months ago, and all they wanted were vouchers towards the cost of the honeymoon. How boring is that?'

I have to admit that she has a point. Most of my friends who have married recently were all living together first, and buying a suitable present for them was surprisingly hard.

'Do you have anyone special in your life?' Anita continues. 'A boyfriend, or maybe a girlfriend?'

'No boyfriend at the moment,' I tell her, smiling at her political correctness. 'My job makes dating difficult.' Across the table, I'm aware that my mother has overheard me and is listening carefully.

'Really? Why?' Anita looks genuinely surprised, and I realise I have to tread very carefully here. I take a moment to frame my answer. I don't want to lie, but I don't want to incur my family's wrath either.

'Quite a lot of what I do involves talking to couples about the, erm, *physical side* of their relationship,' I begin. 'In order to do that, I have to know what I'm talking about. Men seem to find that knowledge intimidating.' I think I've managed to dodge the bullet, as I can see Mum drop her eyes back to her plate.

'Do you? I thought marriage guidance was more focused on helping a couple to resolve conflicts and see the world from the other person's point of view. Dealing with the physical side, as you put it, seems to me to be straying more into sex therapy. Is that what you are, a sex therapist?'

Somehow, Anita's words have fallen during one of the lulls in the general conversation, and I don't even need to look up to know that my mother and Lily are glaring at me. What am I supposed to say? Anita looks genuinely interested as she waits for my answer, so I decide to lance the boil.

'That's exactly what I am,' I tell her.

'How fascinating,' she continues enthusiastically, completely unaware of the waves of displeasure coming from the other end of the table. 'I could have sworn you told me Poppy was a marriage guidance counsellor, Hazel?'

My mother flushes deep scarlet but, is cut off by Evie, Rose's eight-year-old daughter, before she has a chance to answer.

'What's a sex therapist?' she asks.

'Someone who helps people when they can't get it up,' Freddie replies, with a smirk.

'Freddie!' my mother exclaims. 'Not in front of the children.'

'When they can't get what up?' Evie continues, unwisely.

'Their willies, silly,' her older sister Olivia chips in. 'A man needs to make his willy hard to give his wife a baby. That's what Charlie Pottle told me, anyway. That's right, isn't it, Mummy?'

Rose takes another huge swig from her glass before answering. 'That Charlie Pottle is a nasty little boy, Olivia. I don't want you hanging around him, do you understand?'

'So Aunty Poppy helps people with their willies?' Evie adds, evidently baffled.

'Leave it,' Rose snarls at her.

'What's wrong with Aunty Poppy's job?' Sarah asks. 'I looked it up when Mum and Dad told me and Freddie about it. It's pretty cool actually.'

'Can we all just stop talking about this, please?' Lily implores. 'There's plenty more, go and help yourselves to seconds if you'd like.'

Rose, Lily and Mum are all shooting daggers at me now. Dad is concentrating very hard on his plate, as if all the answers to life's questions are there. Dan's parents just look bemused. Despite my best efforts and tact, all of this is obviously my fault.

That went well, then.

5

'I thought we agreed you weren't going to talk about your job,' my mother hisses at me. Dinner is finished and we're clearing up before Lily's icebreaker game starts. All those under the age of twenty have been excused from the game, so Olivia and Evie have skipped off to watch the Disney Channel somewhere, and Freddie and Sarah have also vanished.

'What was I supposed to say?' I reply, keeping my voice low so as not to be overheard.

'You were supposed to stick to the script, and tell them you're a marriage guidance counsellor, not announce to the whole room that you're a, well, you know. Thank goodness Anita and Richard seem to be OK with it, but it could have made things very awkward with them. Why do you have to be so inconsiderate?'

'If you remember, it was Anita who first mentioned sex therapy, not me.'

'That's not the point. You led her on with all your talking about physical relationships. You should have been more discreet.'

'I was as tactful as I could be! I wasn't going to lie to her when she asked directly. I'm sorry my job makes you uncomfortable, but there's actually nothing shameful about it.'

'Of course there is! Look at what happened with Evie and Olivia. Poor Rose is going to have to have some uncomfortable conversations with both of them now. That would never have happened if you had a normal job, like an accountant or something. You need to apologise to her. You'd better apologise to Lily as well. I'm sure she's very upset that you ruined our first meal together. This is Lily's week, and you would do well to remember that, rather than drawing attention to yourself all the time.'

I can feel my temper starting to rise, and I concentrate on keeping a level head. If I tell my mother what I really think, it'll only escalate into a full-scale row that will definitely upset Lily. Thankfully, the situation is defused by Anita, who chooses that moment to wander into the kitchen.

'That really was a delicious dinner, Hazel. Thank you so much,' she says.

'It was nothing, really,' Mum replies, blushing slightly. She's trying to be modest, but I know she's secretly lapping up the praise. She's shifted from being narrow-eyed and furious to delighted in a matter of seconds. If only I had that knack; I'm still seething with resentment. I'm sorely tempted to rush back out to the hallway, grab my bags and go home. I know it's impractical, and I'm probably over the drink-driving limit anyway, but my family seems to be uniquely equipped to get under my skin and irritate the hell out of me. I'm so busy simmering with fury that I almost miss the next part of the conversation. It's only when I hear my name that I register it.

'...Poppy. You must be so proud of her,' Anita is saying. Shit, what have I missed? If she's genuinely prompting my mother to agree with her, I fear she's in for a disappointment. I take a swig of wine and force myself to carry on with the washing-up, so Mum doesn't spot that I'm eavesdropping.

'I'm proud of all of them. You can't help it, can you? It comes with being a mum. You must be the same with Dan and Stuart,' Mum replies smoothly.

She's unbelievable. I take a deep breath to steady myself, but this unfortunately results in some of the wine going down the wrong way. The results are immediate. As the coughing fit begins, I spray the tiles behind the sink with the wine I haven't yet swallowed and then brace myself against the counter alternately gasping for air and hacking away. The timing couldn't be worse, and I'm aware of my mother looking at me suspiciously.

'Goodness, are you OK?' Anita asks, swiftly stepping forwards to pat me firmly on the back. I'm not sure why people do this; it never seems to help, in my experience. I am grateful, though. At least she's doing something, unlike my own mother, who is standing back with a look of disdain on her face, as if I've done this deliberately as part of my apparent attention-seeking campaign. Eventually, the attack begins to subside and I reach for a piece of kitchen towel to mop up the tears from my streaming eyes.

'Sorry about that,' I croak. 'The wine went down the wrong way.'

'Don't you just hate it when that happens?' Anita agrees. 'Why don't you get yourself a top-up and I'll finish up here.'

'I'm sure Poppy is quite able to finish the washing-up,' my mother declares firmly. 'We don't want to mess up Lily's rota, do we?'

That reminds me. As Mum and Anita walk off together, leaving me alone, I take the opportunity to cast my eyes over the famous rota. I assume we're responsible for our own breakfasts and lunches, as there's nothing on the rota for them. Dan's parents are cooking tomorrow evening, which I already knew, and Andrew and

Zoe are washing-up. I'm washing-up again on Tuesday after Rose and Steve have cooked, and I'm cooking on Wednesday. Conveniently for her, Lily doesn't appear to be cooking at all, although she and Dan are washing-up after me on Wednesday. For a moment, I'm tempted to cook something fiendishly difficult that uses all the pots and pans, but I realise I'd just be cutting off my nose to spite my face. There's no way I'm doing a separate meal for Sarah though, so I'll just do something vegetarian for everyone.

Once I've washed, dried and put everything away, I top up my glass and head off in search of the others. My bags are still in the hallway but, as nobody has told me where I'm sleeping yet, they'll have to stay there for the time being. I decide to take the opportunity to have a nose at the rest of the ground floor while I'm here. This place really is massive; there's a TV room with an enormous flatscreen television mounted on the wall, and comfy sofas to spread out on while you watch. This room is currently occupied by Sarah, Olivia and Evie. There's also a games room with a full-sized snooker table at one end and a table tennis table at the other. I might see if I can tempt Andrew to a few games of table tennis while we're here; we always used to play at the caravan park Mum and Dad took us to every summer when we were growing up, and the games would get fiercely competitive.

The final room is the sitting room, where I find everyone gathered. This is almost a mirror of the kitchen and dining room, in that it's huge and also has bifold doors looking out into the garden. There is a mixture of squishy leather sofas and armchairs, most of which are already occupied. I slot myself into the middle seat of one of the sofas, between Andrew and Zoe.

'Did you see the games room?' I ask Andrew.

He smiles. 'I may have done.'

'Fancy a grudge match while we're here?'

'Absolutely!'

Zoe sighs dramatically. 'Does this mean I'm going to be a ping-pong widow this week?'

'Cheer up,' I tell her. 'At least he doesn't play golf.'

'I suppose I should be grateful for small mercies. Anyway, how are you, Pops?'

Once again, I don't get the chance to answer, because Lily is on her feet again and clapping her hands for attention.

'OK, everyone. It's time for the icebreaker game. Dan and I have put you all into pairs, which I will reveal in a moment. When we start, you and the person you're paired with will have ten minutes to find out as much as you can about each other. At the end of the ten minutes, you will then introduce the person you've been paired with to the group. Any questions?'

Oh great. I'm not a fan of icebreaker games at the best of times, and this sounds positively excruciating. Maybe I'll be lucky and get Anita; she seems easy to talk to. I suspect that's unlikely, though.

'Can we take notes?' my father asks. 'My memory isn't what it was.'

'If you like. Any other questions before I pair you off? No? Right, let's begin!'

Any lingering hope that I might get paired with Anita goes up in smoke when my mum is paired off with Dan's father, and vice versa. Andrew gets paired with Rose's husband, Steve, and Zoe and Rose are also paired off. I get Dan's younger brother, Stuart.

'Hang on a minute, Lily,' Rose calls, and I can't help noticing a slight slur in her voice. 'That means you're paired with your own fiancé! That's hardly fair.'

'Bride's privilege,' Lily replies, looking smug.

'Don't be bolshy, Rose,' my mother admonishes her. 'Lily has put a lot of work into this. You might like to slow down on the wine, too.'

'Funny you should say that,' Rose replies, bullishly. 'Last time I looked, I was a fully grown adult and perfectly capable of deciding for myself how much to drink.'

My antennae are twitching now. This is more than Rose being a bit feisty after a few glasses of wine. There's definitely something eating her. Maybe she's jealous that Lily is the centre of attention, but it's not exactly new. Whatever the circumstances of her conception, my parents have doted on Lily from the moment she was born. I'm not saying the rest of us were neglected, but Lily has always enjoyed special treatment.

'OK everyone, time to get into your pairs,' Lily calls, and we begin shuffling around. I join Stuart on one of the other sofas just as Lily announces that the ten minutes have begun.

'So, sex therapist, eh? That's pretty cool. What made you want to get into that?' Stuart begins.

I give him the sanitised version, that I helped my friends at uni and realised it was what I wanted to do. I tell him about my training, first as a psychotherapist, and then an extra two years to get my psychosexual therapy diploma. I can tell he's not really taking any of it in, a fact confirmed by his response.

'You must know, like, *everything* about sex though, yeah? All the positions, everything. You're like the Wikipedia of doing it! How come you're here on your own? Someone like you must be able to have any man you choose.'

I can't help laughing. 'If only!' I tell him.

'I'd totally do you,' he replies.

I'm not sure whether to laugh or slap him. I decide to give him the benefit of the doubt; this is probably just youthful lack of tact, rather than a serious proposition.

'You're a little young for me.'

'Young is good. Think about it; a bloke your age is going to need a day or two at least to recover, whereas I can be raring to go after half an hour or so.'

'Post intercourse recovery time, which is what I think you're talking about, varies from person to person and, if you don't mind me saying, sex every half an hour sounds rather chafe-y from a female perspective.'

'I'd keep you so turned on there wouldn't be any chance of chafing.'

This has gone far enough, I decide. 'Well thank you, kind sir. I do have to point out that, apart from the age gap, I usually expect a little more romance before a proposition like that. You haven't even bought me dinner, let alone flowers. Now, tell me some non-sexual stuff about you.'

I learn that he's still at university, studying Economics. When he leaves, he's hoping to take a year out to travel the world before getting a plum job at a think tank somewhere and buying his first Aston Martin before his thirtieth birthday. I can't fault his self-belief, but I suspect he's in for a rude awakening down the line. He's just telling me how he had to dump his ex-girlfriend because she was getting too heavy and serious and he didn't want to be tied down, when Lily claps her hands again to indicate that our time is up, and it's time to present back what we've learned.

Dad goes first, adjusting his glasses and clearing his throat before he begins. He tells us that Anita was a stay-at-home mum while Dan and Stuart were growing up, but that she now volunteers in a charity shop in Newquay and has joined the University of the Third Age, which she's really enjoying.

Most of the presentations follow a similar vein, although it's difficult to make out parts of Rose's precis of Zoe, because she mumbles bits of it and slurs others. Mum's irritation is palpable, but it's obvious to me that, as well as being drunk, Rose is utterly miserable for some reason. This is not a jealousy thing; this is something much worse. I make a mental note to draw her aside at some point this week and see if I can find out what's going on.

Eventually, it's Stuart's and my turn. I go first, sharing what I've learned with the group, and then hand over to Stuart.

'Erm, yeah, this is Poppy,' he begins. 'She's got a shitload of qualifications that I don't remember, but basically she's a walking encyclopaedia of sex. However, if you want to find out what she knows, you have to buy her flowers or dinner first.'

I can sense Mum bristling, but Rose pipes up before anyone else has a chance to say anything.

'That's a turn up for the books,' she remarks acidly, probably much louder than she means to. 'You weren't so choosy at school, were you, Ceejay? Tell me, were there any boys in your year you didn't sleep with?'

Mum's response is immediate. 'That's *enough*, Rose,' she says, so sharply that Rose blinks a few times, as if she's been slapped.

I haven't heard my school nickname for fifteen years, but it still hurts like hell. Mum's immediate response and the fact that she doesn't appear to be shocked by Rose's question tells me that she knows much more about the whole Ceejay debacle than I thought. I feel the heat rushing to my cheeks as I stare at Rose in disbelief. To think that I was actually planning to try to help her! She can go and fuck herself, for all I care.

6

I'm woken up by the sunlight pouring into my room. The evening wrapped up fairly quickly after Rose's barbed remark to me. I tried to hide how upset I was, but I don't think I did a particularly good job, as Dan's family made their excuses pretty much within minutes, and Rose stormed off to bed after a furious altercation with Mum about how much she'd had to drink. Steve traipsed after her, muttering his apologies as he left, and then it just felt a bit awkward. Mum and Dad went to bed at around ten, leaving Andrew, Zoe, Lily and me nursing our glasses of wine. Lily tried to paper over the cracks with some forced jollity, wittering away about how much she thought Dan's parents liked us, but nobody was really buying it and she gave up after a while.

She did at least remember to show me where I was sleeping, and I'm not at all unhappy with my room. It's large, like the rest of the house, and has a king-size double bed with that cool, crisp bed linen that makes you sigh with delight as you slide under the duvet. It also, and this is the best bit for me, has a beautiful view out towards the beach and the sea. When I went to bed last night, I opened a window and didn't draw the curtains, so I could lie in bed and let the sight and sound of the sea soothe away the hurt of having the past dragged up.

I know I brought it on myself to some extent; schools are cruel places, after all, but it's not a phase of my life that I'm particularly proud of, and it's certainly not who I am today. I thought I'd left all that behind me, but Rose kindly brought it along with her and shoved my face in it last night. The fact is, there weren't just a few boys I slept with at school; it's more honestly described as 'quite a few'. The nickname Ceejay, short for Chlamydia Jane, was dreamt up by idiot extraordinaire Oliver Stone, who also publicly accused me of having given him an STD. Mia, his equally cretinous girl-friend at the time, was convinced he'd given her chlamydia because neither of them had paid the slightest attention in our (admittedly woeful) sex ed classes, and therefore didn't realise that the itching and soreness were much more likely to be thrush. Add in the drama club's upcoming production of *Calamity Jane*, and the nickname was born. It wasn't even true but, even after their itching was confirmed to be thrush and therefore nothing to do with me, the accusation still stuck and I became a pariah more or less overnight. Even people that I considered close friends suddenly wanted nothing to do with me. It was at this point that Rose told Mum what was going on. That's the real irony in all of this: I always believed that Mum thought she was intervening before I made a name for myself. Now I know that Rose obviously didn't spare her any of the gory details, and I feel hot tears of shame pricking behind my eyes. I'm tempted to pop out to the pharmacy when it opens and buy a bottle of Deep Heat. A good dose of that inside all her knickers would certainly give her something other than my past to think about. The thought makes me smile. I know I won't do it, but it's fun to imagine.

I don't know how long I lay there last night, brooding on the past, staring out of the window and listening to the swish of the waves on the beach, but it felt like hours before sleep came. I glance at the clock on the bedside table, which tells me it's half past six in the morning. Amazingly, I do feel refreshed even though it must have been a short night. The bed is so comfortable that I briefly contemplate closing the curtains and going back to sleep, but it's also a beautiful morning outside and I need to get away from this house and my family for a while, so I decide to throw on some clothes and go for a walk along the beach.

The house is completely quiet as I make my way downstairs; everyone else is obviously still asleep. The key for the front door is hanging on a hook in the hallway, but that presents a problem. If I take the key and lock the door behind me, then I'm effectively locking my family inside the house. If I don't lock the door, I face a potential roasting for leaving them at risk of burglary. In the end, I let myself out through the bi-folding doors in the kitchen and lock those behind me instead. The air is pleasantly cool at this time of the morning, although the sun is already high in the cloudless sky, so it won't be long before the heat starts to build. I walk up to the end of the lane and follow the main road for a short distance before turning on to the beach. As soon as I get there, I sit down, take off my socks and shoes, and relish the feeling of the cool sand against my feet. I focus on my breathing as I walk towards the sea, curling my toes into the sand with every step.

I'm less than twenty-four hours in and my family have already got completely under my skin. How on earth am I going to survive them for the rest of the week? I try to distract myself by enjoying the view. The beach is pretty much deserted at this time of the morning, although there are a couple of surfers already out on the water. The waves aren't particularly large to my untrained eye, but obviously big enough to make it worth their while being out there. I watch them for a little while as they paddle out, wait for a wave and then ride it back towards the shore. Maybe I should have some surfing lessons while I'm here, I think to myself. It would be a great way to get me away from my toxic family, and give me something other than them to focus on. I make a note to check out whether there are any surf schools here.

As I get close to the water's edge, my eye is drawn to a man standing a little way down the beach from me. He has a large black dog with him and is throwing what looks like a tennis ball into the water for it to fetch. It's obviously some sort of training exercise as much as a game, because the dog doesn't react immediately when he throws the ball. It sits patiently by his side until he gives it a command, at which point it rushes into the water, swimming out confidently and returning with the ball, which is the trigger for the game to begin again.

The last vestiges of an incoming wave wash over my feet, making me gasp from the sudden icy coldness of the water. By the time the next wave comes in, I'm prepared and, before long, I've rolled up my trouser legs so I can enjoy the sensation of the water bubbling around my feet and ankles as I paddle in the shallows.

'Beautiful morning for it, isn't it?' One of the surfers is carrying his board out of the sea. He doesn't sound local, but I can't place his accent. He's obviously been here for a while, because his face is tanned and his floppy blonde hair is bleached from the sun. He's got one of those faces which make it impossible to work out his age. He could be late twenties, but he could equally be mid-thirties. He keeps in shape, if the silhouette of his black wetsuit is anything to go by.

'Yes, very,' I reply. His eyes are the most extraordinary shade of blue. They're light, but the colour is intense. For a moment, I wonder if he's wearing contact lenses, but quickly realise he can't be, because the sea would have washed them out.

'It's going to be hot later,' he continues, as he unzips the top of his wetsuit to reveal his smooth, sculpted chest. I'm having to try very hard not to stare at it. He really is a beautiful physical specimen and, for a moment, the 'holiday fling' part of my brain lights up as I clock the lack of wedding ring on his left hand. Thankfully, the sensible part of me quickly shuts it back down again. Attractive as he is, he's probably staying in a camper van or a hut somewhere, and my days of sex in uncomfortable locations are long behind me. He also looks like exactly the type of person who would take full advantage of single women over the summer season. I can see it now: the declarations of love and promises to stay in touch and see where 'this' goes, only for the poor smitten girl to be forgotten and replaced with another the moment she's on her way home. However, I realise he might be able to help me with my surf school question, so I drag my eyes from his chest back up to his face.

'Have you been here long?' I ask him.

'A few weeks. You?'

'I arrived yesterday. Do you happen to know if there are any surf schools here?'

'There's one, but I think it's pretty busy. How long are you staying?'

'Just a week.'

'Shame. I don't think you'll get in there then. Most people book their place before they actually come.'

'Oh, right. Thank you.' I start to walk on but, after a couple of steps, I'm aware of him walking next to me.

'I could teach you, if you like,' he offers. 'I'm pretty sure I've got a wetsuit that would fit you back at my place, and I've got a beginner's board as well.'

'Oh yeah? And what would you want in return?' I ask with a smile. I know exactly where this is going.

'Nothing,' he replies. 'You could buy me a drink if you like. My name is Sam, by the way.'

'Poppy,' I reply. 'It's a lovely offer, but I think I'll have to pass.'

'Why? I'm a good teacher, I promise.'

'I'm sure you are, but I think we both know what you'd be looking to get out of it, and I'm not interested in a holiday fling.'

'Who said anything about holiday flings?' He's doing a good job of looking confused, but I can see straight through him. I stop walking and turn to face him.

'Look, Sam. Let's stop pretending, OK? I know your type.'

'Really? And what type might that be?'

'You're here to relax, get out on your board, maybe smoke some weed, and have plenty of casual sex, probably with women that you offer to teach to surf. That's fine, I'm not judging you at all. But it's not my thing. So thank you for the offer, but no.'

Despite the directness of my brush-off, he smiles, and I can't help noticing how white and even his teeth are.

'Fine,' he replies. 'Just so you know, it was a genuine offer without any of the strings attached that you've just described. I'll see you around, yeah?'

As he strides away, I can't help giggling. There's obviously something in the air here that either makes me irresistible to men or puts them all on heat. First there was Stuart's deeply unattractive proposition last night, and now this. I continue walking along the waterline for a while, enjoying the sensation of the water and the shifting sand against my feet as the waves come in and recede. I can feel the heat from the sun starting to build already, and a glance at my watch tells me it's not yet eight o'clock. Sam's right about one thing, at least: it is going to be a scorcher.

When I get back to the road, one glance down at my sand-encrusted feet is enough to convince me that putting my shoes back on isn't an option. I remember Mum making us all put our shoes on for the journey from the beach back to our holiday caravan when we were little, and the agony of having our feet effectively sandpapered as we walked. The sand used to get absolutely everywhere, too. Even though we'd hang our towels on the line to dry, Mum would shake them vigorously before bringing them in, and we'd bang our shoes together several times to empty all the sand out of them, it still found its way into the caravan. How the plughole in the shower didn't clog up from the amount of sand that went down there is a mystery. There would even be sand in the boot of the car when we got home. Thankfully, Mum isn't here, so I pad down the road barefoot. The tarmac is already warm where the sun has been shining on it, and it's a lovely contrast to the cold of the sea earlier.

By the time I get back to the house, my feet are pretty much dry and most of the sand has dropped off. I decide to have a quick explore of the garden before going in to shower. My arrival yesterday was so rushed that I never got the chance to look around out here last night. Like the house, the garden is fairly large, but the swimming pool takes me by surprise. I'm not sure why; on reflection it's obvious that a house like this would have a pool, even though it seems utterly pointless when the sea is so close by. I can't help noticing that the pool is pretty much the same shade of blue as Sam's eyes but, unlike him, it's an inviting prospect and part of me wants to plunge right in. It's surrounded by a large sun deck with chairs, umbrellas and loungers laid out. Whoever designed the garden obviously put a lot of thought into this area because, although it's in plain view of the house, there are walls on two sides that mean it's not possible for passers-by to see in. I plonk myself on one of the sun loungers and brush the remaining sand off my feet, before closing my eyes, turning my face to the sun and enjoying the warmth on my face. If the weather stays like this for the whole week and I get plenty of time by myself either down on the beach or sitting here, I think this trip could just about be bearable.

With my mood restored, I feel brave enough to go back inside and cope with my family. However, as I approach the bifold door to let myself back into the kitchen, I can see that I'm no longer the only one up. A solitary figure is sitting at the dining table.

It's Rose, and she doesn't look happy at all.

7

'Where have you been so early in the morning on a Sunday?' Rose demands, as I close and lock the door behind me.

'Not that it's any of your business, but I've been walking on the beach. Why?' I reply. I'm determined not to let her upset me again, but her tone of voice is a dangerous mix of sullen and aggressive, so it's impossible to predict which way she'll go. If she kicks off, I'll just go back to my room. I need a shower anyway, so I can use that as an excuse. After last night, I don't really want to spend any more time in her company than I absolutely have to.

'No need to be antsy, I was just asking. Everyone else is still asleep,' she tells me. 'God, I feel dreadful. How much did I have to drink last night?'

'You were putting it away, that's for sure. I expect Mum will want another word.'

I can almost hear her brain processing what I've said. It takes several seconds before she replies.

'What do you mean, "another word"?'

'Don't you remember? You had quite the row with her just before you went to bed.'

She groans. 'Shit, really? Were Dan's parents there? She's so keen to make a good impression, for Lily's sake. She'll be livid with me if we argued in front of them.'

She really can't remember how vile she was? That's too much to bear, and there's no way I'm letting her get away with it.

'No, they went after you dropped the Ceejay bomb and basically accused me of being a slut in front of everyone,' I tell her angrily. So much for not letting her upset me. 'Thanks for that,' I continue, my voice shaking with rage. 'I'm not sure what I did to deserve it, but you certainly ripped that particular wound wide open and poured a truckload of salt into it. I hope it was worth it, but I'm sure you'll understand that I'd rather be anywhere else than in your company right now.' The look of shock on her face leaves me completely unmoved. Too bad, you don't get a 'get out of jail free card' simply because you were too plastered to remember what you said.

'Poppy, wait!' she calls after me as I stride towards the hallway, but I don't turn back. She can stew.

My room feels like a refuge as I close the door behind me and walk over to the window to take deep breaths of the ozone-rich sea air. I'm shaking and tears are silently running down my cheeks. There are a few more people on the beach now and I focus on them, trying to bring back the feeling of calm and well-being that I had until my conversation with Rose just now. I take some comfort in the fact that I think I managed to make my point in a reasonably mature, adult manner, even if I don't feel particularly mature and adult right now. I remember the intensity of the fights we used to have when we were little. Nothing was off limits: hair-pulling, kicking, scratching and even biting on occasion. I feel the same rage towards her as I used to during those fights, but without the cathartic outlet.

When the shaking subsides enough that I feel reasonably steady on my feet, I strip off and step into the shower. I've never been more grateful for an en-suite bathroom; apart from meals, I could be completely self-contained up here and not have to spend much time with any of them. There's a balcony outside my room with a chair and a table on it, so I could always just sit there and read. I'd rather be by the pool or on the beach, but it's reassuring to know that there's somewhere I can be alone if I need it.

I stand under the shower for longer than normal, letting it wash away the tears, before wrapping myself in the predictably large and fluffy white towel and wandering out onto the balcony with my book. I've barely settled myself in the chair before there's a thunderous pounding on my bedroom door. With a sigh, I walk back into the bedroom. I'm not ready for another skirmish with Rose yet; I'll just tell her to go away.

'Who is it?' I call through the door.

'Are you awake?' my mother's voice answers. 'You need to get going. We're leaving for church in half an hour.'

'I'm sorry?'

'Church, Poppy. It was in Lily's email. Didn't you read it? The vicar is going to say some prayers for them, and we're all going.'

I open the door to find her fully dressed and ready to go.

'It said church was optional,' I tell her, and I'm embarrassed to note the petulant note in my voice.

'It is, technically, but what else are you going to be doing? We've got ground to make up with Dan's parents after last night, and a good showing at church is a step in the right direction. It'll cheer Lily up, too. Coming to church is the least you can do to make it up to her after you and Rose put on your little spectacle.'

'Surely you're not blaming me for that? She just went for me for no apparent reason. It was totally unprovoked!' With dismay, I realise that this is pretty much the same conversation I've had with my mother after every one of Rose's and my fights. It's official: I've regressed to being a teenager.

'Was it? Why did Stuart say that you'd leap into bed with him in return for a few petrol station roses if you're so innocent?'

'That's not what I said! He propositioned me, and I was trying to let him down gently by making light of it. Do you seriously think I would go to bed with him? I hardly know him, and he's thirteen years younger than me, for goodness' sake!'

'Why does Aunty Poppy need to go to bed with Stuart, Nanny? Hasn't he got a bed at his own house?' Mum and I have been so engrossed in our argument that we never noticed little Evie coming down the corridor.

'Good point, Evie,' I tell her, before Mum has a chance to say anything. 'See, Mum? There's no need for me to go to bed with Stuart, because he has a perfectly good bed at his house. I'm going to get dressed now, and I'll think about whether I want to come to church or not. OK?'

I close the door and lean against it. Once again, I'm sorely tempted to pack my bags and leave. I'm still deciding what to do when there's another knock at my door. Someone else coming to have a go, no doubt.

'*What*?' I explode as I fling open the door. I really am at the end of my tether.

'Sorry, Poppy. Is this a bad time?' Zoe asks. 'I was looking for a hairdryer because I stupidly forgot to pack mine.'

'Oh, right. Yes, of course you can borrow mine. Come in.'

I close the door quickly behind her, before grabbing the hairdryer out of my case and handing it to her.

'Bring it back when you're done, will you?' I ask her.

'No problem. I'll just dry it here, if that's all right with you. Are you OK? You seem a little rattled this morning, if you don't mind me saying.'

'It's just the usual. Rose got to me last night, and then Mum had a pop this morning. Honestly, Zo, I don't really know what I'm doing here. Nobody seems to want me. I was just wondering whether it would be easier all round if I went home and left you all to it.'

'Oh, Poppy. You know that's not true,' she says as she wraps her arms around me. 'Rose was bang out of order last night, and I'm going to tell her as much. As for your mum, she's just a bit uptight because she's so desperate for Dan's family to approve of us. You know what she's like.'

'I do, but it just seems like I haven't been able to do a single thing right since I got here. She basically accused me of coming on to Stuart, because I'm clearly some sort of nymphomaniac who throws herself at any single man, and now she's demanding that I come to church, presumably to atone for my slutty behaviour. It's like she's determined to make me into the bad person, no matter what I do. It's exhausting, and I don't really see why I need to put up with it. I'm thirty-three, for God's sake! I'm a bloody adult, with my own house and everything, but she somehow manages to turn me back into a child again.'

'I think she's a little bit insecure. She was just the same with my parents when they first met. In fact, that one was even more awkward, because I was pregnant and she and your dad felt they had to apologise for Andrew's behaviour, as if it was nothing to do with me.'

I can still remember that time. Zoe and Andrew had only just left university and started work when she discovered she was pregnant with Freddie. It's the only time I've ever known Mum to properly hit the roof with Andrew. She was convinced that they were too young to cope with a baby, even though she was exactly the same age as Zoe when she had Andrew. She was also horrified that Zoe would basically be parading around the evidence that she and Andrew were having sex once the pregnancy began to show, and tried to persuade them to have an abortion, but Zoe stood firm on that one and Andrew supported her. Zoe's parents offered to let them live at their house, but they pooled their resources and managed to rent a tiny house in Paddock Wood instead. The funniest thing was that my mother's attitude changed completely the moment Freddie was born. She was so proud of her first grand-child that you'd think she'd been in the room urging them on during his conception.

'Aren't you angry with her?' I ask. 'She was pretty hard on you both, from what I remember.'

'No. She just wanted what she thought was best for us at the time, and we were very young. It was difficult, and we had no idea whether we were mature enough to be parents, but I've never regretted having Freddie, not for a moment. And, on the plus side, having them so young means we'll still be relatively young when they hopefully leave home and give us our lives back. With any luck, they'll be gone by the time we're fifty, and then we can start checking into all those adult-only hotels that you see advertised on the TV.'

'You don't mean that,' I reply, with a grin. 'You'll be devastated when they go. You'll sit there, staring at Andrew, who will probably be fat and bald by then, wondering how on earth you're going to stand being alone with him without Freddie and Sarah to keep you sane.'

'Do you think?' she laughs. 'I'm not so sure. I can tidy the house until it's immaculate, but Freddie is like a hurricane. He literally only needs to be in a room for a minute and it looks like a bomb has gone off in there. And Sarah? She's fourteen going on twenty-four, that one. Honestly, she's got a comeback for everything. If you ever have a couple in therapy who think becoming parents will solve all their problems, you're welcome to borrow my children to show them how wrong they are.'

'Thanks, I'll remember that. So, what about this church thing? Are you and Andrew going?'

'Yes. Freddie and Sarah are coming too, although there was quite a lot of whining and sulking. It's not really my thing, but it means a lot to your mum, and I know Lily will be really pleased if we're all there. It's a small sacrifice to buy brownie points in case we need them later. Don't tell your mum, but we've promised the kids ice cream afterwards as a bribe.'

'Can I have ice cream if I come?'

'Absolutely! In fact, there's room in our car if you want to squeeze in with us. It'll save you having to find somewhere to park, and then we can all sneak off to the ice-cream shop afterwards. What do you think?'

'That would be brilliant, if you're sure you don't mind.'

'Of course I don't mind! You can sit in the middle between Freddie and Sarah, and stop them fighting.'

I narrow my eyes at her. 'Is this a stitch-up?'

Her gaze is steady as she answers. 'If it is, it's only a tiny one. They don't actually fight in the car that often any more. Don't expect much in the way of conversation, though. They'll be glued to their phones the whole way. I'll have to confiscate them before the service starts, otherwise the vicar's sermon is going to be punctuated by pinging.'

Zoe has really cheered me up, and I'm just about to tell her so when we're distracted by the muted sounds of a commotion coming from downstairs. I can hear my mother shouting and Rose yelling back. After a few moments, a door slams and someone thunders up the stairs, slamming another door behind them. Zoe turns to me and smiles.

'Looks like you're not the only one having a difficult morning,' she observes, as she turns on the hairdryer.

'Why is ice cream from the supermarket never as good as ice cream from a proper shop?' I ask, after I've groaned with pleasure at my first mouthful. I've got a scoop of vanilla and one of white chocolate, and they're both heavenly. Zoe practically herded us out of church at the end of the service before anyone could talk to us or invite us to stay for coffee, and we're now sitting in the ice-cream parlour digging in to our treats.

'There's a difference between gelato, which is what we're eating here, and ice cream that you'd buy in the supermarket,' Andrew replies. 'Gelato has less air whipped into it during the churning process and it's got a lower fat content, which intensifies the flavour and gives it a silkier texture. Ice cream has to be stored at a colder temperature to keep it firm.'

'How come you're such an expert on ice cream all of a sudden?' Zoe teases.

'It was one of the questions at your work Christmas quiz last year, don't you remember? Is there a difference between ice cream and gelato, or is gelato just the Italian word for ice cream? It niggled me, so I looked it up.'

Zoe turns to me. 'I've known your brother for over half my life now, and I still have no idea how his mind works sometimes.'

'I just like to understand things, that's all. There's nothing suspicious about it,' Andrew replies.

'I know. It's part of your charm,' she tells him as she pats his arm affectionately.

The church service wasn't actually too bad. As predicted, Lily was delighted that most of us came. Rose, Steve and their two girls were the only absentees: Rose flat out refused to come, and Steve said it would probably be too much for the girls and they'd only spend the entire time wriggling and fidgeting, so they stayed behind at the house. I had to stifle a giggle when the choir processed in at the beginning. I say 'processed', but it was more of a shuffle. Anita has to be the youngest chorister by at least twenty years. One of them was so ancient, I actually worried that he'd died during the sermon. Thankfully, it turned out he was just asleep, as his neighbour nudged him at the end to wake him up. I didn't know any of the hymns and, although they gave us books with the words of the service in them, they kept darting back and forth between different pages so I just gave up in the end, and stood and sat when everyone else did. Given that most of the congregation were probably well beyond retirement age, I was surprised to see that the vicar was probably under forty. He was certainly energetic, dashing up and down the aisle asking people questions during the sermon. I felt quite vulnerable as I was at the end of the pew, but he must have realised that I wasn't really into it and left me alone. He was very attentive to Dan and Lily, though, and the prayers he said for them were heartfelt. He was pretty easy on the eye too, which helped.

'I think we've done our duty for today,' Zoe continues, after a few more mouthfuls of gelato. 'What are everyone's plans for the afternoon?'

'I thought I might go back to the beach and make the most of this glorious weather,' I reply.

'It'll be busy,' she warns.

'I know, but I quite like that. It gives it a bit of a party atmosphere, and I can always dip in the sea if I get too hot.'

'Don't forget that we've got the official beach day tomorrow as well,' Andrew tells me.

'That's not a problem. I think I could happily spend the whole week on the beach. Do you guys want to come with me?'

'I will,' Sarah replies instantly.

'Yeah, I don't mind,' Freddie agrees.

'It looks like we're going to the beach this afternoon, then,' Zoe smiles. 'I think there are some folding chairs and umbrellas in the storage cupboard by the pool. We can take those down so we've got something to sit on. Sand has a nasty habit of getting into your bikini bottoms if you sit on the ground, and I don't fancy that. There are some parts of a woman's anatomy that don't mix well with sand.'

'God, Mum, you're so embarrassing!' Sarah complains.

'Who, me?' Zoe laughs. 'Shall I tell Aunty Poppy about the time you got sand in your bum crack when you were little, and you wouldn't stop crying until I'd washed it all out?'

Sarah looks like she wants the ground to open up and swallow her, which only makes Zoe laugh harder.

'I hate you sometimes,' Sarah mutters.

'Aww, no you don't,' Zoe replies, putting her arm around her. 'I'm just teasing.'

'What about you, Freddie? Any embarrassing beach stories?' I ask, trying to divert attention away from the furiously blushing Sarah.

I get no response. Freddie obviously thinks his contribution to the conversation is finished, as he's making workmanlike progress through the most enormous sundae I think I've ever seen while watching something on his phone.

'I think we need a game of table tennis after we get back from the beach, don't you, Poppy?' Andrew murmurs conspiratorially.

'We could probably squeeze in a couple before dinner,' I whisper back.

'I can hear you, you know. I'm sitting right here,' Zoe mock-admonishes us. 'I will allow one match. Any more than that usually results in you both getting uber-competitive, and then we'll never get you out of there.'

'Competitive? Us?' Andrew holds up his hands, trying to look innocent, but we both know she has us bang to rights.

* * *

'Where did you lot all scuttle off to?' Mum asks when we get back to the house. 'I turned around after the service and you'd vanished!'

'I'm sorry, Hazel,' Zoe replies. 'We would have stayed and chatted, but we felt we'd already used up our goodwill ration with Freddie and Sarah, so we thought it best if we didn't hang around.'

'At least you came, unlike some,' she sniffs. 'Rose is still sulking in her bedroom, and Steve and the girls are out by the pool.'

I know this makes me sound like an awful person, but I'm quite enjoying the fact that Rose is in the doghouse rather than me for once. It won't last, I know, but it's a nice change.

'We thought we might head to the beach this afternoon. Do you and Dad want to come?' I ask her, keen to maximise my advantage by making them feel included.

She considers for a few moments. 'It might be a bit too hot for us,' she replies. 'You young things go. Your dad and I will stay here in the cool. Besides, someone has to be around to let Dan's parents in.'

'OK, as long as you're sure.'

'I am, but thank you for asking.'

In the end, everyone apart from Rose, Mum and Dad decides to come to the beach. We locate the folding chairs and umbrellas that Zoe mentioned and pack bags with drinks, snacks for the children, beach towels and sunscreen before setting off. Zoe's prediction was right; the beach is pretty crowded, but we manage to find a space and set up our camp. Lily and Dan stretch out in the shade under one of the umbrellas while Zoe and I help Steve try to rub sun cream into Olivia and an extremely wriggly Evie. I can't help raising my eyebrows as, out of the corner of my eye, I glimpse Sarah stepping out of her T-shirt and shorts to reveal the skimpiest bikini I think I've ever seen.

'I know,' Zoe mutters. She's obviously seen my expression. 'She had a full-on meltdown about privacy when I walked into her bedroom without knocking a few weeks back. But this is different somehow. Go figure.'

Thankfully, Sarah seems oblivious to the amount of male attention she's picking up as she and Freddie rush down to the sea, diving straight in and squealing at the cold. Some of the men casually shifting position to keep her in view are probably older than me, and I've got half a mind to go and tell them they should be ashamed of themselves, leering at a fourteen-year-old. Sarah and Freddie are followed by Steve, Olivia and Evie at a slightly more sedate pace. They've got buckets and spades and it's not long before a sandcastle is well under way.

Having applied my own sunscreen with a little help from Zoe, who kindly did my back, I recline the chair as far as it will go and settle down to read. I'm about halfway through my novel, and it's just the tonic I need today. I'm feeling slightly more benign this afternoon than I was last night and this morning, so I've mentally downgraded my family from 'toxic' to 'difficult'. I'm definitely having a much easier time than the main character in my book, however, whose life is so chaotic I'm amazed she's able to function at all. After a couple of chapters, Freddie and Sarah reappear, their bodies glistening with water droplets. There's a bit of a skirmish where they try to drip water on their parents, completely ignoring their threats of dire retribution, and I can't help but smile. I'm sure this is a scene played out between parents and children on every beach around the world; it's practically a ritual. I remember Mum and Dad having it particularly bad, because there were four of us to torment them.

'Do you remember that time when you tipped a bucket of sea water over Mum when she was sleeping in the sun?' I ask Andrew.

'I'll never forget it!' he laughs. 'She went properly mental, didn't she?'

'It was a bit over the top, to be fair.'

'Yeah, you're probably right.'

Freddie and Sarah have flopped down on their towels like exhausted puppies and have picked their phones back up, but it's obvious they're listening to our conversation.

'Don't even think about it, you two,' Zoe warns them.

'What, us?' Freddie replies, trying to sound innocent. 'Sarah, shall we go and help Evie and Olivia with their sandcastle? It looks like they might need a hand bringing water up for the moat.'

'I mean it,' Zoe says.

'Yeah, yeah. Come on, Sarah.'

'We're doomed, you know that, don't you?' Andrew tells her, as Freddie and Sarah set off towards the spot where Steve, Olivia and Evie are still working on their very impressive sandcastle.

'Mm. Perhaps I should pre-empt them by taking a dip before they can get to me. You might want to come too, otherwise they'll just target you instead.'

'I'll come as well, if you don't mind,' I say.

The three of us wander down to the sea. The sand is hot under-
foot now, and the coolness of the water is a relief after the initial
shock. I take my time wading in; it really is cold and I gasp repeat-
edly as the water makes its way slowly up my body. By the time it's
up to my midriff, I can take it no more and plunge forwards. As I
turn on my back, I can see Zoe and Andrew are still in the shallows,
edging their way in.

'Go, Aunty Poppy!' Sarah yells in encouragement, as I roll onto
my front and start to swim away from the shore. I've always loved
swimming and my body goes into autopilot as I power through the
waves. Now that the initial shock is over, the sea is refreshing and I
feel energised by it. There are quite a few surfers out on the water
as well, so I check regularly to make sure I'm not straying out of the
area designated for swimmers. The last thing I need is to be
knocked unconscious by a surfboard. After a while, I stop and tread
water. I'm near the edge of the swimming area and have a good view
of the surfers. There are people of every ability here, and my eye is
drawn to one guy who is riding a wave and making it look no
harder than walking down the street. It takes me a moment or two
to realise that it's sleazy Sam from this morning. Not far behind him
is another surfer. She also has blonde hair and evidently knows her
way around a surfboard. When they reach the shore, they hop off
their boards and high-five each other before turning around to
paddle back out to sea. I've got to hand it to him; he's a fast mover. I
only hope the poor girl knows what she's letting herself in for. She
looks much younger than him, not that he appears to have any
qualms about that.

I'm starting to shiver, so a leisurely breaststroke takes me back
to the shallows. Evie and Olivia appear to have completed their
sandcastle and are taking turns running down to the sea to fill
buckets of water for the moat. Steve is keeping an eye on them

while collecting shells for them to decorate the castle with. Andrew, Zoe, Freddie and Sarah are splashing around in the shallows.

'That's quite a sandcastle, girls. Well done!' I tell Evie and Olivia, after admiring their work for a while.

'Thank you,' Olivia replies, solemnly. 'Daddy says he's going to take a picture of it on his phone to show Mummy. Mummy isn't feeling very well, so hopefully it will cheer her up.'

'I'm sure it will,' I reassure her.

I'm just about to set off back to my reclining chair and my book when Sam and his companion walk out of the sea, clutching their boards. She's definitely a lot younger than him, and I feel suddenly protective towards her, for some reason. Maybe she's naïve and doesn't realise what he's up to. I decide, probably against my better judgement, to intercept them.

'Hello, Sam,' I say when I get close to him. He stops and studies me for a minute before recognition dawns.

'Poppy, isn't it?' he replies as the young woman stops next to him, also eyeing me curiously.

'That's right. From this morning. You hit on me, remember? Although I see you've moved on already. Are you going to introduce me to your new friend?'

I'm expecting him to look embarrassed, or annoyed, but instead he bursts out laughing.

'I'd be delighted!' he tells me. 'Jessie, this is Poppy. I met her on the beach this morning. She was asking about surfing lessons and I offered to teach her, but I think she took that as some sort of come-on. Poppy, this is my daughter, Jessie.'

9

His *daughter*? I'm mortified, and I can feel the flush of embarrassment flooding across my cheeks. Now that I look at her again, the family resemblance between Jessie and Sam is obvious. Apart from her blonde hair, she also has the same piercing blue eyes.

'I'm so sorry,' I stammer. 'I saw you together and assumed—'

'Don't sweat it,' she reassures me. 'So, Dad offered to teach you to surf, did he?'

'You know what that surf school is like; you have to book months in advance for a summer slot. So, when Poppy asked, I offered,' Sam tells her before turning to me. 'I was a little surprised by your reaction, I have to admit.'

'If you want to learn, you should definitely let Dad teach you,' Jessie enthuses. 'He's a really good instructor. He taught me, so I should know.'

'I don't think I can, after all the awful assumptions I made!' My nervousness makes me laugh. 'I really am sorry, Sam.'

'It's fine, honestly. I was a little taken aback, but I can see why you thought I was coming on to you. If it's any help, I can assure you that I don't make a habit of offering to teach random strangers to surf, my weed-smoking days are long behind me, and Jessie here would have plenty to say if I were being even remotely disrespectful to a woman, single or otherwise!'

'You're probably the first woman apart from me and Mum that he's spoken to in years,' Jessie explains. 'You need to work on your chat-up lines, Dad.'

Jessie's mention of her mother suddenly makes me feel uneasy again. Maybe I misread the lack of a wedding ring this morning. I'm tempted to take Sam up on his offer, to make up for my earlier rudeness if nothing else, but I don't want to cause any marital strife. Some women are fiercely possessive of their men and, if Jessie's mum is one of them, she won't be at all happy about Sam spending time with me, even if we are in plain view all the time.

'What would your mum think about your dad teaching me?'

'Oh, she's not here,' Jessie replies, matter-of-factly. 'She and Dad split up years ago, when I was tiny, and she's happily married to someone else. So I don't think she's likely to have any opinions about it, beyond being pleased that he might make a new friend.'

'I'm not sure which is worse,' Sam interjects. 'Poppy deciding that I'm some sort of sexual predator, or your description of me as a sad, lonely old fart who needs to make some friends!'

'Dad's a spy, so he can't form meaningful relationships in case the person he falls for works for a foreign superpower,' Jessie tells me, conspiratorially.

'Behave, Jessie. She only says that because she thinks my actual job is so boring it must be a cover.'

I'm intrigued. 'What do you really do, then?'

'I'm a data scientist.' Sam obviously spots my nonplussed expression. 'I work on data models that we feed into machine-learning algorithms, and then interpret the results.'

'See? Told you. Obviously a spy,' Jessie retorts, and I can't help smiling. She can't be more than seventeen or eighteen, but she has the self-confidence of someone much older. The way the gentle banter is flowing between them shows me that they're evidently incredibly close, and I feel a slight pang of envy. I'd love to have that sort of relationship with my parents.

'So, would you like me to teach you? The offer is still there if you want it,' Sam says to me.

'Do you know what? I'd love that,' I reply.

'Great. I'll be working during the day, so it'll either have to be early morning or after I finish. What suits you?'

'Mornings would probably be better. I'm here with my family, so I probably ought to spend some time with them in the evenings.'

Now it's Sam's turn to look uncertain, and it takes me a moment to twig what the problem is.

'When I say my family, I mean parents, brother and sisters, not husband and children.'

His face clears, 'Ah, OK. So, half past six tomorrow?'

'If you're really sure.'

'Yes, it's no problem at all. I'd be out here anyway.'

'Great, I'll see you in the morning. Are you coming as well, Jessie?'

'Not likely!' she replies. 'I don't like to get up at silly o'clock when I'm on holiday. I'm only here for a couple more days, so I intend to make the most of my final lie-ins.'

Now that I've realised he's harmless, I'm looking forward to spending more time with Sam. If he's half the teacher Jessie makes him out to be, it should be fun. As I walk back to my chair, I briefly imagine him catching me in his strong arms when I fall off, and holding me as I gaze into those blue, blue eyes.

'Who are your new friends?' Zoe thankfully interrupts my train of thought before it tips over into fantasy. 'He's quite the specimen, I noticed. Shame about the girlfriend.'

'His name is Sam,' I tell her. 'I met him on the beach this morning and he offered to teach me to surf. I thought he was coming on to me, so I was quite rude to him, but it turns out he's a really nice guy. The "girlfriend" is actually his daughter.'

'You're kidding!' Zoe turns her eyes back to where Sam and Jessie are unzipping their wetsuits. 'He can't be older than, what, thirty? And I'd say she looks older than Freddie, so he must have been about twelve when she was born. And we thought we were young. Bloody hell.'

I follow her gaze and realise she's right. Either he's hiding his true age incredibly well, or there's a story there. Sam's torso out of the wetsuit is even more distracting than it was this morning, and I force myself to look away.

'It's just surfing, Poppy,' I mutter to myself.

* * *

By the time we get back to the house, Dan's parents have arrived with Stuart. They're all sitting on the sun deck around the pool, and my heart rate quickens slightly when I notice that Rose is with them. I've had such a lovely afternoon that I really don't want another fight now. I can't avoid her for the rest of the week, though, so one of us is going to have to make the first move. I'm not ready to forgive her yet, and she's looking determinedly at everyone except me, so it looks like the standoff is set to continue for a while. Fine, I'll just chat with everyone else until she grows up and admits what she's done.

'How was the beach?' Dan's father asks. 'You all look like you've caught the sun.'

'It was busy, but we managed to find a spot,' Lily replies as we start to put the chairs and umbrellas back in the cupboard.

'We made a sandcastle,' Evie tells him proudly. 'And Freddie and Sarah helped us to put water in the moat.'

'Daddy took a picture of it,' Olivia adds. 'Show Mummy what we made, Daddy.'

Steve fiddles with his phone and then hands it to Rose.

'Very nice, girls,' she tells them, after examining the photos. 'Well done.' I can't help noticing her lacklustre tone, but thankfully Olivia and Evie are oblivious and start wittering away happily to their mother about the various details of the sandcastle. I can tell from her glazed expression that she's not listening to a word they're saying.

'Are you feeling better, Mummy?' Evie asks, once they've run out of steam.

'Yes, thank you darling. Mummy just had a bit of an upset tummy earlier.'

'Is that what we're calling hangovers now?' Freddie murmurs, just loud enough for everyone to hear. Rose shoots him a filthy look, and Zoe places a warning hand on his arm.

'It's such a lovely evening, we thought we'd have a barbecue,' Dan's father announces. 'Anita and I have raided the supermarket for burgers, sausages and kebabs. We've got hotdog buns, burger buns, all manner of sauces and various salads. How does that sound?'

Uh-oh. In my experience, barbecues are universally disastrous. What usually happens is that the men congregate around the barbecue, drinking beer, prodding the coals and offering 'helpful' advice to whoever is nominally in charge, when in reality none of them have the first idea how to cook anything and all the food is either burned to a cinder or raw in the middle.

'That sounds lovely, Richard,' my mother enthuses. Hopefully he hasn't picked up her overly bright tone, which is exactly the same one she used to use when we came home from primary school brandishing our latest hideous masterpiece from art class.

'I don't mean to be difficult, but did you happen to pick up something vegetarian for Sarah?' Zoe asks.

Richard's face falls. 'I'm so sorry. We completely forgot. I'll run down to the store by the beach and see if they're still open and have anything.'

'Don't worry. I think we've got some veggie sausages in the fridge,' Zoe replies. 'Let me know when you need them and I'll get them for you.'

'Thank you. Shall we aim to eat at about seven?' Richard asks. Mentally, I gear myself up to eat nearer nine, after we've taken pity on the men and taken the food inside to cook in the oven. I'll have to watch how much I have to drink, as I could get into serious trouble if I'm drinking on an empty stomach for too long. I can't afford a hangover like Rose's if I'm to be bright-eyed and bushy-tailed for my first surfing lesson tomorrow, and I certainly don't want a repeat of last night, with me as the drunken embarrassment this time. I don't think Mum would be able to take us disgracing ourselves in front of Dan's parents again. A glance at my watch tells me that I have an hour and a half to kill before Richard thinks dinner will be ready.

'I think I'm going to go and have a shower. Wash the sun cream and sand off. I'll see you all a bit later.'

'That's an excellent idea,' Zoe remarks. 'We'll do that too. Freddie, Sarah, put your phones down and go and shower please.'

'Let me know when you're done,' Steve says to them. 'The girls could probably do with a bath as well, so we'll come in after you.'

When I get to my room, I close the door and breathe deeply. A whole hour and a half of peace and quiet stretches before me, and I'm tempted to sink down onto the bed immediately for a luxurious doze. I can still feel some residual sand between my toes though, and the last thing I need is sand in the bed, so I strip off and head for the shower. I'm not sure how well the house's plumbing system is going to cope with so many people needing hot water at the same time, but it turns out I have nothing to worry about. At home, I have to make sure the washing machine is off and the loo isn't refilling before I step into the shower, otherwise I'm alternately boiled and frozen as the pressure changes. Here, it's just one constant temperature and pressure, and I take my time, enjoying the sensation of the jets on my scalp and skin.

When I'm done, I dry myself, wrap a towel around my wet hair and another around my body and head out to the balcony again with my book. Hopefully, unlike this morning, I'll actually get some peace to read it. The heat is beginning to go out of the day now, although it's still comfortably warm. The beach is also starting to empty, as people head home for their evening meals. My mind turns back to Sam, and I scan the houses that I can see, wondering if he and Jessie are in any of them. He is very nice to look at, but I tell myself sternly that I really don't need the emotional complication of a holiday romance. I've been there before, and it's very nice while it lasts, but heartbreaking when it ends.

* * *

After a few chapters, I get up and wander back inside to get dressed. I'm just about to go downstairs to find Andrew so we can begin our table tennis match, when there's a tentative knock at my door. As soon as I open it, I realise that the table tennis is probably going to have to wait for another day.

'Come in,' I say to Rose, as she steps over the threshold.

I close the door behind her, and for a moment, there's an awkward silence. I wait for her to speak; I'm not going to make this easy for her.

'Poppy, I'm so sorry for what I said last night,' she begins. 'I honestly didn't remember it this morning, so I couldn't work out why you were so angry with me. I was a bit pissed off with you, if I'm honest, but Zoe has just filled me in, and I'm mortified.'

'It was really cruel, Rose. You know how difficult that time was for me, and I've worked so hard to move on from it and leave it in the past. When you said what you did, it was like I was straight back there, with everyone laughing at me and making jokes about me. Why did you do it? Have I upset you in some way?'

'God, no! Look, I really am sorry. I'm just in a shitty place at the moment, I had way too much to drink, and you know as well as I do that I'm not a nice drunk, so I guess I just lashed out at you. You didn't deserve it, and I feel really bad about it, if that's any consolation.'

'You've never been a good drunk,' I tell her. 'Do you remember the time when you came home from Tania's party, and you were absolutely slaughtered?'

'Was that the time I told Mum I wanted a party like Tania's, accused her of being an evil bitch when she said no, and then vomited all over the carpet?'

'That's the one.'

'I was grounded for weeks after that,' she smiles. 'I'd probably be grounded now if Mum reckoned she could get away with it. I really am sorry, Poppy.'

She's so contrite that I can't stay angry at her. We may have fought like cat and dog for most of our lives but, when we did declare a truce, we always somehow believed that it would last this time. Today would appear to be no different.

'I forgive you,' I tell her. 'Don't ever do it again, OK?' I reach out and draw her into a hug.

As we stand there, with our arms around each other, I become aware that she's shaking. Very gently, I detach myself a little from her, and I'm surprised to see tears pouring down her cheeks. I draw her back in and just hold her while she lets it out. I feel slightly awkward – this is the most physical contact I've had with her in years – but she obviously needs this as she's clinging on to me. Eventually, the sobs begin to subside and she loosens her grip on me.

'Do you want to tell me what's going on?' I ask her.

'It's Steve,' she says baldly. 'He's having an affair.'

10

'Bloody hell, Rose. No wonder you're in a state. How did you find out?'

'Oh, it's all the usual things. The first clue was when he started coming home late. I assumed he was working, but I needed to ask him something so I called his office phone one evening and got no reply. When he got home, I asked him where he'd been and he lied and told me he'd been at work.'

'Did you confront him?'

'No. I thought maybe there was an innocent explanation at first. But it keeps happening. He's also been incredibly distant recently, like he's distracted by something. The girls have noticed it too. It's like he's checked out of our family. Presumably because he's spending all his time thinking about *her*.'

'Are you sure it's not just a mid-life crisis?'

'He's thirty-nine! It's hardly middle age, is it?'

'No, but men can be funny about these things. As soon as they start to feel they're getting older, they panic.'

'It doesn't explain him coming home late so often, though, does it? Also...' she tails off, evidently embarrassed about what she was about to reveal.

'Come on, get it all off your chest.'

'Well, things have never been particularly fiery in the bedroom,' she confides, 'but lately he's completely lost interest. I wondered if it was my fault, if I should be trying to make more of an effort, so I tried. I even bought some of that horrible scratchy lacy underwear, but he just said he was tired and went to sleep.'

'Has he been having any difficulty getting or maintaining an erection? Sometimes, if men are depressed—'

'I don't need you sex therapising me, OK?' she interrupts. 'That's not what this is. He's not depressed, he's up to something.'

'Fine. What about his phone?'

'What about it?'

'Quite often, when men are having an affair, they suddenly become very possessive about their phones. They might put a passcode on it for the first time, or they never leave it anywhere, because there are incriminating messages and so on. Does that sound familiar?'

'No. He's pretty relaxed about the phone, actually. You saw how he just handed it to me earlier.'

'And is that his only mobile? He doesn't have another one for work, for example?'

'He's a financial controller at a garden centre company, not a high-flying executive!' She thinks for a moment and I can see from her facial expression that the seed of an idea is taking root before she continues. 'I guess he could have a second phone, what do they call it?'

'A burner phone.'

'Yeah, one of those. If he has, then he's doing a brilliant job of hiding it. Maybe he keeps it at work.'

'OK, before you go all Miss Marple on me, remember that this is all speculation at the moment. Have you asked him anything at all about how he is?'

'Of course not! I already told you that. What would I say? He'd probably just deny everything and tell me I'm imagining things. It's tearing me apart, though, Poppy. I can't sleep at night, because I keep trying to imagine who she might be and what she looks like. Is she someone from work? What does *she* have that I don't? And then there are the girls to consider. What if I confronted him, he admitted it and then left me to be with her? I'm not cut out to be a single mother.'

'You can't carry on like this, Rose. It sounds like it's already affecting your mental health.'

'I know. It's worse being here, because I see Lily and Dan all loved-up and then there's me, alternating between wanting to do whatever it takes to stop Steve from leaving me and wanting to smash his face in.'

'Somehow or other,' I tell her firmly, 'we're going to find out what's going on, and we're going to do it this week. I admit that he's acting a little strangely from what you've described, but there's still every possibility that this is a mid-life crisis and nothing more.'

'Even if it's a mid-life crisis, it doesn't mean he's not having an affair. He could be seeing some pert twenty-something who reminds him of his youth, rather than drab old me.'

'You're not old or drab, and it doesn't mean he is having an affair either. Innocent until proven guilty, remember?'

'That's easy for you to say. You're not the one being cheated on.'

'I still think there might be another explanation. Can you think of anything you can do this week, short of confronting him, that might shed some light? You can't spend the whole week tying yourself up in knots. It's not good for you and, as we discovered last night, it's not good for the rest of us either.'

'I said I was sorry, don't labour the point. I'll think about it, but it doesn't seem very likely, does it? He's hardly going to be sneaking off to meet her here, unless she's come too and is staying close by...'

'Listen to yourself. You're starting to sound like a madwoman. He'd be much more likely to be texting or sneaking off to call her, if she exists.'

'You're right. Maybe the burner phone is here somewhere. I just have to find it.'

'That is something you could do but maybe try to give him the benefit of the doubt as well.'

She sighs. 'Thanks for listening, Poppy, and I really am sorry about lashing out at you last night. It does feel a bit better, now that I've told someone.'

'Good. Now, why don't we go downstairs and see what's happening with this barbecue? I have low expectations.'

'Oh yes, me too,' she replies, and I'm relieved to hear that her voice is a lot brighter. 'Steve used to insist on having them and inviting the neighbours round, and I always had to take the meat inside and cook it in the oven. I don't get the attraction at all.'

'I think it's a caveman thing. Staring into the fire and all that. It makes them feel all masculine, as if it's some magnificent beast that they've hunted and are cooking over an open fire, rather than a few manky sausages.'

* * *

When we get downstairs, I'm surprised to see that the barbecue is completely unattended and the lid is closed. It's obviously alight because I can see smoke snaking out from underneath the lid, but nobody is paying it the slightest attention. Given that it's now twenty minutes to seven, I think my prediction that dinner is going to be considerably delayed is probably accurate.

'Table tennis?' I ask Andrew.

'Absolutely! Lead the way,' he replies.

'I'd better come too, to supervise you,' Zoe adds.

By the time we begin our first game, a small crowd of spectators has gathered. Zoe has appointed herself the referee, but Lily, Dan, Sarah, Freddie and Stuart have also come to watch. By the end of game three, Andrew is ahead by two games to one, and there have already been a couple of disagreements over the rules. Andrew was adamant that the serve had to go into the opposite quadrant, like in tennis, and tried to claim a point when one of my serves didn't do that. Freddie immediately Googled the answer, and the point came to me because, not only was I right, but Andrew hadn't returned it as he thought it was a foul serve.

By the end of game four, we're level again. Lily, Dan and Stuart have wandered off, but Freddie and Sarah are cheering their father on. I'm just about to serve for the first point of the deciding game when we hear my mother calling us to dinner.

'You're kidding me!' I exclaim to Andrew.

'We can play the decider afterwards,' he offers.

'Not bloody likely! You're just trying to take advantage, because you know I'll have a couple of glasses of wine to help the charred food go down.'

'I'll be drinking too,' he offers.

'No. This is far too serious. If I lose to you after dinner, I'll always wonder whether it was because of the alcohol. We'll have to play the decider tomorrow.'

'You two really need to lighten up,' Zoe says. 'It's only a game.'

'And you knew what you were letting yourself in for when you offered to referee!' Andrew counters.

Zoe sighs. 'You're right. Come on, let's go and eat.'

To my surprise, the food actually looks OK. The burgers are still recognisable, rather than the charred discs I'm used to, and the sausages have an even brown tinge. The salads look good too.

There's a potato salad, some coleslaw and the obligatory green salad.

'Help yourselves!' Dan's father booms.

'Hang on, Richard. We haven't said grace yet,' Anita reminds him.

'Oh yes! Sorry. Thank you Lord for this food, and may nobody get food poisoning. Amen,' he intones.

'This is amazing!' I tell him, after I've tried a few bites of a burger, cut into the sausage and discreetly tested the centre with my tongue to see if it's hot. 'What's your secret, Richard?'

'No secret,' he smiles. 'Keep the lid closed and leave the damned thing alone. If you have the lid open, you've only got direct heat from the coals and nothing cooks properly, particularly if you keep fiddling with it and turning the food over. If you close the lid, it's more like an oven so everything cooks through properly. Plus, you keep the smoke inside, which gives a better flavour.'

'Richard loves to cook,' Anita explains to me. 'He says he finds it therapeutic. When he first started, we had to have a couple of difficult conversations about not leaving the kitchen looking like a bomb site, but he's much better now.'

'Lucky you,' my mother replies. 'I let Bill cook once, when I was ill. It was only soup from a carton, so hardly haute cuisine. He managed to burn the bottom of the pan so badly that, not only was the soup inedible; I had to throw the pan away!'

'It's a fair cop,' my dad answers good-naturedly. 'I got distracted by an article in the paper, and completely forgot about it until I smelt burning.'

'Dan's a brilliant cook,' Lily boasts. 'What was that dish you made me the other week? The salmon one.'

'Salmon en croûte,' Dan answers. 'I served it with dauphinoise potatoes and creamed spinach.'

'That does sound impressive,' Anita says to him, with a smile. 'Was it Waitrose?'

'Shut up, Mum. It might have been,' he replies, blushing.

'It was still delicious,' Lily comforts him.

As we eat, I can't help watching Steve for signs of shiftiness, but I can't see any. To be fair, I don't know him that well, but he seems a perfectly ordinary, genuine guy. He's always been quiet in family situations like this, but he's attentive to his children and is also making sure that Rose's glass is kept topped up. Thankfully, she's drinking a lot more slowly tonight, so hopefully there won't be any repetition of last night's episode. I can see Mum is also watching her like a hawk, pursing her lips in distaste every time Rose accepts more wine.

As soon as we've finished the main course, Richard and Anita bring out the puddings. They're definitely going to be a hard act to follow, as there's a fresh fruit salad and an Eton mess, as well as ice lollies for those who don't fancy either of them. I hope this week isn't going to turn into some sort of competitive cook-off, otherwise the bar is going to be impossibly high by the time it's my turn on Wednesday. Incredibly, despite the size of the puddings, they are completely devoured, and I smile as Evie and Olivia attack the Eton mess bowl with their fingers, determined not to let a single morsel go to waste.

Darkness is beginning to fall as Zoe and Andrew start to carry plates and glasses into the kitchen to clear up. Most of the rest of the group head inside, but I decide to stay out a little longer and enjoy the cool evening air. Rose announced to Steve that she was going to put the girls to bed; I suspect she's going to take the opportunity to go through his stuff and see if she can find the burner phone she's now convinced he has. I wish I'd never mentioned it, but I will try to help her get to the bottom of whatever's going on. I have to admit, having watched him this evening, that I'm struggling to see Steve as the type of person who would be unfaithful. I'm just telling myself off for being so ridiculously unprofessional, that I know perfectly well there isn't a cheating 'type', when I become aware that I'm not alone.

'I've come to get a drink,' Stuart tells me, indicating the bottles still stacked next to the barbecue. 'Would you like a top-up?'

I glance at my glass, slightly surprised to find it empty. 'Yes, that would be lovely, thanks, Stuart.'

When he returns with the full glasses, instead of going back inside to join the others, he plonks himself down on the sun lounger next to me.

'Sorry if I caused a problem between you and your sister last night,' he says. 'I was only trying to be funny.'

'Don't worry about it,' I tell him. 'She'd had a bit to drink, and she always gets aggressive when she drinks.'

'I've been doing some thinking, though, and I'm afraid you do have to sleep with me,' he grins.

Not this again. 'How have you figured that one out?' I ask him.

'Simple,' he replies. 'I'm the best man, and you're the only one of the bridesmaids here who isn't under age or already attached in some way.'

'Nice try, but I'm not going to sleep with you to fulfil some ridiculous cliché.'

'Fair enough. It was worth a go. You're missing out, though. My ex-girlfriend had an orgasm every time. What do you say to that?'

I know I ought to shut this conversation down, but I'm intrigued.

'Really? That's quite the achievement. What's your secret, beside your incredible recovery time?'

'Lots of positions. Women love a bit of variety. Finish up with doggy style, which is my favourite. Are you sure you aren't tempted? A bit of the old Stuart magic?'

'Quite sure,' I smile. 'So, let me get this straight. Your formula is based entirely on penetrative sex, with regular changes of position, is that right?'

'Yup.'

I desperately want to laugh, but I force myself to keep a straight face. 'I have some bad news for you, Stuart. I think she may have been faking it.'

'I don't think so,' he says belligerently. 'What makes you say that?'

'Basic mechanics,' I reply. 'Have you got a pen?'

'I think I saw a biro in the kitchen.'

'Right. This is a vagina,' I tell him a few moments later when he's retrieved the biro and I've done a basic sketch on one of the leftover napkins. 'This is the opening here, where your penis goes, and this up here is the clitoris, which is the main female pleasure centre.'

'I know how female anatomy works,' he says, but I notice the cockiness has gone out of his voice.

'Good. So, in order for a woman to stand a chance of having an orgasm, can we agree that there needs to be some stimulation of the clitoris? There are a lot of other factors involved, but that's probably one of the most important ones.'

'What's your point?'

'My point is that most penetrative sex positions do nothing for the clitoris, because all the action is here,' I jab the biro at the opening, 'and not here.' I colour in the clitoris to emphasise. 'Doggy style is one of the worst positions, because there is no clitoral stimulation at all. Furthermore, you flipping her over like a burger to change positions every couple of minutes is going to interrupt the flow and stop her pleasure building. It might be fun for you and help you last longer, but I doubt it's doing anything for your partner. Imagine you're pushing a car uphill. If you stop and let go of it for a few seconds, what is going to happen?'

'It'll start to roll back.' He's looking quite deflated now, and I'm starting to feel a bit sorry for him.

'That's what changing positions does. It's the sexual equivalent of letting the car roll back down the hill. Do you see?'

'What are you two whispering about out here?' Mum enquires suspiciously, as she marches out of the kitchen. She'll see if I try to conceal the napkin now, so I leave it where it is and brace myself for the inevitable explosion when she spots the drawing.

'Nothing, we were just chatting,' Stuart tells her. He's trying to sound innocent, but the flush in his cheeks tells a very different story.

She picks up the napkin and examines it for a moment.

'What is this?' she asks, turning it around and looking at the drawing from several angles. 'It looks a bit like an avocado, but you've put the stone too far down and it's much too pointy.'

'That's exactly what it is,' I tell her, seizing my lifeline. 'Well done. Stuart couldn't work it out at all.'

'I'm not surprised,' she observes, putting the napkin back down on the table. 'It's a terrible drawing. Give me the pen.'

I watch with a mixture of horror and amusement as she carefully draws a much more recognisable avocado next to my vagina diagram.

'There,' she announces. 'Art was never really your thing, was it, Poppy? Anyway, fun as your little game of Pictionary is, I just came out to tell you that your parents are about to leave, Stuart.'

As she wanders back inside, I catch Stuart's eye and we both snort with laughter.

11

'Right, the first thing we need to do is get you used to the balance of the board,' Sam tells me.

'How come my board is so much bigger than yours?' I ask. Whereas his looks compact and manageable, the board he's brought for me is enormous.

'Believe it or not, that's a beginner's board,' he explains. 'It is larger, but that makes it more buoyant and stable.'

I don't have any option but to believe him, but I'm pretty sure the surfboard is longer than the *Titanic* and I'm already starting to wonder if this whole learning to surf thing is going to turn out to be one of my not-so-good ideas. When I was getting ready this morning, I realised I had absolutely no idea what people wore under wetsuits and hadn't thought to ask Sam. I did a bit of internet research and discovered that my options were either to wear nothing (umm, no thanks) or a one-piece swimsuit, which is what I opted for. Thankfully, Sam seemed to approve, but then just getting into the damned wetsuit proved to be quite the challenge. I'm borrowing Jessie's as we're both roughly the same size, and it fits very snugly, but it took quite a long time wriggling and shoving to get me into it, and I suspect I'll find out how reptiles feel shedding their skins when I have to try to get the bloody thing off again.

'OK, so the first thing we need to do is attach the leg rope to you. If you fall off, which you will, it basically stops the board from floating away.' He takes a piece of rope that's attached to the board and wraps the Velcro strip at the end of it around my ankle. 'How does that feel?'

'Fine, I think.'

'Good. I've waxed the board for you already, so I just need to take you through a couple of safety protocols before we hit the water.'

'Waxed it? Won't that make it really slippery?'

'The opposite. It makes it much easier for your feet to grip – not that I think we'll have you on your feet today. We're going to start off getting you confident paddling the board, and then we'll look at how to catch a wave with you lying on the board. Does that make sense?'

'Not yet, but hopefully it will.'

Sam laughs. 'By the time I'm finished with you, it'll all make perfect sense, don't worry.'

He shows me how to protect my head if I fall off, so the board can't ram me and knock me unconscious, and then we head out into the water.

'Umm, Sam?' I say, as we start to wade out. 'I don't think this wetsuit is working. I can feel cold water coming in.'

'It's supposed to do that,' he smiles. 'Don't worry. It will feel cold for a short while, and then the wetsuit will trap a thin layer of water against your body, and you'll be warm again.'

'Really? I thought the whole point was to keep the water out.'

'Then it would be a drysuit, not a wetsuit.'

'Oh.'

Once the water is deep enough, Sam helps me to lie on the

board and shows me the effects of being either too far forward or too far back. We practice this for a while, until I'm comfortable that I can get on the board in the right place each time.

'Right, let's see if we can get you catching a wave,' he says, after we've worked our way up and down the beach a few times, with me getting onto the board and paddling. He leads me out until the water is up to my waist.

'This ought to do it,' he tells me.

'But the beach is literally feet away!' I exclaim. 'As soon as I catch the wave, it'll be over.'

'Trust me, this is where you want to be to begin with. See how the waves have broken? That makes them easier to catch.'

He explains to me about how to catch the wave by pointing the surfboard at the beach and paddling as it comes up behind me. An hour later, I'm exhausted but I have caught a couple and belly-ridden them in on the board. It's a lot harder than it looks, that's for sure, but Sam is very patient and I do feel like I've made some progress.

'I reckon that's enough for this morning, don't you?' he says to me, after I successfully catch my third wave and ride it to the beach. 'You've done really well. Have you enjoyed it?'

'I think so. I wasn't prepared for how difficult it would be to catch the wave,' I reply. 'I suspect my arms are going to ache from all the paddling.'

'They might do, but it should be short-lived.' We're walking up the beach with the boards and Sam is unzipping his wetsuit, which is incredibly distracting once again. 'Do you fancy some breakfast before I start work? I reckon you've earned it.'

I'm about to make my excuses and head back home, but the physical exertion and the sense of achievement have made me hungry, and the idea of breakfast with Sam sounds much more appealing than going home.

'Sure, why not? I think the café is open. I just need to get out of this and into some clothes.' I unzip my own wetsuit and start trying to wriggle out of it while Sam watches with a smile.

'There's a technique. Here, let me show you.'

He helps me to get the suit off my shoulders and remove my arms, and then rolls it down over my waist and thighs. Even though he's being careful so that he's only touching the suit, it feels incredibly intimate, and I'm conscious of my heartbeat picking up and my mind secretly willing his hands to slip, so I can feel them against my skin. I give myself a stern mental talking to, but it's not really going anywhere. My body, deprived of male attention for so many years, is threatening to rebel against all the rational things my mind is trying to tell it.

'There you are,' he says, once he's rolled the suit past my knees. 'You should be able to use your hands to push it off now. Make sure you point your toes, that will make it go over your feet more easily.' His eyes meet mine and something melts inside me. *For God's sake, Poppy, get your hormones under control.*

'So, café?' I ask, when I've dried myself and put on my shorts and T-shirt. The dampness from my costume is already seeping through, but there's nothing I can do about that until I get back to the house and change. At least I'm decent, and the shape of the damp patch clearly indicates that it's a swimsuit and not a bladder accident.

'We could do, but I'm thinking of something a bit healthier. Are you happy coming back to mine? Jessie will probably be up by now, so we won't be alone.'

I know he's trying to reassure me, but part of me is a bit disappointed. Now that I know how to remove a wetsuit, I wouldn't mind helping him with his. What on earth is the matter with me? An hour and a half in the sea, and I'm having almost pornographic thoughts about a man I barely know. It must be some sort of allergic reaction to the salt water, I tell myself. I glance sideways at him as we amble along the road; he really is very easy on the eye and the idea of a holiday fling is starting to feel more and more appealing, even though I know I'd pay for it dearly in emotional heartache next week.

Sam's house is nowhere near as large or grand as ours, but then it's only him and Jessie living in it, so it doesn't need to be. It's nice, though, less showy and rather more homey than ours. Jessie has obviously only just got up, because her long hair is at the dishevelled end of 'tousled' and she's sitting on the sofa in the sitting room in short pyjamas with her legs tucked up against her, sipping a mug of coffee.

'Morning, Dad. How was— oh!' she exclaims when she sees me following behind her father. For a moment, I wonder if she's going to be upset about me invading their privacy, but her face breaks out into a huge grin.

'I invited Poppy to have breakfast with us before I start work. You don't mind, do you?' Sam asks her.

'Mind? Of course not!'

'Great. I'm just going to jump in the shower and then I'll get breakfast on. Can you get Poppy a tea or coffee, or whatever she likes to drink please?'

Thankfully, even though she's just woken up, Jessie is excellent company and keeps my mind from wandering and imagining what is going on the other side of the wall. I learn that she's just finished school and is starting a psychology degree at Durham University in the autumn. She asks me about my family, and I'm explaining how we're here for Lily's wedding and glossing over some of the family dynamics when Sam reappears, freshly showered, smelling faintly of aftershave and wearing a white T-shirt over jeans. I can't help watching the muscles on his arms moving as he sets about preparing breakfast.

'Is this your house?' I ask him, as he cuts sourdough bread to put under the grill, mashes avocados and heats the water for poached eggs.

'No!' he laughs. 'I live in Swindon, about half a mile from where I grew up. However, one of the best things about my job is that I can literally do it from anywhere with a half-decent internet connection. So, I rent this house for a month every summer and surf before and after work. Jessie usually comes for a week or two, so I take that time off, and it all works pretty well.'

'Have you never been tempted to move down here permanently?'

'I've thought about it, but I'm not sure whether I'd want to live here full-time. I love it for the month I'm here, but it's probably a lot less fun in the middle of winter. Plus, I've been tied to Swindon up until now, because that's where Jessie and her mum live and I couldn't have been far away from her. Now that she's all grown up and heading off to university, I might start looking around, though. Swindon isn't where I see myself long-term. I wouldn't mind being closer to the sea but not as far away as here. Dorset, maybe, or somewhere like that. Anyway, breakfast is only a couple of minutes away so, if you need the loo, now would be a good time to go.' He aims this remark at Jessie.

'Dad gets annoyed because I usually decide I need a wee just as he's announced that a meal is ready, so this is his latest thing,' Jessie smiles.

'Actually, I could do with using the loo as well,' I admit.

'Poppy can use my bathroom,' Sam tells Jessie. 'Can you show her where it is while I deal with the eggs?'

Jessie leads me into Sam's bedroom and shows me the door into the en-suite. I can't help glancing at the bed as I go, and my mind instantly starts filling with images of the things that Sam and I could get up to in it. The en-suite smells of shower gel and Sam's spicy, woody aftershave, which doesn't help my raging hormones.

'You have got to pull yourself together and stop this, Poppy,' I firmly tell my reflection in the mirror as I'm washing my hands after using the loo. 'He's teaching you to surf and being friendly. Nothing more, OK?'

Confident that I've regained my composure, I walk back to the living area and take my seat at the table.

'Wow. This is delicious, Sam,' I tell him, as I take my first mouthfuls of toast, avocado and egg. He's poached the eggs perfectly, with firm whites giving way to rich, runny yolks.

'He's always been a brilliant cook,' Jessie tells me. 'He probably uses food to soften up enemy agents. Who knows how many secrets he's prised out of people, simply from a well-made hollandaise, eh? To be fair, I'd be more inclined to spill the beans if I were tied up and Dad were force-feeding me something yummy rather than all that shining a light in your eyes stuff you see on TV.'

Sam rolls his eyes at his daughter before turning to me.

'Do you see what I have to put up with?' he smiles. 'I'm glad you like my cooking, Jessie, but it's honestly just breakfast. After this, I'm going to do my very ordinary day job, and nobody is tying anyone up, force-feeding them or pumping them for information, OK?'

Shame. That sounded like a lot of fun to me.

12

'Creeping in first thing in the morning again!' Rose remarks, as I let myself into the kitchen through the bifold doors. 'You're going to get a reputation at this rate.' She obviously realises that her remark is unfortunate, given the whole Ceejay debacle earlier in the week, and has the grace to look a little embarrassed. I decide to let it pass; she doesn't mean anything malicious this time, I reassure myself.

'It's not first thing in the morning, and I'm hardly creeping!' I retort good-naturedly. 'I've been having a surfing lesson.'

'If you say so,' she replies, smiling and turning her attention back to her cereal.

'Morning, Poppy,' Zoe says as she wanders into the kitchen from the other end. 'How was the surf lesson? Did you fall in the sea and have to be rescued by the handsome blond hunk?' She heads for the fridge, singing 'Summer Nights' from *Grease* under her breath, although I notice that she's modified the lyrics so they go, 'I saved her life. She nearly drowned/He showed off, surfing around.'

'I can hear you, you know,' I tell her. 'And that's not how the song goes.'

'It does now,' she smiles. 'Perhaps I'll rename you Sandy for the rest of the week, after Olivia Newton-John's character in the film.'

'What on earth are you two going on about?' Mum has now joined us and, in typical form, thrust herself into the conversation.

'Nothing, Hazel,' Zoe replies, grinning widely at me as she dobs me in. 'Just that Poppy's started having early morning "surfing lessons" with a *very* attractive man.' She actually does the air quotes, and I start casting around for things to throw at her.

'Have you, indeed?' Mum eyes me sceptically. 'I hope this is a strictly *professional* arrangement.' She emphasises the word 'professional' and raises one eyebrow as she speaks, to let me know that she's firing a warning at me. 'You know what men are like. I'd hate to think you were being taken advantage of.'

'It's fine, Mum. I'm thirty-three; I think I can look after myself. Anyway, he's here with his daughter, so we're chaperoned, OK?'

'Hmm.' She looks far from convinced, but has obviously decided to let the matter drop for now.

'Who's looking forward to another be-yewdiful day on the beeeeaaach?' Lily trills, as she sashays into the kitchen in a pair of short pyjamas that remind me a bit of Jessie's. It's weird to think that Jessie is actually five years younger than Lily; I know I don't know her nearly as well as my sister,, but she seems more mature somehow. Lily can be surprisingly babyish at times, probably because Mum still mollycoddles her to death, even though she's supposed to be a fully functioning adult. Marriage is going to be a rude awakening for her in a lot of ways. I watch as she saunters over to the fridge, opens it and proceeds to stare gormlessly into it, presumably in the vague hope that it will recommend something suitable to her for her breakfast.

'I think your father and I will probably stay here again, darling,' Mum tells her, and I note that there's none of the reproachfulness in her tone that there is when she's speaking to me. 'It's going to be another hot day, and your father gets terrible heat rashes.'

'Don't drag me into this!' Dad exclaims. Typically of my father, he's managed to enter the room without anyone noticing. 'I can think of nothing better than to spend the day building sandcastles with my flower girls.'

That's a phrase I haven't heard for a while. When we were growing up, Dad always used to refer to us as his 'flower girls', on account of us all being named after flowers. Andrew used to think it was hysterical and bullied us remorselessly about it. We decided he was just jealous that he wasn't in our club, and teased him back just as hard.

'I think we're probably a bit old for that now, Dad,' Rose informs him. 'I'm sure Olivia and Evie would like it, though, if you're in the mood.'

'Don't come running to me when you're hot and irritable and itching from head to foot,' my mother warns him, and I notice she's pouting with disapproval again.

'If I start to get hot, I'll just take a dip in the sea to cool down again. Come on, Hazel. I'll bring the umbrellas so we've got shade. We're supposed to be spending time together as a family this week, aren't we? There won't be much of that if we're stuck up here while everyone else is down there.'

'Fine,' she huffs. 'We'll come to the beach as well. But no funny business from you lot, OK? That goes for your children too, Zoe and Rose. I don't want to be splashed, dripped on or covered with sand, do you understand?'

Zoe and Rose look at each other and raise their eyebrows. 'Fine,' they chorus in unison.

'Right. Now that's settled, what does everyone want for breakfast?' Mum continues, barging Lily out of the way and rummaging around in the fridge. 'We've got bacon, eggs, yoghurt...'

'I'm OK thanks, Mum,' I tell her. 'I've already had breakfast.' Out of the corner of my eye, I can see Zoe's eyes widen until they look like they're about to pop out of her head, so I flee before she can say anything.

* * *

Once I reach the safety of my room, I slip out of my damp shorts, T-shirt and swimming costume and head for the shower. As I wash, I reflect on the events of the morning. Yes, the surfing was fun and I could feel that I was making progress. Sam is a good teacher; Jessie was completely right about that. But I think I probably enjoyed the breakfast even more, sitting and chatting with him and Jessie. I've got to face facts, though: I'm ludicrously attracted to Sam, and that's a problem. The memory of him easing the wetsuit over my hips causes my stomach to fizz in a way that I haven't felt for years, and I find myself fantasising about the feel of his hands on my body, and his lips on mine. At the same time, my rational brain (what's left of it) is telling me not to fool myself into thinking I can compartmentalise this into a holiday fling and leave it behind when I go home. For some reason, I'm suddenly reminded of one of my psychology lecturers talking about the id, ego and superego when we were studying Freud. She told us that the id, which represents our basic urges, was effectively like a gorilla in the basement of a house; the superego, which represents our moral conscience, was a demanding maiden aunt in the attic; and the ego (the realistic part that mediates between the other two) was an exhausted bank clerk running up and down the stairs between them, trying to keep them both pacified. My fantasies here are definitely id-driven, and I fear that the demanding aunt (who for some reason always had my mother's face when I imagined her) may be going to lose out here. It's like those cartoons, where a character has an angel sitting on one shoulder and a devil on the other, both giving conflicting advice.

In the end, the superego wins out by pointing out that nothing can happen because Jessie is there. I'll just have to enjoy Sam from afar as a guilty pleasure. It's probably for the best. Although didn't Jessie say she was going home soon? I'll have to make sure I get over this ridiculous crush before she leaves, somehow, otherwise the gorilla in the basement might escape and run amok.

I've just finished dressing in a fresh pair of shorts and T-shirt, with a bikini underneath ready for the beach, when there's a firm knock at the door.

'Come out. I know you're in there,' Andrew calls sternly.

'What's got into you?' I ask, after I've opened the door to him.

'Don't play the innocent with me,' he growls. 'You've made a commitment, and I'm here to make sure you don't back out.'

I stare at him blankly. I literally have no idea what he's talking about. He must sense that I'm not following him, as his expression softens a bit.

'Table tennis, idiot,' he tells me. 'We've got a match to decide.'

'Are you serious? I've just got back from my first surfing lesson, and I can already feel my shoulders tightening up. Can't we do it later?'

'Absolutely not! You promised that we'd play the decider today. It's not my fault you've gone out and deliberately handicapped yourself, is it? In fact, I'm doing you a favour, because you'll probably be worse later.'

I sigh. 'Fine. Give me a couple of minutes to dry my hair and brush my teeth, and I'll be with you.'

When I get downstairs, Andrew and Freddie are already at the table tennis table, knocking the ball back and forth between them.

'Unfair!' I cry. 'You're having a warm-up session.'

'Nonsense,' he replies. 'For all you know, I've just used up all my best shots on Freddie here.'

'I'm not getting involved,' Freddie states, placing his bat on the table. 'You two are seriously mental, you know that?'

Unsurprisingly, the game goes decisively in Andrew's favour, and he revels in his victory, dancing round the room bellowing 'We Are the Champions' horrendously out of tune. Freddie Mercury must be spinning in his grave, poor man.

'I'll get you next time,' I tell him.

'I don't think so,' he gloats. 'You've lost your killer instinct, that's your problem. All that sitting around in your treatment room empathising with people has made you soft.'

* * *

Andrew is still full of himself an hour later, when everyone is finally ready and we set off for the beach. Dan has texted to say that he will meet us there, along with his parents and Stuart.

'Do knock it off,' Zoe tells him as he swaggers down the road, still humming the Queen tune. 'Nobody likes a bad winner. At least Poppy is being gracious in defeat.'

'Yeah, well, she should be,' he sniggers. 'She gets enough practice!'

'Enough, Andrew,' my mother barks, catching us both by surprise. 'You're thirty-eight, not thirteen.'

'That's not fair,' he whines. 'Poppy would be crowing just as much if she'd won.'

'And I'd be telling her off exactly the same,' my mother replies. 'If you two can't play that damned game nicely, I'm not going to let you play it at all.'

Now it's my turn to snigger.

'And you can cut that out as well,' she tells me. 'Stop winding each other up.'

Thankfully, Mum is soon distracted by other things once we get to the beach and set up the chairs and umbrellas. My poor father is slathered in such a thick layer of sun cream that he looks as if he's been smeared with lard before he's allowed to step out into the sunshine, and she dollops a similar amount over her face, legs and arms before settling in the shade of the umbrella with a magazine. I hope they've brought plenty of bottles with them because they're going to get through it at quite a rate if they keep plastering it on like that. The rest of us apply it rather more sparingly before the different family groups split up much as they did yesterday. Lily and Dan recline their chairs to soak up the sunshine, Zoe and Andrew follow Freddie and Sarah down to the water, and Steve goes off to help Olivia and Evie build another sandcastle. After a few minutes, Dad announces that he'd like to be part of it too, and follows them down to the water's edge.

'How are you feeling this morning?' I ask Rose, once I've checked that Mum is buried in her magazine and unlikely to be eavesdropping.

'Still shit,' she replies. 'Ever since you mentioned it, I'm convinced he must have a burner phone somewhere but whenever I try to look for it, he's there. I need an hour or so alone, so I can go through all his pockets, check his socks, make sure his shaving foam canister doesn't have a hidden compartment, all that sort of thing.'

'He might not have a burner phone. Innocent until proven guilty, remember?' I'm really regretting saying anything about the possibility to Rose; she's fixating on it in an unhealthy way.

'Yeah, I've thought about that. It doesn't work in a marriage. In a marriage, there's no smoke without fire. He's guilty until proven innocent.'

'And how can he prove his innocence? If you're convinced he's clever enough to modify a can of shaving foam to hide a phone, when will you ever be satisfied that you've covered every base and searched every possible hiding place? Look at him, Rose. He's happily playing with his children and it doesn't look to me like he has a care in the world, let alone some enormous secret that he's hiding from you.'

'Something's going on, Poppy. I know it is, and I can't rest until I've uncovered it.'

'So what are you going to do?'

'I think the sun is going to give me a headache. I think I'm going to have to go back to the house soon. He'll offer to come too, but I'll tell him he needs to stay here and look after the girls. When I get back there, I'm going to go through every item of clothing, every pocket of every bag, and I'm even going to search the car. I'm going to find that bloody phone, and then I'll have the smoking gun to confront him with.'

'And if you don't find it?'

'I will.'

13

Sure enough, after an hour or so of staring vacantly at the same page in her book, Rose announces that she has a headache and is going back to the house. As predicted, Steve offers to go with her, but she tells him she just needs to lie down in the cool for a while. She's a good actor, I'll give her that.

Dan, his parents and Stuart arrive late morning, and I'm amused to see Stuart wearing a pair of highly reflective aviator-style sunglasses.

'Nice pair of perving shades,' I remark, as he sets up a chair next to me.

'I don't know what you mean!' he replies, looking slightly embarrassed.

'Of course you don't,' I goad him. 'You didn't choose them deliberately so you could check out the female talent on the beach without being spotted at all, did you?'

'You really think I'm that much of a cliché?'

'Let's see. You've hit on me every evening that I've been here so far, including suggesting that I have to sleep with you because I'm a bridesmaid and you're the best man. Yeah, I'd say you were pretty clichéd.'

'Whatever. I'm going to go for a swim. Do you want to come, or would you rather stay here and draw me another avocado?' he whispers, so my mother can't hear.

'I'm fine here for the time being, thank you mister orgasm-every-time and ready again in ten minutes,' I reply equally quietly. 'Go and enjoy yourself.'

I watch him as he saunters down to the sea. Unlike Freddie and Sarah, who rushed in a straight line, his path is more meandering and seems to involve passing nearly every female sunbather on his way. Subtle, he is not. When he reaches the sea, I lower my gaze back to my book, occasionally glancing up to see what the other members of my family are doing. Lily and Dan have gone into the water to cool off and have a bit of a canoodle if the proximity of their heads is anything to go by. Sarah and Freddie have returned from their swim and are stretched out in the sun to dry. Steve, Olivia and Evie are splashing around in the shallows. Everyone else is either reading or chatting quietly.

Shortly after midday, Mum announces that she's going to go back to the house and make sandwiches for everybody. She looks pointedly at me as she says this, so I'm left in no doubt that I'm expected to volunteer to help. Anita and Zoe also offer, so I pull on my shorts and follow them. If nothing else, it will give me an opportunity to check how Rose is getting on.

The cool of the house is a stark contrast to the warmth outside, and it takes us all a moment before our eyes adjust to the comparative gloom of the hallway. As we make our way into the kitchen, Mum and Anita happily chatting wedding stuff, I catch sight of Rose sitting at the table.

'Oh, hello love,' Mum says to her. 'How are you feeling?'

'A bit better, thanks,' Rose replies. 'I think the sun and the heat

caught me by surprise a bit. I've taken some painkillers, so hopefully I'll be able to come back down after lunch.'

'I think that would be a good idea. Those girls are running poor
Steve ragged,' Mum tells her, before diverting her attention to the
fridge and bringing out packets of ham, blocks of cheese and
various other bits and pieces.

'Did you find anything?' I whisper to Rose, once I'm sure that
the others are far enough away.

'Not a thing. I went through all his clothes, his suitcases, his
shoes, even his washbag. Every place I could think of to look, I
looked. The car came up blank as well. I can't think where he's
hiding it.'

'It probably doesn't exist. Maybe there's another reason for his
behaviour.'

'I'd love to believe you, but I can't. I'm sure he's having an affair.
There's no other explanation that fits.'

'OK, well let me know if there's anything you need me to do.' I give
her shoulder a squeeze and go to do my part in the kitchen. The more
I watch Steve, the less convinced I am that Rose is right, but it's their
marriage and maybe she sees things that I don't. Mum and Anita have
set up a sort of production line, and it's not long before we've made a
mountain of ham, cheese and pickle sandwiches, remembering to do
one without ham for Sarah. Mum pulls various soft drinks and non-
alcoholic beers out of the fridge, as well as a selection of fruit, and we
pack it all into cool boxes before setting off to re-join the others.

After lunch, I pick my book back up and turn on to my front to
let the sun warm my shoulders. The exertions of the morning are
starting to take their toll and they're a bit sore, so hopefully the heat
will help.

'I want to go back in the sea,' Evie whines, somewhere to my
right.

'Not yet, Evie,' Rose tells her. 'You need to wait twenty minutes after eating, otherwise you might get cramp.'

I can't help smiling. We used to have the exact same conversations when we were little. To date, I've never found any evidence that going swimming immediately after eating does give you cramp, but the folklore persists nonetheless.

'But I'm bored,' Evie persists.

'Read your book. It won't kill you to read for a bit.'

'Reading's boring,' Olivia joins in.

'Come and sit with me for a minute, girls,' I tell them, flipping back over and sitting up. 'I'll play a game with you.'

Evie is by my side in an instant, but Olivia takes her time, eyeing me warily as if this might be some sort of trap. As soon as their backs are turned on her, Rose mouths 'thank you' at me, and suggests to Steve that they go for a wander around the beach together. I suspect she's planning to gently grill him and see if she can get him to give anything away.

'What's the game?' Evie asks excitedly.

'I hope it isn't anything babyish or dumb,' Olivia adds, obviously keen to emphasise that she's two years older than her sister.

'What you have to do', I tell them, 'is look around the beach and find a family. Without pointing, you have to tell the rest of us which family you've chosen. So, for example, you could use a clock face. Twelve o'clock is straight in front, six o'clock is behind and so on, do you understand?'

'Yes,' they chorus.

'So, when you've found your family, you then have to tell us a story about them. Who they are, where they've come from and whether they're having a nice time or not. You can use different voices for the different people in the family if you like. Shall I go first, so you get the idea?'

They both nod. Evie is already scanning the beach for her family, but I can see Olivia isn't hooked yet.

'OK,' I say, after looking around for a few seconds, 'ten o'clock, under the red and white stripy umbrella. A man, a woman and two older children. Got them?'

It takes Evie a moment to work out where ten o'clock is. 'Do you mean them?' she asks.

'No pointing, Evie!' Olivia hisses.

'That's the one. So the mother is actually a princess from a magical kingdom and, when she was born, everybody marvelled at how beautiful she was.'

'She doesn't look that beautiful to me,' Olivia observes. 'She looks kind of mean and grumpy.'

'There's a reason for that,' I tell her. 'Let me finish. As I said, everyone thought she was the most beautiful princess ever and her parents, the king and queen, boasted that she was the most beautiful girl that had ever lived.'

'Uh-oh,' Olivia interrupts again. 'That never ends well.'

'You're right, Olivia. The queen's sister was jealous, because she also had a daughter, and nobody had ever commented on how beautiful she was.'

'Was she beautiful?' Evie asks.

'No. I'm afraid she wasn't. So the queen's sister was jealous and cast a spell on the child. On the princess's tenth birthday, the king and queen threw a big party for her but, when it was time for the party to start, nobody could find her.'

'Where was she?' Evie is totally immersed in the story.

'She'd been spirited out of the kingdom, stripped of her magical powers and transformed into a perfectly ordinary ten-year-old girl, being brought up in our world by a perfectly ordinary couple called Brian and Marjorie.'

'That doesn't sound too bad,' Olivia counters. 'She could have been sent to sleep for a hundred years like Sleeping Beauty, or turned into a toad or something.'

'Here's the thing,' I reply. 'Most of the time, she doesn't remember that she was a beautiful princess, but once a year, on her birthday, she has a dream where she remembers, and she sees her frantic parents searching the castle for her. And that's why she looks grumpy. It was her birthday yesterday.'

'And what about her husband?' Evie asks, staring at the family. 'Is he really a prince in disguise?'

'No, he's an ordinary man called David and he works in a bank.'

'What happened to the king and queen?'

'Oh, they died of broken hearts and the queen's sister took over the kingdom. But everybody hated her and there was a big war where everyone was killed.'

'That's a terrible ending!' Olivia exclaims. 'You need a happy ending, not everyone dying.'

'Why don't you see if you can do any better, then?' I challenge her.

After a couple of false starts, they really get into it, with ever more outrageous suggestions and ideas. At one point, Olivia invents a highly elaborate pirate story involving a couple of surfers and some buried treasure being guarded by a pair of elderly pensioners snoozing under an umbrella, which has us all laughing.

'You look like you're having fun,' Rose observes as she and Steve return from their walk. Rose is trying to sound jolly, but failing, and Steve looks confused, so I guess she didn't find anything out. 'I was going to suggest that you can go back in the water now, but perhaps you'd rather stay here with Aunty Poppy!'

'No!' they chorus.

'We want to swim,' Evie tells her. 'Aunty Poppy can come with us.'

Rose laughs. 'I think you've made a rod for your own back there, Poppy,' she tells me, before turning back to her girls.

'Mummy will come with you. Aunty Poppy probably needs a rest.'

'It's fine. I could do with cooling off anyway,' I tell her, so the four of us make our way down to the water. Olivia and Evie are filling Rose in on the game, but I can tell she's not really paying attention. I can't help noticing the dynamics between the two girls; Olivia is definitely the dominant child, and Evie is very much in her shadow. It's been fun spending time with them, even if I do feel a little drained.

My plan to abandon them for a swim quickly unravels, as it turns out I'm the girls' new favourite person, so I resign myself to paddling around in the shallows with them for a while, before hopefully detaching myself and maybe having a proper swim later. At least it gives me the opportunity to watch the surfers, studying their techniques now that I know a little bit more about it. It doesn't take me long to spot Jessie, and I'm filled with admiration as she makes it look so effortless. After a while, she spots me too and waves, before riding a wave in and coming over.

'Hi Poppy, how are the shoulders?' she asks.

'A bit sore, but I'll live,' I reply. 'This is my sister Rose, and her two daughters, Olivia and Evie.'

'Hi, I'm Jessie,' she tells them. The girls are staring at her as if she's some sort of magical mermaid. She'd have made a brilliant subject for one of our stories, I realise.

'Jessie's father, Sam, is the one who's teaching me to surf,' I explain to Rose, who is obviously struggling to work out what my relationship to this complete stranger is.

'Dad'll be down in a bit,' Jessie informs me. 'I'm about to head back to the house. Would you like me to ask him to bring down the board so you can have another go? I'm done for the day, so you can use my wetsuit again if you like.'

'I'm not sure,' I tell her. 'I had a hard enough job getting into it this morning, and that was when it was dry. I'll never get into it now it's wet!'

'There's a knack,' she tells me. 'As long as you're also wet, it'll go on fine.'

'Really?'

'Trust me. I've been around wetsuits since I was little, so I know.'

'OK, thank you. Why not?'

Sure enough, an hour or so later, Sam appears with Jessie by his side. He's wearing his wetsuit but she's changed into shorts and a bikini top, and is carrying hers. Sam is also carrying the *Titanic*-sized board for me. I'm very aware of Mum, Rose, Zoe and Lily all watching carefully as they come over and I stand to greet them.

'Mum, this is Sam and his daughter Jessie,' I tell her, before she can make any caustic remarks. 'Sam is teaching me to surf. Sam, this is my mother.'

'Pleased to meet you, Poppy's mother.' Sam smiles at her, offering his hand to shake.

'Poppy told me she was having lessons,' Mum replies, a little frostily. 'I assume you're a qualified instructor?'

'As a matter of fact, I am,' he replies smoothly. 'Although I don't instruct professionally any more. I'm teaching Poppy purely for fun.'

'Are you?' she replies, and there's no doubting the suspicion in her voice.

'Shall we get started, then?' I suggest quickly, before my mother can interrogate Sam any further about his intentions towards me, which she clearly still believes are dishonourable.

Ten minutes later, after I've wrestled my way into the wetsuit with a bit of help from Jessie, Sam and I are on the water again. It's safe to say that, although Sam didn't manage to completely charm my mother, Stuart is completely enchanted by Jessie. He may be wearing his pervy glasses, but there is no doubt that his eyes are out on stalks behind them. He's managed to persuade her to occupy my chair, next to him but, if her bored facial expression is anything to go by, I'm not sure she shares his enthusiasm.

Despite being very aware of my family watching, I do manage to catch a few waves, and they're gracious enough to give me a little round of applause when Sam and I emerge from the sea. Jessie helps me back out of the wetsuit, which is probably just as well as I'm sure Mum would spot the hormonal meltdown that I'd have if Sam did it.

'It's my last night,' she tells me as I push the wetsuit legs over my feet. 'I was talking to Dad earlier, and I asked if I could invite you round for a drink.'

This sounds suspiciously like she's trying to set me up, and I'm not sure what to do. If she's giving her tacit blessing for me to take things further with Sam then that's a big green light but, tempting as he is, I'm still just about rational enough to know a relationship with him will not be good for me. Also, what if he's not interested? I may be harbouring the biggest crush I've had for years, but he's not given me any indication that he feels the same way. It might all end in embarrassing humiliation for me, and that would be even worse than the inevitable heartache of a fling.

'I'd love to, but I'm eating with my family at seven, so there probably isn't time,' I say, trying to let her down gently.

'You could come afterwards,' she smiles.

'Wouldn't you rather spend your last evening with your dad?'

'I've just spent the whole week with him!'

'You're not going to take no for an answer, are you?'

'I wasn't planning to.'

'Fine,' I concede. 'I'll see you at nine.'

'Perfect,' she beams. 'We'll look forward to it.'

I must be losing my touch. Unless I'm very much mistaken, I've just been expertly outmanoeuvred by an eighteen-year-old. I'd happily lay money that she will decide that she's tired and needs to go to bed while my glass is still full enough that I can't escape, leaving me and Sam alone.

14

'Who *was* that guy on the beach?' Jessie asks, once we've all got glasses of wine and have sat down. Jessie has bagged the only armchair, so Sam and I are sharing the two-seater sofa, which I'm sure she's engineered deliberately, and I'm very aware of the closeness of him. It's delicious and absolute torture all at the same time. Despite the cool of the evening, he's wearing shorts and his thigh is so close to mine I can almost feel the heat of it through my thin summer dress.

'That's Stuart, my soon-to-be brother-in-law,' I reply. 'His brother is marrying my sister on Saturday.'

'Do you like him?'

'I don't really know him,' I tell her. 'I only met him for the first time on Saturday. He's a bit immature, I suppose, but harmless enough. Why?'

'I thought he was a creep. Sorry!' she laughs as Sam's eyebrows shoot up. 'I know he's about to join your family and everything, Poppy, but I'd barely sat down before he started coming on to me. It wasn't quite as cheesy as "what's a girl with a nice face like yours doing in a place like this", but it really wasn't far off.'

'Oh no, really?'

'Yeah. As soon as he found out I was about to start uni, he started bragging about his experiences and telling me how much better I'd find it if he "took me under his wing". I'm not sure how he figured that was going to work, given that he's not even at the same university as me. Then he told me how a lot of the second and third-year students refer to freshers' week as "fuck a fresher" week, but he'd come and protect me if we were together.'

'Jessie, I'm so sorry.'

'Don't worry about it. I'm a big girl; I can handle myself.'

'What did you do?'

'I thanked him and told him that my boyfriend already had my back. That shut him up.'

'What boyfriend?' Sam asks. 'This is a new development.'

'Relax, Dad. You know as well as I do that I'm not seeing anyone at the moment, but he doesn't need to know that, does he?'

'I suspect that his swagger is all bravado, with nothing to back it up,' I tell them. 'He's come on to me a couple of times as well, so we're either his two dream women or he's so desperate he'd chat up a dustbin if it was wearing a skirt.'

Jessie giggles and puts on a Disney-style French accent. 'You are looking very beautiful tonight Mademoiselle Dust-been. What is zat 'eavenly perfume you are wearing? Eau de Poubelle, you say? It suits your *personalité* perfectly. And your eyes, zey are like stars. I want to cover your beautiful *plastique* body with *petits bisous*.'

'Someone used that line on me once,' Sam tells us, after we've finished laughing.

'Used what line?' Jessie asks.

'What's a boy with a nice face like yours doing in a place like this,' he replies.

'No! Who was it? Was it Mum?'

'No. I was with your mum at the time, though. She was pregnant with you, and we'd had to go to London for something – I forget what. Anyway, as soon as we got to Paddington to catch our train home, she decided she needed the loo and rushed off. I think you must have been pressing on her bladder, as she seemed to need the loo every five minutes back then. Anyway, I was standing around, staring at the departure boards and trying to work out which platform our train was leaving from, when this old guy came up to me and gave me that line.'

'What did you do?'

'I was so shocked, I didn't really know what to do. I said the first thing that came into my head.'

'Which was?'

'I'm waiting for a train.'

'A perfectly reasonable response, given where you were,' I reassure him, after we've finished laughing.

'So, what happened next?' Jessie presses. She's obviously never heard this story before, and is sitting on the edge of her seat.

'He started telling me how he'd been in the military, how he'd been bullied because of who he was, and then he asked me to go to the gents with him.'

'Ugh.'

'Thankfully, your mother chose that moment to reappear, which obviously confused him. He'd clearly been hoping to snag a lone teenage boy, so the heavily pregnant girl in the mix completely threw him. I've never been so pleased to see your mother. I was still shaking when we got on the train.'

I sense my opportunity. 'So, if you don't mind me asking, how old were you at the time?'

'Seventeen,' Sam replies.

'I'm the child that wasn't supposed to be,' Jessie cuts in, picking up my unasked question. 'A disastrous mistake by two love-struck adolescents, who only made it into the world because my mother didn't discover she was pregnant until it was too late to do anything about it.'

I don't know what surprises me more: the baldness of Jessie's words, or the fact that she says them completely without rancour. Jessie obviously senses my discomfort, as she smiles and continues.

'Don't get me wrong, I'm not complaining. I've grown up with as much love as any child, probably more, in a lot of ways. But you don't have to be Einstein to look at how old Mum and Dad were and work out the story.'

'Although I don't like the way she tells it, Louise and I have always been honest with Jessie. As she says, she'd have worked it out anyway, and I think she'd only have resented us if we'd tried to sugar-coat it.'

'How would you tell the story?' I ask him.

'Jessie's mum, Louise, and I were both sixteen when she got pregnant; we'd been going out for a while and were in love. We were always careful, but the condom came off one time. Louise went to get the morning-after pill and we didn't think any more about it. We had exams and stuff to focus on, so it was a few months before she realised that she hadn't had a period. Yes, she'd put on a bit of weight, but we thought that was probably because of all the late-night snacks while she was revising. When we found out she was pregnant, her parents tried to haul her off to get an abortion, but the scan at the clinic showed she was over six months gone, so that was out of the question.'

'What happened next?'

'I did what I thought was the right thing and stood by her. She moved into my bedroom – she was so far along there wasn't time to do much else. My parents weren't exactly delighted, but her dad was absolutely livid and told me in no uncertain terms that he'd castrate me if I so much as set foot in his house again, so we didn't really have any other choice. When Jessie was born, Louise's parents wouldn't have anything to do with her to begin with, but thankfully my mum and dad offered to help with childcare so we could finish school.'

'That must have been hard.'

'It was. My parents were brilliant, but not well-off. We didn't have any money either, so we had to rely on charity shops and hand-me-downs. And looking after a newborn baby is exhausting, even with help, so yeah, it was tough. We were determined to make it work, even though everyone said we were too young and didn't stand a chance.'

'But you're not together any more.'

'No. It turns out that everyone was right. We did really well to begin with, but we were too young and I think it just got too much. We were tired all the time and fighting about whose turn it was to do things, and whose schoolwork took priority. Louise accused me of being selfish, and started to feel that it was me, rather than the baby, that was holding her back. Mum and Dad began to get annoyed with her because they felt she was taking advantage of them, and the whole situation became toxic. In the end, we accepted the inevitable, agreed it wasn't working, and split up.'

'Where did she go, if her parents had thrown her out?'

'Ah, well here's the first occasion where Jessie played a blinder. Louise's dad was adamant that he'd have nothing to do with her or the baby, but her mum couldn't resist her granddaughter for long. She came to visit a few months after Jessie was born and, of course, she was smitten. She knew that Louise's dad would be too, if she could only engineer a meeting. She tried various things to persuade him, but he just dug his heels in, so in the end she borrowed Jessie, took her back to their house and forced him to hold her.'

'What happened?'

'Jessie smiled at him, and that was that. He's been besotted with her ever since.'

'So when you split up...'

'Louise went home. I think we were all relieved, and having her parents on hand to help as well as mine made everything a lot easier. Jessie was a very sunny baby who never seemed to mind being passed from pillar to post, which was another bonus.'

'I was lucky, in many ways,' Jessie cuts in. 'I had these two amazing families that loved me, that still love me.'

'You did try to divide and conquer a few times, too,' Sam admonishes her.

'Well, yes. But who wouldn't?' she smiles. 'When your dad says you can't have something, you're going to try it on with your mum, aren't you?'

'Luckily, Louise and I stayed good friends, so she never got away with it,' Sam tells me.

'Not true!' Jessie laughs. 'What about the car? Mum was adamant she didn't want me to have a car, as she'd never know where I was, but you caved pretty much straight away.'

'That's not quite how it happened, though, is it? You came in ranting to me about how you were going to use the money from your holiday job to save up and buy a car, so I had a chat with your mum, and we agreed it would be better if we bought you something, rather than you buying a total death trap with your savings, just because it was cheap wheels.'

'Whatever. I got a car out of it,' Jessie grins.

'And Louise is married now? Do I remember that right?' I prompt Sam, eager to hear the whole story.

'Yes, to a really nice bloke called Neil. They invited me to the wedding, actually.'

'Did you go?'

'They wanted me to, but I didn't think it was a good idea. It was their day, and I thought that they should be looking forward into their future together without me there as a reminder of the past.'

'Very thoughtful of you. I'm sure they appreciated it.'

'They didn't, actually. They were very nice about it when I turned down the invitation, but then they suggested to Jessie that she should invite me as her plus one.'

'I was eleven,' Jessie remarks. 'I don't know who else they thought I was going to invite!'

'They played us both. Don't worry, I'm keeping score. Anyway, I ended up going, and it was a really lovely occasion. I'll probably invite them to my wedding if I ever get married.'

'Anyway, enough about us,' Jessie cuts in again. 'What about you? What do you do for a living?'

'I'm a sex and relationship counsellor,' I tell them, watching Sam's reaction carefully. His response surprises me.

'Oh, wow,' he says. 'That must be really intense. How do you manage to switch off, when you're carrying so many intimate secrets and people are relying on you to help them fix their relationships?'

I've never been asked this question before, and I take a moment to consider before I answer.

'I think I'm just really good at compartmentalising and leaving work problems at work. It can be pretty intense sometimes, and I'd probably go mad if I brought it home with me. I'm lucky with my colleague, too; we support each other.'

'You could do something like that when you finish your degree, Jessie,' Sam tells her. 'I expect psychology is a really good base for counselling of all sorts.'

'It was for me,' I agree. 'But there are lots of different things you can do besides being a therapist, if counselling isn't your bag. Have you had any thoughts?'

'Not really. One thing at a time, I reckon. I need to get the degree first.'

'You'll be fine,' Sam tells her. 'With genes like yours, how could you fail?'

Jessie laughs and gets to her feet. 'Thinking of Mum, I've got to be up early if I'm going to miss the traffic on the way home.' I glance at my watch to discover that it's a quarter to ten already.

'I'd better be off as well,' I say to them. 'Thank you for a lovely evening, but I have to be up for my surfing lesson tomorrow.'

'That you do,' Sam says, and I notice a mischievous twinkle in his eye that makes my stomach flip.

'It's been really lovely to meet you, Poppy,' Jessie says, stepping forward and enveloping me in a hug. 'Take care of him, won't you?' she whispers in my ear, just before releasing me. As I look at her, a little dumbfounded, she grins and winks at me and I realise she's seen straight through me. A flush of embarrassment starts to spread across my cheeks, but thankfully she's already turned away towards her bedroom and doesn't see it.

'Thank you for coming. I'll see you in the morning,' Sam also wraps his arms around me and I breathe in his aftershave as my insides fizz at the close contact. In the cartoon version of my life, this is the moment when the angel on my shoulder disappears in a puff of smoke, leaving the devil victorious. Freud's gorilla has definitely escaped from the basement.

* * *

'How was the handsome surfer?' Zoe asks me when I get back to the house. 'Were you overcome? Did he have to give you mouth to mouth after you fainted in his arms?'

'Behave!' I reply. 'Chaperoned by the daughter, remember?'

But I won't be tomorrow, I think as I climb the stairs to bed.

15

As soon as I arrive on the beach and we get started, it's clear to me that Sam is as distracted as I am. Having learned to catch the waves reasonably reliably, he's now trying to teach me to 'pop up', which is the bit where you move from lying on the board to standing up.

It seemed reasonably straightforward on the beach, but is proving next to impossible in the water. I'm grateful for the training he gave me right at the beginning on how to protect my head, as I reckon the surfboard would have knocked me out at least twice so far. I've also swallowed much more seawater than I'm sure is good for me. After forty minutes or so, we decide to call it a day and head up for breakfast. I'm pretty sure neither of us are thinking about food, though. My heart is thumping away in my chest, and it's got nothing to do with the exertions on the surfboard. As he helps me out of the wetsuit, Sam's hands brush my thighs, sending tingles to my core. He's definitely on the same page as me, because his hands linger for just longer than is necessary, and his blue eyes hold mine for what feels like an age.

'Don't worry, you'll get there,' he encourages me on the way back to the house, although there's a definite catch in his voice. 'It's the hardest part, but when you get it, you'll feel like you're king of the world!'

'Or queen,' I prompt him.

He smiles apologetically. 'Or queen. You're quite right.'

When we reach his house and step inside, the atmosphere is so charged I can practically hear it crackling. Sam takes his time hanging the wetsuits up to dry, and I'm embarrassed to admit my legs are quivering with anticipation as I wait in the kitchen, trying to lean nonchalantly against the counter. Normally, the sensation of the damp swimsuit against my skin would be a total passion-killer, but I'm not even aware of it when he steps back into the room. All I can see is those eyes and his mouth, which is curved up in a gentle smile. It seems to take an age for him to close the gap between us, and there's a moment when we just stand completely still, mere inches apart. Every fibre of my being is screaming at him to kiss me, but neither of us speaks. Very slowly, he reaches up to brush a stray lock of hair from my face and tucks it behind my ear. As I lean forward to make it easier for him, our lips finally meet and any last traces of doubt about where this is going to end fall away. Freud's gorilla in the basement has not only escaped; she's tied up the bank clerk and thrown the maiden aunt out of the window. All I know is that I want this man. I want him so much that nothing else matters. The future will have to take care of itself.

* * *

'I have a confession to make,' Sam says, half an hour or so later. We're lying on top of the duvet in his bedroom completely naked, and he's gently running a finger from between my breasts, down over my stomach to my knicker line or, at least, where my knicker line would be if I were wearing any knickers. Even though I'm completely satisfied, it's still an electric sensation and I have my eyes closed to make the most of it.

'Oh yes?' I murmur.

'You know when I first met you, and you thought I was hitting on you?'

'Mm-hmm.'

'I kind of was. Well, when I say that, I mean I was attracted to you and wanted to find a reason to spend time with you. It's been a long time since I've felt like that about anyone, so I'm sorry if I came across as clumsy.'

I open my eyes and turn to look at him, propping myself up on my elbow.

'It's been a while for me too. I reckon we figured it out in the end, though, didn't we?'

Things had heated up pretty quickly in the kitchen; Sam's shirt and my T-shirt are still in there. When we moved to the bedroom, though, something strange happened. The certainty and the confidence that we both felt slipped away, and there was a moment where we just stood and looked at each other in a kind of 'are we sure we want to do this?' way. I felt conflicted as he eased my shorts down and slipped the straps of my swimsuit off my shoulders. On the one hand, my body was responding to every touch and every kiss, revelling in the feel of his lips on me as he slowly uncovered me, but on the other, I felt very self-conscious. I was about to be naked in front of a man for the first time in years: what if he didn't like what he saw? What if I'd forgotten what to do? I could see the same doubt in his eyes when my turn came to undress him, although his body was obviously as keen as mine. Thankfully, as soon as we were both naked, the awkwardness vanished and it was all fine again. The urgency returned in full force and, although we occasionally whispered to each other to slow it down and take our time, we just couldn't help ourselves. It was, as Rachel would put it, more fast food than banquet but, now that we've satisfied our initial hunger, maybe we can have more of a banquet next time.

'I'd love to stay here all day with you,' he begins.

'But you have to work, I know.'

'Have dinner with me this evening. I don't trust myself to feed you here, but I can book a table somewhere.'

'I can't,' I tell him. 'I'd love to, but Lily has this rota, and it's my turn to wash up tonight. I can come round straight after, though.'

I can tell he's disappointed, but there's no way I'm going to be able to persuade anyone to take my washing-up slot. I have an idea.

'I could bring some things and stay over, if you like?'

He smiles and pulls me to him. 'I like that very much,' he says into my hair. 'Would you like something to eat before you go?'

I realise that I'm actually starving now that I'm no longer sick with nervous anticipation. Also, I've had quite a workout this morning, one way and another. We haul ourselves out of bed and I shudder as I pull on the still damp swimsuit. For a moment, I'm tempted to go commando under my T-shirt and shorts, but I think that might give the game away and I don't want to give my mother any reason to interrogate me when I get back. As Sam moves around the kitchen, arranging smoked salmon and scrambled eggs on top of the sourdough bread, I watch him with an idiotic grin on my face. Every so often, he glances at me and returns my smile. When he sets the plate down in front of me, we kiss for so long that there's a real danger the food will go cold.

'I'm not sure how much work I'm actually going to manage to get done today,' he tells me as we begin to eat. 'I think I might be rather distracted.'

'Really?' I ask him, mock surprised. 'Why?'

'Oh, you know. I might be thinking about this gorgeous woman I met on the beach a few days ago.'

'If it's any help, I think she might be thinking about you too,' I smile.

When we've finished eating, I help Sam clear up, and then he pulls me into another long kiss. I can feel the tension building between us again, but I manage to detach myself from him.

'Let's wait until later, when we've got more time,' I tell him.

'I'm so not going to get any work done,' he replies.

* * *

I practically skip the half-mile or so back to our house, and even the sight of my mother bustling around the kitchen when I let myself in isn't enough to pop the balloon of happiness that has settled itself in my chest.

'Do you need breakfast after your exertions?' Mum asks.

'I've eaten, thank you,' I reply, trying not to grin at her inadvertent double-entendre.

Rose is sitting at the table, brooding over a cup of tea. 'You look very pleased with yourself this morning,' she observes. 'Did the surfing go well?'

'Yes, very,' I lie. 'Sam reckons it won't be long before I'm standing.'

'Well done.' I can tell she's trying to be encouraging, but her mind is far away. I sit down at the table next to her and put my hand over hers.

'How are you doing?' I murmur, so that Mum can't hear.

'I'm no further forward. You know we went for a walk yesterday, while you were looking after the girls? I gave him so many openings to tell me what's going on, but he didn't bite. I even made up a friend who suspected her husband was cheating on her and asked his opinion about what she should do.'

'And what did he say?'

'Nothing, really. In fact, he didn't say anything of any consequence during the entire walk. We used to talk about everything and anything, but it's like he's somehow checked out. It's as if I'm married to an automaton; he looks like Steve, sounds like Steve and does Steve-y things, but something vital is missing. I just can't seem to get through to him any more, and I literally have no idea what to do. Have you got any more ideas? You're my only ally at the moment'

'Which is a strange turn of events, given our history, don't you think?'

I'm glad we've been talking *sotto voce*, because my mother chooses that moment to stride over and interrupt.

'You can't sit around in your pyjamas all day, Rose. We're leaving in just under an hour. You too, Poppy. Go and get changed.'

As she hurries off to find someone else to bully, I turn to Rose and raise my eyebrows.

'Shopping,' she tells me. 'We're all going into Newquay for the day; had you forgotten?'

If anything is going to ruin my mood, a day of shopping with my family is pretty much guaranteed to do it. I love shopping normally, and spending the day at Bluewater with a couple of friends, browsing the stores and stopping every so often for something to eat or drink is one of my favourite pastimes. But shopping with my family, especially en masse, is soul destroying. I know; I've had years of it growing up. What will happen is that we will amble along a street until someone declares that they need to look inside some darling little boutique or other. Because there are so many of us, we can't all fit in at once, so the rest of us are forced to stand around outside, bored out of our minds, until the person who wanted to visit the shop in the first place eventually comes out empty-handed. Then we'll move a couple of yards on, and the whole process will repeat itself. It's purgatory.

'Surely we're not inflicting that on the kids?' I ask Rose. The idea of dragging four grumpy under-twenties with us only makes the prospect worse.

'Steve said he'd stay behind and watch them. Freddie and Sarah don't exactly need a lot of supervision, and he's used to our two, so it's no hardship for him.'

I think fast. 'Even still, it might be an idea to have a second adult around the place, in case something goes wrong, don't you think?'

'Like what?'

'Well, what if one of them trod on something, and Steve needed to rush to the pharmacy for plasters? He'd either have to take them all with him or risk leaving them unsupervised.' As I speak, I'm aware how implausible I sound. Rose is bound to have a healthy stock of plasters, painkillers and pretty much everything else that's available over the counter from a pharmacy. She's that kind of organised person.

'You don't want to come, do you?'

'Of course I do!' I lie. 'It's just that I think it would be better if there were two adults here, that's all.'

'Rubbish. This is me you're talking to,' she counters. 'OK. I'll play along, on one condition.'

'What?'

'You try and find out what the hell is going on with my husband.'

16

Mum and Lily are decidedly less than impressed when Rose and I present them with our plan, and the whole thing is nearly scuppered when Andrew offers to stay behind so I can go. Thankfully, Rose heads him off by telling him that she thinks it would be a good idea for me to spend some more time with Olivia and Evie before the wedding, because they don't know me quite as well as they do him and Zoe. I'm aware of my mother's scrutiny throughout the conversation; she's pretty shrewd when it comes to her children, so her decidedly non-maternal second daughter offering to babysit is ringing alarm bells in her head, I'm sure. Freddie and Sarah aren't likely to give me any problems, but I must admit that the prospect of a whole day with Olivia and Evie is making me a little anxious. It's still better than the shopping trip, though, and I won't be alone as Steve will be here too.

As soon as the front door closes and the cars pull out of the driveway, I sigh with relief. Freddie and Sarah are still in bed and Steve is fixing breakfast for his children, so I head up to my room to shower and change. A series of delicious images from this morning plays through my mind as I wash, pull on a dry bikini and apply some sunscreen. It's as if my skin is still tingling where Sam touched it, and I'm already yearning to see him again. Freud's demanding aunt has obviously found her way back to the attic, because I do have a niggle of doubt about the wisdom of jumping into bed with a man I only met the day before yesterday. After my disastrous experiences at school, I've generally been careful not to start a physical relationship with someone until I know them really well, so this is definitely out of character for grown-up me. However, the aunt is soon silenced by the gorilla, who is definitely still in charge where Sam is concerned. Her view is very much, 'You've had sex with him now, so what difference will more sex make? You might as well make the most of it while you can.'

By the time I get back downstairs, Sarah is up and mooching around the kitchen, helping herself to cereal and making a surprising amount of mess in the process.

'What do you fancy doing today?' I ask her, as I wipe up a puddle of milk from the counter.

'Not a lot,' she replies. 'I thought I might just lie by the pool and work on my tan, you know?'

'That was just what I had in mind too,' I tell her.

Steve is already on the sun deck, supervising Olivia and Evie in the pool, when I wander out and settle myself on a sun lounger with my book. I have no idea how I'm going to try to prise any information out of him, and part of me is kicking myself for being stupid enough to agree to Rose's condition, but I've got plenty of time to come up with something, so I decide not to worry about it for now. Sarah has gone off to shower and get changed, and there's still no sign of Freddie, so I have nothing to do for the time being. Sighing with contentment, I take a sip of my coffee and start to read, breaking off every so often to have a little daydream about Sam. After a while, Sarah reappears with her earbuds firmly inserted in her ears, and lies down on the lounger next to me. By the time Freddie shows his face, it's nearly midday. Evie and Olivia are still in the pool, battling over a lilo. As soon as one of them manages to climb onto it, the other tips them off. There's lots of squealing and splashing, and I'm tempted to go and get my earbuds as well to drown it out. If I do that, though, I might miss my opportunity to chat with Steve and see if I can get any closer to figuring out what's going on with him.

'Where's everyone else?' Freddie asks, having ascertained that we're the only occupants of the house.

'Shopping,' I remind him. Sarah is completely oblivious, still plugged into her phone.

'Ah yes. I forgot, sorry. Shall I make my own breakfast?'

'I wouldn't bother, if I were you. It's nearly lunchtime.'

'Fair enough. I'll go and get some trunks on, then.'

Delighted that I've managed to dodge the bullet of cleaning up after Freddie as well, I sink back into my book. A few minutes later, he reappears and jumps into the pool with the most enormous splash that causes both the girls to squeak.

'Careful, Freddie,' Steve admonishes him, but I don't think Freddie hears, as he's churning up the water with a powerful crawl. Out of the corner of my eye, I'm aware of Sarah removing her ear buds and sitting up.

'Stop showing off, Freddie!' she calls, when he finally surfaces after a couple of full lengths of the pool.

'Come and race me, then,' he replies.

'What's the point? We both know you're faster than me. Why don't you race Aunty Poppy instead? She's a good swimmer, I reckon she could beat you hands down.'

'Hey, don't drag me into this!' I exclaim.

'No, Sarah's right,' Freddie agrees. 'What do you say, Poppy? Fastest over four lengths?'

'I'll be the referee,' Sarah continues. 'To make sure there's no cheating.'

I realise I'm cornered. 'Fine. I'll race you, but no getting all sulky and upset if I beat you, OK?'

'Girls, get out of the pool. I don't want you being run over,' Steve says to Olivia and Evie as Freddie and I line up on the side at the deep end. Once the pool is clear and the lilo has also been removed, Sarah shouts, 'Ready, steady, *go!*' and we both dive in. Competitive swimming was very much my sport at school, and it was one of the things that kept me sane after the whole Ceejay scandal. It's not a team sport, as such; even in relay races, it's just you and the water against whomever you're racing. I can feel my mind emptying and becoming calm as I focus completely on my stroke, my breathing, and timing the flip turns. I'm aware of Freddie, but only vaguely. I can also just make out the muffled shouts of encouragement, but I have no idea whether they're directed at me or Freddie. At the end of the fourth length, I raise my head to see that Freddie is some distance behind me.

'Bloody hell, Aunty Poppy, that was amazing!' Sarah says, as Freddie reaches the end of the pool, breathing hard.

'Yeah, well I used to do a lot of competitive swimming when I was your age,' I tell her, as I pull myself out of the pool. 'I guess it never really leaves you. Are you all right, Freddie?'

'I'm fine,' he puffs. 'Good race. Well done.'

'Why don't we play a couple of games of pool volleyball before lunch?' Sarah suggests. 'There are six of us, so three on each team. I think there's a ball in the storage cupboard.'

It takes a little while to find the ball, blow it up and organise ourselves into teams, but eventually we decide on me, Sarah and Olivia in the deep end versus Steve, Freddie and Evie in the shallows. I'm not sure anyone is keeping the score very accurately, but it's good-natured and even Steve looks as if he's enjoying himself. I must find a way to talk to him, I realise, as time is starting to run out.

'Right, I'm going to get lunch ready,' I announce after we've played a few games. 'Steve, do you fancy helping me?'

'I'd better stay out here and keep an eye on the girls, if you don't mind,' he replies. Damn. I'll have to up my game. Rose won't be at all pleased if I haven't even spoken to him by the time she gets back.

I wander inside and start bringing out the cold meats and cheeses that Mum has set aside for today's lunch. There's a loaf of fresh bread that I cut into slices, and I'm halfway through assembling a salad when Olivia appears in the kitchen.

'Are you OK, Olivia? Do you need a drink or something?'

'I'm fine,' she replies. 'I just wanted to ask you a question without Dad listening in.'

'Oh yes?' I'm only semi-engaged in the conversation. It's probably something trivial.

'You know lots about sex, don't you? It's your job, isn't it?'

Now she has my full attention, and I put down the knife to focus completely on her. I'm aware that I'm on very dangerous ground here as I have no idea how much Steve and Rose have talked to their children about the facts of life, and I don't want to say anything I shouldn't.

'Well, sex isn't my job, but I help other people when they're having trouble. Why?'

'Does it hurt?'

'Does what hurt?'

'Sex.'

'It shouldn't do. Why?'

'This boy at my school, Charlie Pottle, he showed me some people doing sex on his phone. There was a man lying down and a woman squatting on top of him. You could see his willy going in and out of her minnie, and she was moaning like it hurt. She was saying, "Yes, yes, yes", but you know how people sound when they're really desperate for the toilet? It sounded like that.'

Despite the seriousness of the situation, I can't help but smile at her description. I do need to be very careful here, though, and I'll definitely need to have a chat with Rose when she comes back so she knows what's been going on. First, however, I need to reassure Olivia.

'OK, Olivia. What Charlie Pottle showed you was actors performing sex, which is not the same as how sex is in the real world. Have you ever been in a play at school?'

'I was the Virgin Mary in the nativity last year,' she tells me proudly. 'My teacher said I was a natural.'

Of course she was the Virgin Mary. Of all the characters to have to use to explain this.

'And did your teacher tell you to project your voice when you spoke, so that people at the back of the hall could hear?'

'Yes. I had to speak clearly and loudly, but not shout.'

'So you had to exaggerate your speech.'

'Yes, I suppose so.'

'That's what the lady on the film was doing. She was exaggerating how much fun she was having. She was acting.'

'But why would you want to act something like that?' she asks. 'She could get an acting job on TV or something, and then she wouldn't even have to take her clothes off.'

'I don't know,' I tell her. I'm not going to get into a detailed discussion of the porn industry with a ten-year-old. Congratulating myself on handling it so sensitively, I pick up the knife and resume my work.

'Charlie said it made his willy go hard watching it,' she continues after a short pause. 'He wanted to show me, but I ran away.'

'That sounds very sensible,' I reply as I cut into a tomato. I'm rapidly coming to agree with Rose that Charlie Pottle is a nasty piece of work and Olivia should stay as far away from him as possible.

'Is sex the only way to make a baby?' Olivia obviously isn't quite finished with the subject yet.

'It's the normal way to make a baby, yes. Sometimes people who can't make a baby through sex can have special medical treatments to help them, but that's how most people do it.'

I'm braced for the next question; I think I'm still handling it pretty well, and I haven't said anything that Rose or my mother could castigate me for. When no question comes, I glance down and I'm horrified to see Olivia is crying.

'What on earth is the matter?' I ask, crouching down and wrapping her in a hug.

'I really want to have a baby when I'm older, but I don't want to do sex. It looks horrible,' she sobs. 'Does that mean I can't have a baby?'

'Listen to me,' I tell her firmly, as I wipe the tears from her cheeks. 'It's completely normal that you don't want to have sex now; you're ten years old. When you grow up, though, it's quite likely that you will change your mind. The important thing to remember is that you don't have to do anything until you feel you're ready. And if you still don't want sex when you're grown up, that's fine too. It's your choice and nobody else's.'

'But how am I going to have a baby if I don't have sex?'

'There are other ways to have a baby besides having sex and giving birth. You could adopt one, for example. Sometimes people have babies and they aren't able to look after them, so they put them up for adoption.'

Her face brightens. 'My friend Lois is adopted. Charlie Pottle said it was because her real parents didn't want her, but she told him she didn't care what he thought because the mum and dad she has now chose her. Thank you, Aunty Poppy. You're the best.'

As I watch her skip out of the kitchen, I can't help thinking that I'd like to find this Charlie Pottle and throttle him. I'm sure Rose will feel the same, and she's much scarier than me. The poor boy doesn't have a clue what's about to hit him, I realise with a smile.

17

'That was delicious, Poppy, thank you,' Steve says as we finish eating.

'It was only a few things from the fridge and a salad,' I reply. 'Not exactly Cordon Bleu.'

'I've never been much of a cook, but I'm pretty good at washing-up. Why don't you go and relax, and I'll bring you a coffee in a bit?'

'There isn't much to clear up. I'll give you a hand.' I'm thinking we could have a bit of a chat while we wash up, and then I'll have something besides Charlie Pottle to report back to Rose.

'I'd feel more comfortable if you were out by the pool keeping an eye on these two.' Steve indicates his daughters. 'I don't want them swimming without adult supervision.'

'I'm sure Sarah wouldn't mind watching them. You're not going to go in the pool, are you, girls?'

Both of them shake their heads solemnly.

'See? It's all fine,' I tell him. 'Sarah, Freddie, take the girls and keep a close eye on them. Nobody is to go in the pool, OK?'

'Yeah, yeah, we get it,' Freddie drawls. 'Come on, you lot.'

As they troop out after him, Steve and I start to clear the table. Now's my chance.

'So, Steve,' I begin, 'how are things? Rose says you've been a bit preoccupied lately. Is everything OK?'

Instantly, I can tell I've said the wrong thing. Steve's whole demeanour changes in an instant. He's suddenly oozing tension from every pore and, when he looks at me, his face is blank.

'I'm fine,' he says tightly. 'I don't know what Rose is talking about.'

'If you don't mind me saying, you don't look fine. I know it's none of my business, but—'

'You're right,' he snaps. 'It's none of your business. Look, Poppy, thank you for making lunch and everything, but I'd honestly be much happier clearing up on my own.'

'OK. Sorry, I didn't mean to make you uncomfortable.'

He sighs. 'No, I'm sorry for biting your head off. The truth is that I have got a lot on my mind at the moment, but it's nothing you can help with. Thanks for asking, though.'

'I'll leave you to it,' I tell him, and head out to join the others. I've never seen him like that before, and I'm glad I didn't bring up the conversation I had with Olivia; he's obviously in no fit state to deal with his daughter's issues as well as his own. At least I can tell Rose that I tried now.

The girls have been as good as their word, and are currently watching something in the TV room with Freddie. Sarah has taken up position on her sun lounger again, and her earbuds are in place, so I turn my attention to my upcoming stay with Sam. It was a bit impetuous of me to suggest it, and now I've either got to be up front about where I'm going to spend the night, with all the accompanying recriminations, or I'll have to sneak out after dinner and hope I'm back early enough in the morning that nobody realises I've been out all night.

After a little while, Steve appears with two mugs of coffee.

'I really am sorry I snapped at you in there,' he says, after checking that Sarah is still plugged in. 'I'm just wrestling with some stuff at the moment, and need space to figure it all out. Would you mind very much watching the girls if I go for a walk after my coffee?'

'No, that's fine, Steve. Just know that I'm here if you need to talk and feel you can't talk to Rose, OK?'

'I think I'll be all right, but thanks for the offer.'

So that's all as clear as mud, then. I can't help wondering what it is he's wrestling with that he can't tell his wife. I can see now why she thinks he's having an affair, but I'm still not convinced. I try to think about other things it could be, but every one of them is a dead end until I remember an article I read a few months ago about gambling addiction. I wonder how Rose would react to that, if that's what it turned out to be. Would she think it was better or worse than him having an affair? I could easily see it being a gambling problem, the more I think about it. Maybe they're about to lose the house, and he can't think how to break it to the family, or maybe he's planning some last-ditch bet to try to hold off the bailiffs. There aren't any betting shops within walking distance of the house, but he could be doing it online, I suppose. I glance over at him. Whatever is on his mind is obviously big, because he's just staring morosely at the sparkling water in the pool, and lifting his mug to his mouth occasionally like an automaton. The more I think about it, the more convinced I am that the gambling fits. If he's chasing big losses then that's going to impact his libido for sure, and it would also explain where he was when Rose phoned him at the office.

Whatever the problem is, he's said as much to me about it as he's going to, so interrogating him further is probably just going to get his back up. I'm definitely going to mention my idea to Rose when she gets back; I reckon it's just as plausible as her theory. Olivia and Evie reappear just as we're finishing our coffees and, having ascertained that at least twenty minutes have passed since we finished eating, Steve agrees that they can go in the pool.

'I'm going to head off, then,' he tells me. 'Give me your mug and I'll pop it in the dishwasher on my way out.' He turns to address his daughters. 'Girls, I'm going out for a while, so be good and do whatever Aunty Poppy tells you, OK?'

Having extracted solemn promises from his daughters that they will be complete angels in his absence, Steve takes the coffee mugs inside and I hear the front door closing shortly afterwards. Maybe I haven't thought this through, I suddenly realise. I'm now the sole adult in charge of four children that I really don't know that well. To be fair, Freddie and Sarah shouldn't present any problems, but I'm going to have to watch Olivia and Evie closely. Rose will never forgive me if anything happens to her precious daughters on my watch. I set my book aside with a sigh and give the girls my complete attention. They've found another lilo, and are happily floating around and splashing each other whenever they're in range. At least they get on reasonably well together; unlike Rose and me at that age. Once again, I notice that Olivia is clearly in charge but, unlike me, Evie seems quite happy to follow her older sister's lead.

My attention is briefly drawn away from them by movement in the corner of my eye. Sarah has removed her earbuds and is sitting up dead straight, staring at her phone. Her face is a mask of absolute horror.

'Are you OK?' I ask, but she completely ignores me.

'Sarah,' I raise my voice a little to get her attention. 'Are you OK?'

'Oh, umm. Yes, I'm fine,' she replies, although it's perfectly obvious that she isn't. 'I'm just going to go inside for a minute.'

She grabs her stuff and disappears indoors, and I return my attention to Olivia and Evie. As time goes on and Sarah doesn't reappear, I start to worry. Something has obviously spooked her, but what to do? I know she's not my daughter, but I feel like I ought to check on her at least. However, if it's something with a long and involved story, as most things with teenaged girls tend to be, I can't leave Olivia and Evie unattended either. I look at my watch; Steve has been gone for an hour. Maybe he'll be back soon. I decide to give it another thirty minutes, and if neither Sarah nor Steve have reappeared, I'll have to do something. I'm also becoming aware that I haven't seen or heard anything of Freddie since lunch but, on reflection, I think I'm more relaxed about that. He's sixteen, so he can look after himself.

Twenty minutes pass and I'm starting to feel quite cross with Steve. It's not exactly fair for him to swan off and leave me holding the can like this, problem or no problem. A knot of irritation and worry has formed in my stomach, and even trying to think about Sam isn't shifting it. In fact, I'm not even able to think about Sam properly, because I'm worried about both Steve and Sarah now. I'm starting to wonder if I've underestimated Steve's level of distress. Suddenly, my mind is filled with images of Steve trying to end his life in various ways. Perhaps I should have insisted he stayed here; he could be under a bus for all I know.

'Come on Poppy, leave the doomsday scenarios alone,' I murmur to myself, as I start to make a plan. First, I need to find Sarah and check she's all right, and then if Steve still hasn't reappeared by the time I've dealt with her, I'll have to go looking for him too. But what to do about the two girls? Suddenly, inspiration strikes. I'll get Freddie to watch the girls while I talk to Sarah, and then hopefully they can both keep an eye on them if I need to go looking for Steve. They'll have to watch a film or something if that happens; even though Freddie and Sarah seem fairly sensible, they'll be powerless if one of the girls has an accident.

It's no good. I'm now in full-on disaster mode. In my mind, Steve's lifeless body is lying somewhere in Mawgan Porth, Sarah's popping tranquilisers upstairs and will surely die unless I intervene soon (not sure where the tranquilisers are supposed to have come from, but welcome to the inside of my head), and Freddie is wringing his arms and crying as Olivia and Evie bleed to death from serious head wounds inflicted when he turned his back on them for a moment. I should never have agreed to babysit. Everyone is dying on my watch, and I'll probably never see Sam again, because I'll be arrested for neglectful abuse and go to prison.

'Olivia, Evie!' I call. 'I need to go inside for a few minutes. Can you both get out of the pool, please?'

'Do we have to?' Olivia replies. 'We're only floating on the lilos. We'll be careful, won't we, Evie?'

'Yes, Aunty Poppy. We won't even splash or anything.'

'I'm sorry girls. I need you to come out of the pool and promise that you'll stay out while I go to fetch Freddie. I'll be as quick as I can. OK?'

'OK,' they sigh, and reluctantly paddle to the shallow end, where they slide off the lilos and slowly make their way up the steps. Their drooped shoulders clearly convey their disappointment.

'Thank you. Right, stay here and don't move a muscle until either I or Freddie come down. Promise?'

'We promise,' Evie tells me.

I trust that they will do as I've asked, but I still hurry inside as quickly as I can. There's no sign of Freddie in the sitting room, games room, TV room or kitchen so, after surreptitiously checking that the girls haven't moved, I head upstairs. The door to Freddie's room is closed, so I knock. No response.

'Freddie, are you in there?' I call. Still no response, so I knock again, a bit harder. I'm completely stressed out now. Every second that Olivia and Evie are on their own increases the chances of something going wrong, but now I'm wondering whether something has happened to Freddie as well and I should have checked him earlier.

There's nothing else for it. I grasp the handle and fling open the door.

18

Whatever doomsday scenarios I've constructed in my head, nothing has prepared me for the reality in front of me.

'Oh, fuck!' Freddie exclaims, throwing his phone on the duvet and hurriedly trying to cover himself up. The scene on the phone is not at all dissimilar to the one Olivia described earlier, although the lack of sound makes it seem even more unreal.

'It's not what it seems,' Freddie continues, yanking out his earbuds and pulling up his shorts. The poor boy looks absolutely mortified.

'Let's not kid each other, OK?' I tell him. 'We both know what you were doing.'

I didn't think it was possible, but his cheeks flush even more deeply.

'Please don't tell my mum. She'll go spare,' he pleads.

I pick up the phone and watch the scene for a few seconds before I reply.

'Is this the kind of thing you normally use to get yourself off?' I ask.

'Umm, no,' he replies. 'I hardly ever use it, just very occasionally.' He looks like he wants the earth to swallow him, and I'm fighting the urge to laugh.

'Come on, Freddie. This is me you're talking to. Do you think I don't know the stats on how much porn sixteen-year-old boys watch? Or girls, for that matter? What I'm asking is whether this is your normal thing, or whether you prefer something a little more extreme.'

I see comprehension dawn and, although I didn't think it possible, he goes even redder. 'I'm not into violence, or kiddie porn, or any of that stuff, if that's what you're asking.'

'Fine. I think we've said all we need to on the subject, then. You might want to lock the door next time, though. I could have been Olivia or Evie.'

'There isn't a lock on the door.'

'Go into the bathroom, then!'

An awkward silence descends while we both stare at the phone. Things are hotting up on the screen, and I can just about hear the gasps and moans from the discarded earbuds.

'Was there, erm, something specific you wanted?' Freddie asks, after a few seconds.

'Oh yes. I need you to go downstairs and supervise Olivia and Evie while I talk to your sister. Will you do that for me?'

'Yes, of course,' he replies, grabbing his phone and heading for the door. His embarrassment has obviously killed his arousal stone dead, which is a relief to me.

'Oh, and Freddie?' I call, as he heads down the corridor.

'Yes?'

'Better turn that off before you get downstairs. The last thing either of us need is for the girls to see it.'

He pauses briefly, bringing his phone back out of his shorts and tapping at the screen to close the browser page, before hurrying away from me as fast as he can without obviously running.

Once he's gone, I knock carefully on Sarah's closed door.

'Who is it?' a small voice on the other side of the door answers.

'It's Poppy. Can I come in?'

'Umm. I'd rather be alone, if you don't mind,' she replies.

'I understand that, but I need to check you're all right. I'll only be a moment.'

There's a long pause before she replies. 'OK.'

When I open the door, it takes a moment for my eyes to adjust to the gloom. The curtains are drawn, and I can just make out Sarah's form underneath the duvet.

'What's going on? Are you feeling ill?' I ask.

'I'm fine. I just needed to lie down.'

'I'd be more comfortable if I could see you. Do you mind if I open the curtain for a minute?'

I'm answered by a heavy sigh. 'If you must.'

I stride over to the window and open the curtains, flooding the room with light. When I turn back to the bed, I can see Sarah's pale face staring back at me. Her eyes are red-rimmed and her cheeks are wet with tears.

'What on earth is the matter?' I exclaim as I settle on the bed next to her. I can't put my arm around her because she's under the duvet, so I stroke her hair instead.

'I'm so stupid,' she sobs suddenly, 'and now I've ruined everything.'

'What's happened?' I ask her gently.

'I c-can't tell you,' she stutters through her tears. 'You'll t-tell Mum, and that will make it all even worse.'

'It can't be that bad, can it? You were fine a little while ago.'

'It is!' she wails. 'And it's all my fault.'

My heart goes out to her. I'm no closer to discovering what the problem is, but the intensity of her emotion reminds me of how I felt when Oliver Stone told everyone I'd given him an STD. I remember the black hole of despair and the feeling of utter help-lessness only too well. Very slowly, I push down the duvet and pull her into a sitting position, so I can wrap my arms around her shud-dering body. I guide her head onto my shoulder and coo gently into her ear as I stroke the back of her head. We stay like that for a good few minutes before the shaking starts to subside and I gently loosen my grip.

'I don't want Mum knowing. She'll be really angry,' she says, as she scoots back against the headboard, pulling her knees up into her chest and wrapping her arms around them protectively.

This places me in a dilemma. I can't promise not to tell Zoe. Sarah is a child in the eyes of the law and, depending on what the problem is, there could be all sorts of safeguarding issues to consider. If I can't give her some reassurance, though, she's going to clam up and nobody will be able to help her.

'Sarah,' I say, 'if it's as bad as you think it is, and you can't fix it yourself, you're going to have to trust someone who is on your side. Who could be more on your side than your own mum? Yes, she might be cross and have a bit of a rant, but she loves you and she will help you, I'm sure of it. Why don't you tell me what it is, and then we can make a plan about how to tell your mum together if we need to. What do you think?'

She looks at me for an age, obviously trying to decide what to do, before her shoulders drop and she sighs. 'I guess I don't really have a choice,' she replies.

I sit back and wait patiently for her to begin.

'Early this year, I started going out with this boy at school,' she says, eventually. 'He's one of the cool kids, you know? Good at sports, popular, all that stuff. I couldn't believe it when he came up to me in the cafeteria one lunchtime and asked if I wanted to go to SmoothShakes after school.'

'SmoothShakes?'

'It's a milkshake and smoothie bar. All the cool people hang out there. Anyway, I texted Mum to say I was staying late to do some work in the library and went with him. When he asked if I'd be his girlfriend, I felt like I'd won the lottery. All my friends were so jealous.'

'So far so normal. What happened then?'

'We started hanging around together. I'd go for a milkshake with him and his mates after school sometimes. We'd meet up at weekends too and we started, you know, kissing and stuff.'

I raise my eyebrows questioningly.

'It was just kissing, actually. He wanted more, but I told him I wasn't ready. Sometimes, when we were kissing, he'd start touching me places, and I'd have to tell him to back off. Anyway, he started going on about wanting to have sex with me. He'd say that all his mates were having sex with their girlfriends, so we should be too.'

'That's not how it works, but go on.'

'He started getting a bit nasty about it. Calling me frigid and stuff. He threatened to dump me a couple of times. I was terrified. If he dumped me, I'd go back to being a nobody. In fact, I'd probably be worse than a nobody, because everyone would know I was the girl who wasn't good enough for Harry Oakley.'

'So you gave in?' Although I want to murder Harry, losing your virginity at fourteen isn't necessarily the end of the world. Unless... a horrible thought pops into my mind.

'Sarah, you aren't pregnant, are you?'

She smiles wanly. 'No, I didn't give in and I'm not pregnant, thank God. But I knew I had to give him *something*. Anyway, one day we were arguing about it as usual, and he said that if I wasn't going to have sex with him, the least I could do was give him some photos to, you know, help him along.'

'And did you?'

'Yes.' The tears start falling again.

I raise my eyebrows again and glance at her chest, and she nods. I lower my eyes to her lap, and she nods again.

'Sarah, you've done nothing wrong,' I say to her firmly. 'Lots of teenagers sext. I mean we didn't, but that was probably only because smartphones hadn't been invented when I was at school.' I smile, trying to reassure her.

'Yeah, but it wasn't enough, and we broke up at the end of last term anyway,' she says flatly.

'His loss,' I tell her robustly. 'It's your body, and it was wrong of him to pressure you before you felt ready.'

'I was OK with the break-up, actually. By that time, all we were doing was arguing. He kept calling me a "frigid bitch" when I turned him down, and him going on about it just made me more resistant. I'd been spending less and less time with him, so nobody was particularly surprised when we split, and my friends have actually been really nice about it.'

'If you're not sad about the break-up, what's happened to upset you so much?'

'He just texted me. He said that he wants me to make a video of... no. I'm sorry, I can't say it. Anyway, he says that if I don't do it, he'll share the pictures of me round the whole school.'

As soon as she finishes speaking, the dam bursts again and her body heaves with huge sobs.

'Can I see the text?' I ask gently.

She picks up her phone, enters the passcode and hands it over, eyes brimming with tears. As I read the text, I'm filled with rage. No wonder she couldn't describe it; I'm shocked by the level of explicit detail in Harry's demands. Any woman would feel threatened and degraded by a text like that, and I completely understand and sympathise with Sarah's distress. One thing is for certain: Harry Oakley is not only going to have to go without his video, but I'm going to make sure he deeply regrets the day he ever sent that text.

I hand the phone back. 'First things first. What he's done is a criminal offence because you're underage. You've got more than enough evidence here, so we could report it to the police and he would go on the sex offenders register, probably for life.'

She looks absolutely horrified. 'I'm not going to the police!'

'Why not?'

'Because they could arrest me as well. We've had lessons about this at school and, because I sent him the pictures, I'm technically guilty of sharing child pornography, even though it's my body.'

'Although you're technically right, the law is there to protect you, and the police would know you've been coerced.'

'I'm still not going to the police. Everybody would know! It would be worse than me giving in to him.'

'How would they know?'

'It would get out. He'd tell someone what I'd done, and then they would tell someone else, and so on.'

'OK, so how do we deal with him?'

'I don't know,' she whispers. 'I don't want to do what he wants. It makes me feel dirty and disgusting just thinking about it, but if I don't then he'll share the pictures and I'll die of embarrassment.'

'This is blackmail, pure and simple,' I reply. 'If you give him this, then all he'll do is come back with another demand, but this time he'll have even more to use against you. We have to stop him, and we have to do it now. If you don't want to involve the police, then we need to come up with another plan.'

'But how? He's holding all the cards! If he shares those pictures, my life is over. If I give him what he wants, he'll just come back for more like you said and my life is over. If Mum finds out what I've done, my life is over. If I go to the police, everyone will know what has happened and my life is over. There isn't a way out of this where I don't lose everything.'

'I think you're underestimating your mum, if you don't mind me saying. This is not your fault; you need to understand that. You trusted a boy with something very private and intimate, but it was him that betrayed your trust. Let me ask you a different question. What do you think Harry's mum would say if she found out about this?'

Sarah thinks for a moment. 'She'd totally murder him. She's on the PTA with my mum, and Mum's always saying how nice she is, but how she doesn't take any nonsense.'

'So, if his mum is friends with your mum, then your mum probably has her number. See where I'm going?'

'I'm still not sure about Mum knowing.'

'She's your best chance, Sarah. Let me talk to her and explain what's happened. She'll want to help you. I can't promise she won't give you a lecture, but I might be able to talk her out of that by explaining that you've learned your lesson the hard way already. Do you trust me?'

There's another long pause, but eventually she lifts her eyes to mine and I'm relieved to see that the tears have stopped. 'Yes. I trust you.'

'Good. Now, why don't you wash your face and we'll go down and see if Freddie has managed to prevent the girls from drowning themselves?'

As she disappears into the bathroom, I exhale loudly. This babysitting gig is so much harder than I could have imagined.

19

I'm relieved to see that Steve has reappeared when Sarah and I walk back out onto the sun deck. The girls are playing happily in the pool and Freddie is lying on a sun lounger, trying to look nonchalant, but the way he starts fidgeting when he sees me gives his anxiety away. I'm just about to reassure him again when Steve blocks my path.

'Poppy, can I have a word?' he asks.

There's an unpleasant undertone to his voice which gets my hackles up, but I follow him to the far corner of the sun deck, away from the others.

'What's up?' I ask.

'What on earth were you thinking, leaving the girls unsupervised?' he hisses.

'They weren't unsupervised! Freddie should have been watching them,' I reply. If Freddie wandered off and left them then the porn conversation is going to be nothing compared to the rest of what I've got to say to him.

'Freddie's practically a child himself! What if something had happened? I can't believe you've been so irresponsible,' he seethes, and something inside me snaps.

'Listen to me,' I tell him. I'm whispering, but there's no doubting the fury in my voice and he recoils slightly. I've always got on fine with him, but then he's never questioned my judgement before. 'If you remember, we were supposed to be minding the children together, but *you* decided you needed to go for a walk to deal with whatever your problem is. While you've been swanning around the countryside like something out of *The Sound of Music*, a truckload of shit has been going down here and I've been trying to deal with it on my own as best I can. I mean, where the fuck have you been, Steve? You've been gone for hours!'

'I told you. I needed time to figure some stuff out,' he says defensively.

'Bully for you. I hope you had a lovely time. But don't you *dare* call me irresponsible. At least I was here!'

'But Freddie...' he begins, determined not to lose face.

'Freddie would have come and found me if he needed to. Your girls are fine. If you're that bloody worried about them, I suggest you stick around and supervise them yourself next time. Now, if that's all you wanted, I've got the next instalment of my fabulous afternoon to get on with.'

He says nothing, so I take that as my cue to leave. I'm furious with him, and it takes all my powers of self-control to keep my voice calm as I approach Freddie.

'Are you OK?' I ask him quietly.

'Of course not!' he replies in a strained whisper. 'My aunt just walked in on me when I was in the middle of, you know...'

'Having a wank?' I smile.

'For fuck's sake,' he groans. 'I'm glad you think it's funny. I'm dying of embarrassment here.'

'I didn't see anything, I promise,' I lie.

'You're making it worse.'

'Oh, get over yourself.' I nudge him playfully. 'You're not the only person in the world ever to have had a wank. In fact, I'll let you into a secret. Girls do it too. Surprisingly often.'

'Argh!' he exclaims. 'My ears are bleeding. Make it stop!'

I glance around to make sure nobody else is listening. 'Look,' I tell him. 'What I saw was perfectly normal for someone of your age, OK? If you'd been watching some seriously kinky shit, then I would have been worried, but you weren't so I'm not. Do you mind me asking how often you use it?'

'A couple of times a week, no more. Can we please stop this now?'

'Nearly. As a professional, it'd be a dereliction of duty if I didn't warn you about some of the potential dangers. I'm sure you've got it all under control, but humour an embarrassing sex therapist, would you?'

'Do I have to?'

'Please? I'll be as quick as I can.'

'Fine,' he sighs. 'Can we go inside, though, away from the others?'

I follow him to the TV room and we settle on the sofa.

'Stop looking so miserable,' I tell him. 'Although it's technically against the law, the statistics show that most boys your age are doing exactly what you're doing, even if they're not admitting it. As I said before, it seems that most of the girls are too. And the vast majority of them will go on to have happy, fulfilling sex lives in the real world. Occasionally, however, things don't work out like that. I don't want you ending up in my treatment room, so I just want you to have all the facts, all right?'

He nods.

'Do you know why watching porn feels so good?'

He shrugs. 'It's, well, you know...'

'Apart from the obvious, it's because your brain releases truckloads of dopamine as a response to what you're seeing. Dopamine is your body's feel-good drug, and studies have shown that people your age react up to four times more strongly to it than adults. The problem with dopamine is your body starts to crave it, like natural heroin. So, you're watching your porn a couple of times a week and your body is making you feel good. That's fine, but if it starts to creep up and you find you need it every day, or maybe more than once a day, then that's an alarm bell. What happens with some people, not many, but a few, is that it becomes a cycle of addiction, where they're watching it more and more often, and they need it to be more extreme, to get the same dopamine hit. Does that make sense?'

'I guess.'

'Great. Now, I'm sure you know this, but real-life sex is nothing like porn. In real life, male arousal, particularly at your age, is a bit like boiling a kettle. Flick the switch and you've got boiling water a few minutes later. But female arousal is more like boiling water in a pan over an open fire. You need to take your time building the fire first, starting with nice dry kindling and slowly adding bigger pieces of wood until you've got a healthy blaze. If you rush to dump the big logs on there too soon, the fire will just go out. It's only once you've put the time and effort into building a good fire that you can even think about adding the pan of water to boil. In porn, the women are always turned on and up for anything, and some people don't realise that real life isn't like that, which can lead to all sorts of problems in the bedroom.'

'Do you get many people like that in your clinic?' he asks.

'A few,' I tell him. 'Of course, they never admit it to begin with. When was the last time one of your mates said to you, "Hey Freddie, I've just had a really good wank to some porn and I'm feeling great about it"? I'm going to take a stab in the dark and guess the answer is "never".'

He laughs. 'How do you know who uses it, then?'

'There are tell-tale signs. Sometimes I have to treat people who are so addicted to porn that they can't get turned on in real life at all.'

'I don't understand that. Can't they just take Viagra or something?'

'Viagra will give them an erection, but the sex will still be unsatisfying because the brain isn't aroused. These guys have usually been watching pretty extreme stuff, and they simply can't get excited about normal sex with a real person. If the brain isn't engaged, the sex isn't going to work.'

'So what you're saying is stick to the mild stuff.'

'Stick to the mild stuff,' I agree. 'And in moderation.'

He grins. 'Do you know what?'

'What?'

'You might be the most embarrassing aunt ever, but you're also kind of cool.'

'Why thank you, I think,' I laugh.

At that moment, a commotion in the hallway indicates that the rest of the family have returned from their shopping trip. Freddie obviously decides this is his opportunity to escape and gets up. As he disappears, I reflect on the conversation. I don't know whether any of what I've said to him will make a difference, but I made the point and I think I got through to him a little. I give it a few seconds before following Freddie out of the room. The others have obviously had a good day, if the number of shopping bags is anything to go by. Lily is in great spirits as she waltzes up the stairs with her spoils, humming as she goes, and even Rose looks fairly relaxed.

'You look like you've had fun,' I say to Mum.

'We did, thank you. Was everything all right here? Nobody drowned or had to go to hospital?'

'Incredibly, everyone survived despite my best efforts,' I reply. 'Rose, can I have a quick word?'

Instantly, the tension is back on Rose's face. She follows me to the TV room, which seems to be turning into my impromptu consultation room for the afternoon, and I shut the door behind us.

'What is it?' she asks. 'Is it Steve? Did you find something out?'

'No. I tried, but he just clammed up. It's actually Olivia I need to talk to you about.'

I fill her in on the conversation, and she's predictably furious with Charlie Pottle. I explain Olivia's anxiety about sex and suggest some conversations they could have to help normalise her views and hopefully make her less worried. I tell her about Steve going off for his walk and we discuss my gambling theory briefly, but I leave out the confrontation we had when he returned. Rose isn't convinced that gambling is the issue; she's pretty sure their finances are healthy but she does agree that she'll do some checks when they're back home to be doubly sure.

Sarah is chatting amicably to Freddie when I walk back out onto the sun deck, but I can see she's tense again now that her mother is home. When she sees me approaching, the colour drains from her face and my heart goes out to her. We agreed earlier that it would be best we talked to Zoe together, but she looks like she might bottle it now that it's about to happen. Her eyes are as wide as saucers when I incline my head to invite her to come over.

'Would you rather I talked to your mum alone?' I ask her.

'No. I'll come,' she murmurs. Poor thing, I can see her legs shaking with nerves.

'Come on, I've got you,' I tell her, and put my arm around her as we make our way indoors.

We find Zoe in the kitchen, waiting for the kettle to boil.

'Hello, you two,' she smiles. 'Do either of you want a cuppa? I'm parched after all that pavement pounding.'

Sarah shakes her head. She looks like she's about to throw up. 'I'm fine, thank you,' I say to Zoe. 'Can we have a chat, when you've made your tea?'

'Sure. Is everything all right?' She looks carefully at her daughter. 'You look a bit peaky, love. Are you feeling OK?'

'She'll be fine,' I reply. Sarah's mouth opens and closes a few times, but it looks like she's lost the power of speech, and I can feel her trembling against me. It seems to take an age for Zoe to make the tea, and it must feel like a lifetime for Sarah, but eventually we settle ourselves in the TV room.

'What's this about?' Zoe asks.

'Sarah's got a bit of a problem, and we hope you might be able to help with it,' I begin. 'There's a boy she's been seeing at school...'

Twenty minutes later, the story is told. There was one point where I was worried that I'd miscalculated and Zoe was going to tear into her daughter, but a bit of gentle guidance headed that one off. There have been tears, hugs, and Zoe has told Sarah fiercely how proud she is that she didn't give in to Harry's pressure to have sex.

'Right. Time to end this. I'm going to call Harry's mum.' Zoe says grimly, as she slips her mobile out of her pocket and scrolls through her contact list. We can both hear the faint ringing as she holds it to her ear, and then a woman's voice.

'Hi Stella, it's Zoe. Yes, we're having a lovely time, thank you. I just need to have a quick chat with you about Harry, if that's OK?'

She steps out of the room for the rest of the conversation, but we watch her striding around outside, talking animatedly into the phone.

'Do you think Harry's mum will believe me?' Sarah asks.

'We've got the texts. She has to.' I reassure her.

Nevertheless, I glue my eyes to my sister-in-law, trying to glean any information from her body language, but I can't tell. It could be going either way. There's a long period where she doesn't appear to speak at all, and I'm worried that Stella is laying into her. Eventually, she puts the phone back into her pocket and strides back into the house with a blank expression on her face. My heart is in my mouth as she enters the room, and Sarah is shaking with nerves again.

'I think we can assume Harry is very sorry,' she tells us. 'Stella was absolutely furious. I had to stay on the line while she stood over him to check that he deleted all the pictures. She also made him show her his cloud back-up, to be certain he didn't have any other copies. She made him read the text he'd sent you down the phone, which horrified us both, and he's now composing an apology. When he's done that and sent it, she will delete your number from his phone, and then she will take it away from him. He's also grounded and can't take part in any extra-curricular activities for the next year. If you ever hear that he's done anything like that again, to anyone, you're to tell me, OK?'

As Zoe gathers her daughter into her arms, I sink into the sofa with relief. Sarah leans round her mother, smiles shakily and mouths 'Thank you' at me, before slipping off to re-join the others.

'Thank you so much for being there for her,' Zoe says to me. 'I'm not sure she'd have found the courage to tell me on her own, and who knows where that could have ended up?'

'No problem. I'm glad I could help. You forget sometimes, being an adult, what it's like being a teenager and dealing with all those raging hormones.'

'You're right. It would be easier if they weren't so bloody secretive. I didn't have the first idea that Sarah was even seeing Harry, and Freddie could be running a harem for all I know.'

'I don't think you need to worry about Freddie. He seems like a perfectly normal boy of his age to me,' I tell her.

'I'm sorry,' she says, as we leave the TV room together. 'It sounds like it's been a bit of a busman's holiday for you this afternoon.'

'I'm just glad I could help,' I reply, and we give each other a brief hug.

20

'Just half a glass please, I'm going out after dinner,' I say to my father as he pours the wine. Rose and Steve have cooked an enormous vegetarian lasagne, which is delicious but also what I was planning to cook tomorrow, so I'll have to think again on that one. Dan and his parents are at their house tonight, so it's just our side of the family round the table.

'Where are you going? It'll be dark soon,' my mother asks suspiciously.

'She's probably going to see her handsome surf instructor,' Lily giggles and starts miming passionate kissing. For someone who's about to get married, she really is incredibly immature sometimes.

'Not in front of the children, Lily,' Mum reprimands her, before turning to me. 'I hope there won't be any of that; you barely know him,' she huffs. 'What time will you be back? I don't want to be up late worrying about you.'

I'm really not in the mood for her after the day I've had. 'Mum, I'm thirty-three and perfectly capable of looking after myself,' I tell her firmly. 'I'll be back when I'm back, and whatever I may or may

not do with Sam is nobody's business but mine, OK?' I can see Lily
still miming the kissing behind Mum's back, and I shoot her a filthy
look.

'I'm just trying to save you from yourself. You know what you're
like where boys are concerned,' Mum sniffs. I open my mouth to
reply, but I'm distracted by Rose putting her hand on my arm and
whispering, 'Don't. It's not worth the aggro.'

I'm clearing the plates and stacking the dishwasher after dinner
when Zoe sidles up to me.

'Why don't you leave that and get off? Andrew and I can do it.
It's the least we can do to thank you for helping Sarah.'

'That's very kind of you, but if Mum sees you doing it she'll
assume I'm skiving and then I'll get into even more trouble. It won't
take long.'

This isn't strictly true. While the lasagne was delicious, Rose
and Steve obviously had the oven too high, because there are bits of
it welded to the dish and I suspect it's going to take a lot of soaking
and scrubbing to get it off.

'Don't worry about her. If she says anything, I'll tell her I owed
you a favour. Go on. You deserve a bit of fun after this afternoon.'

I don't need telling again and skip up the stairs to get ready. I'm
just stuffing my swimming costume, make-up essentials and tooth-
brush into the smallest bag I can find when there's a tap at the door.

'I forgot to tell you earlier, the weather forecast for tomorrow is
wind and rain, so the water-sports company have cancelled,' Lily
tells me when I open the door.

'Oh. Have you got something else planned?'

'No. We'll just hang around here. It's only one day, thank goodness. The forecast for the rest of the week is great and it's going to
be perfect on Saturday for the wedding, which is the most important thing.'

'Good. Thanks for telling me.'

'No worries. I thought you'd like to know, in case you want to spend more time with your *boyfriend*.' She grins mischievously.

'Lily?' I ask her, smiling as sweetly as I can.

'Yes?'

'Fuck off, would you?'

I can hear her giggling as she retreats down the corridor. I wouldn't be so annoyed if the idea of spending the day with Sam wasn't exactly what came to mind. He'll be working, though, so I'll just have to take what I can get. As I wander down the road, the daylight is starting to fade and the last die-hard surfers are packing up on the beach. I can't believe it was only this morning that Sam and I were in bed together. It feels like a lifetime ago, and I'm suddenly nervous. What if he's changed his mind, or he's decided it was a mistake? I know it's irrational as he seemed pretty keen, but maybe he'll have lost interest now that he's been to bed with me.

I'm giving myself a stern talking to as I ring the bell, but it's not helping the butterflies fluttering in my stomach. When he opens the door, however, all my anxiety melts away. He's grinning broadly and leans forward to place a lingering kiss on my lips before stepping aside to let me in.

'I wasn't sure you'd come,' he tells me.

'Why?'

'I don't know, I thought maybe you might have had second thoughts or something.'

'I was worried that you had! Have you?'

'No, of course not!'

'Good, because I've had a hell of a day, and I'd really like a glass of wine and a hug.'

He grins again. 'I reckon I can supply both of those.'

He rummages in the fridge before pouring me an enormous

glass of wine and settling on the sofa next to me. I curl into him as he wraps his arms around me and we spend a long time just kissing. I can feel my body responding to him, and I'm aware that he's just as aroused as me. Part of me is tempted to just drag him straight to the bedroom, but I'd also like to enjoy the anticipation for a little longer. I gently break away from him.

'Let's take it slowly this time,' I tell him. 'We've got the whole night, after all.'

'And the morning,' he replies, still grinning.

'And the morning,' I confirm, smiling back at him.

The rest of the evening passes in a bit of a blur. I don't elaborate too much on my day, but we chat about this and that, periodically breaking off for an episode of passionate kissing (Lily would laugh her head off) and trying desperately not to rip each other's clothes off.

'So, how did you end up becoming a sex therapist?' he asks, after we break off to catch our breath for the umpteenth time. 'It's a pretty niche career, if you don't mind me saying.'

I laugh. 'Says the data scientist!'

'Fair point. In my case, it was a maths degree, followed by an internship at an IT firm that led to an offer of employment. I was just a programmer to begin with, but artificial intelligence and machine learning fascinate me, so when a job came up, I went for it and was lucky enough to get it.'

'People always think I must be obsessed with sex to do my job,' I begin. 'But actually, the physical act isn't that important. When people come to me because they're experiencing difficulties with their sex lives, the underlying cause is pretty much always emotional rather than mechanical. My job is to tease out what the real issue is and help them to resolve it. It's a mixture of being a therapist and a detective.'

'In that way, your job isn't so different from mine,' he states, and I raise my eyebrows in surprise.

'Go on. This I have to hear,' I tell him.

'You think I spend all day staring at data, right?'

'Yes, that seems logical. The clue is in the title.'

'Whereas I hardly ever look at the raw data itself. It's training the machine-learning algorithms to find meaning in the data, that's the thing. There's a lot of analysis, which is like your detective work, and problem-solving, which is also part of what you just said you do. I reckon we're probably interchangeable.'

'I don't think so,' I laugh. 'I reckon I'd probably go to sleep in ten minutes flat if I tried to do your job.'

'Maybe you're right,' he smiles. 'Now that I come to think about it, I'm not that interested in listening to people moaning about their sex lives either. Especially not when my own sex life has taken such an exciting turn, anyway.'

He leans in to kiss me again and this time, we don't break off.

When I wake the next morning, I'm momentarily disorientated before I remember where I am. I stretch luxuriantly; there was none of the awkwardness of our first time last night, and it was very nice indeed. I reach over to Sam's side of the bed, only to find it empty. I listen for a moment or two, but I can't hear him moving about in the bathroom either, so I reluctantly get up to go and look for him.

'Morning,' he smiles as I walk out into the living area. He's wearing a tight-fitting T-shirt and boxer shorts, and I savour the sight of him. 'I was just going to bring you a coffee.'

'What time is it?'

'Seven thirty. We won't be surfing today, I'm afraid. The waves are way too big for a learner.'

I look out of the window and I'm rather relieved. Although I can see a few surfers in the water, the wind has whipped the surf into much bigger waves than I've been practising on, and the rain is lashing down.

'Don't let me stop you from going,' I say to him. 'I just need a quick shower and I'll be on my way.'

'I must admit, I'd normally be out there like a shot. But...'

'But what?'

'But I don't normally have a beautiful woman standing in front of me looking absolutely irresistible. I thought we might have a bit of breakfast and then maybe go back to bed, if you don't have any other plans?'

'What about your work?'

He smiles. 'The problem with Cornwall is that bad weather can easily disrupt the power supply, haven't you heard? No power, no internet. It's a crying shame and someone really ought to do something about it.'

'You're making that up.'

'Who's to know?'

* * *

It's nearly lunchtime by the time I disentangle myself from Sam and do the walk of shame back to our house. I'd have happily stayed all day, and I think Sam would have liked that too, but I have to decide what I'm cooking tonight and go to the supermarket to buy the ingredients. I have promised him that I'll be back after dinner, though. Mum isn't going to like it, but I don't care. I'm trying very hard not to fall for him because I know we'll be going our separate ways soon, but I don't think I'm succeeding. Thankfully, I manage to slip into the house and up to my bedroom unnoticed. I had a shower at Sam's before I left, but the rain has soaked me on the way home, so I look distinctly bedraggled. After drying my hair and putting on a long-sleeved top and a pair of jeans, I'm ready to face my family.

'Ah, there you are!' my father remarks good-naturedly as I walk into the sitting room. 'Have you been having a lie-in?'

'Something like that,' I reply, aware of Lily and Zoe desperately trying not to laugh. 'Where is everyone else?'

'The girls are all watching a DVD with Steve. I think Andrew is spoiling for another table tennis match with you, but is passing the time playing snooker with Freddie, and your mum and Rose are in the kitchen getting lunch ready,' Zoe tells me.

'Are we seeing Dan's family today?' I ask Lily.

'Yes, they're coming over this afternoon and staying for dinner. What are we having?'

'I haven't decided yet. I'm going to go to the supermarket in Newquay after lunch to see if inspiration strikes.'

'I'll come with you, if you like,' Lily offers.

I raise my eyebrows. Lily doesn't normally offer to do anything unless there's something in it for her. There's an agenda here.

'I'm not sure, Lily,' I reply. 'Are you just going to make smoochy noises at me all the way there and back, or are you actually planning to be helpful?'

'Oh, ye of little faith!' she retorts, with mischief in her eyes. Smoochy noises it is, then.

'I'll think about it,' I tell her. 'I'd better go and check whether Rose and Mum have murdered each other.'

Incredibly, the kitchen is relatively peaceful when I walk in. Mum is putting the final touches to a salad, and Rose is cutting a baguette into thick slices.

'Where the hell have you been?' Mum snarls as soon as she

spots me, shattering the illusion of peace. 'You were out all night, weren't you? Thank God Dan's parents aren't here; goodness only knows what they'd think of your behaviour.'

'I'm sorry, but what on earth has it got to do with them?' I ask, trying to keep my voice calm.

'In case you haven't noticed, we're trying to create a good impression here!' she exclaims. 'But you seem determined to sabotage us at every turn. You'd barely met Anita before you were assaulting her with all your sex stuff on the first night, and now this.'

'Hang on a minute.' I'm not standing for this, and I'm aware that I'm starting to raise my voice. 'Firstly, I didn't bring that up; Anita did. And, as I've told you more times than I can remember, *there's nothing wrong* with what I do; you just seem to have a massive problem with it, for some reason. Finally, it really is nobody else's business whether I choose to stay over at Sam's or not. It's not your business, and it certainly isn't hers. I doubt very much she'd think anything of it.'

'Of course she would!' Mum shouts. 'They're churchgoers. They have views about things like that.'

'For fuck's sake, Mum, leave her alone!' Rose suddenly bellows, stopping us both in our tracks. Mum looks like she's been slapped for a moment, before she turns slowly to Rose.

'I beg your pardon?' she asks, in an ominously quiet voice.

'You've been on her case from the moment she got here,' Rose continues hotly. 'She doesn't deserve it, so leave her the fuck alone, OK? If anyone is giving us a bad name here, it's you.'

'How dare you speak to me like that!' Mum yells at her, just as the kitchen door opens and Andrew walks in.

'What on earth is going on in here?' he asks. 'We can hear you from the other end of the house!'

'Tell *her* she's been picking on Poppy,' Rose demands, pointing at Mum. I'm still speechless, mainly because I think this is the first time that my sister has ever stood up for me.

'She's right, Mum,' Andrew agrees. 'You have been, a bit.'

'I don't believe this!' Mum shrieks. 'All I'm trying to do is make Dan's parents like us, for Lily's sake, and you're all accusing me of behaving like a playground bully!' With that, she bursts into tears and storms out, slamming the kitchen door behind her.

21

Unsurprisingly, lunch is a fairly tense affair. Dad has done his best to calm Mum down, but she's patently still furious, fixing each of us with baleful stares at various points. Lily initially tried to paper over the cracks with some wedding chatter, but it was obvious that nobody was listening, so she soon gave up. The children have picked up the mood and are wisely keeping their heads down. It's a long time since my mum has lost it like that, and I think we're all a little shell-shocked. I'm really grateful to Rose and Andrew for sticking up for me, but I'm also so used to the way Mum is with me that I hadn't really noticed that it was any worse than normal. Freddie, Sarah and the two girls disappear in the direction of the TV room as soon as they've finished eating, obviously keen to be away from the oppressive atmosphere. It's a sign of how on edge we all are that nobody tells them off for not asking to get down from the table.

'That was delicious, love. Thank you,' my father tries, as we start to clear the dishes, but Mum just harrumphs and disappears in the direction of the sitting room.

'She'll be fine. Just give her a bit of time to calm down,' he tells the rest of us, before following her. Poor Dad: he'll do almost anything for an easy life and I think he deliberately chooses to ignore quite a lot of what's going on.

'I'm not apologising to her. She has been foul to you and, if anyone's going to say sorry, it should be her,' Rose says defiantly, once it's just our generation in the kitchen.

I don't reply. I'm still trying to get used to the whole idea of Rose taking my side rather than throwing me under the bus.

'I think Dad's right,' Andrew chips in. 'Give her time to calm down. Dan and his parents are coming over later, so she'll have to be all smiles and jollity then anyway. I'll try to have a chat with her in a bit and clear the air.'

'I'll do it,' Zoe offers. 'I have the advantage that I haven't fallen out with her so far today. Stick the kettle on and I'll take her a cup of tea and a biscuit.'

'Good luck,' I tell her. 'I think you might need it.'

'Are we going to the supermarket then?' Lily asks, as soon as we've finished clearing up.

'I am,' I reply. 'Don't you think you should stay here to greet Dan and his parents when they arrive? I'm not sure how long I'm going to be, and I don't want you pressurising me to hurry up. I'm bound to forget something important if you do that.'

'They're not coming until late afternoon, and I'm sure they won't mind if I'm not here. Much more important for me to spend some quality time with my sister.'

'Fine,' I sigh. I don't believe a word of the quality time nonsense, but she evidently wants something and it will be a lot easier to let her have her way. I don't have the energy for another fight today.

'Yay!' She claps her hands in delight. 'I'll just pop to the loo and get my purse. I'll meet you back here in five minutes, OK?'

* * *

The weather appears to be improving a little bit as we head towards Newquay. It's still raining, but the sky is not so dark and brooding and the wind has definitely eased off a bit. There are some fairly impressive puddles on the road, so I concentrate on my driving and let Lily's prattling largely wash over me.

'Do you think I should have asked Rose to be chief bridesmaid rather than Amy?' she asks, around ten minutes into the journey.

'Amy's your best friend. I don't think Rose expected you to ask her.'

'Yeah, you're probably right. It's such a juggling act, trying to keep everyone happy and still have the wedding I want, and sometimes I wonder if I've got it wrong.'

'It's your day, Lily. I'm sure everyone understands that you're trying to make it as perfect as possible.'

This seems to be all the reassurance she needs, and I tune her back out as she resumes chattering about the complexities of the seating plan. Although Rose and I have very rarely seen eye to eye on anything, we have always agreed that we can't stand Amy. She's one of the most manipulative people I've ever met, revoltingly saccharine on the surface, but a total control freak underneath. Although we're all bridesmaids together, Rose and I have tried to have as little to do with her as possible, although it's proved hard as she continually harangues us through the WhatsApp group she set up so we could all be 'on the same page'. I have no idea why she felt the group was necessary, because she hasn't once asked our opinion about anything. It's just been a way for her to dictate to us where we need to be and when. I'm just pleased that she's arriving today and staying in the hotel with the other hangers-on. Lily did suggest bringing her for the whole week to stay with us, but Rose and I managed to head her off, saying that we thought it would be better to have some time just as a family. Amy pretended to agree when Lily told her at the next bridesmaids' meeting, but you could see in her eyes that she was really pissed off about not being invited, which was much more satisfying than it ought to have been.

By the time we reach the supermarket, I've decided that I'm going to make a kind of vegetarian cottage pie with Quorn mince and buy a selection of puddings. It will cost a bomb, but at least I know everyone will eat it. Lily pushes the trolley as I load it up with all the bits and pieces I need. We agree that, even though it's summer, the weather has been so filthy today that it might be nice to have a hot pudding to offer, so I buy some apple pies and custard as well as a selection of cheesecakes. I find I'm actually looking forward to cooking; apart from the fact that I genuinely enjoy it, it will give me a legitimate reason to skulk alone in the kitchen for the rest of the afternoon and avoid any further confrontations with my mother.

'Can I ask you a question?' Lily begins, once we're safely out of the car park and on our way back.

'What sort of question?' I reply.

'A sex question.'

Aha. This is the hidden agenda. It's fine; I can deal with this. After Freddie and Sarah, dealing with Lily should be a walk in the park.

'Go on,' I tell her.

'The thing is, although I'm a virgin, Dan isn't. I'm worried that I'll be no good at it and he'll be disappointed.'

'Lily, the only people who need to worry about being "good" at sex are those who do it professionally.'

'Porn stars and prostitutes, you mean?' she interrupts.

'We call them sex workers,' I continue. 'For the rest of us, it's about communicating, exploring and finding what you like. It's a two-way street, you know? As much as you have to learn what Dan likes, he has to put the effort in to please you. That's one of the reasons why sex in a committed, long-term relationship is often more satisfying than in a one-night stand. It gets better the more you learn about each other.'

'Will it hurt, the first time?'

'It might be a little uncomfortable, but it's unlikely. You don't have any trouble putting tampons in, do you?'

'No.'

'You'll probably be fine then. It's not a bad idea to have some lube to help things along, and a glass of wine or two never does any harm. Just don't get paralytic beforehand. However excited Dan will be about seeing you naked for the first time, I don't think you flopping around and vomiting is going to be particularly conducive.'

Out of the corner of my eye, I notice that Lily is blushing. I haven't said anything particularly risqué, so I'm a little confused.

'Are you OK?' I ask her.

'Yes. Well, I have a little confession to make.'

'Go on.'

'Dan has seen me naked before. Although we haven't made love, there's been plenty of...' She dries up, blushing furiously.

'Plenty of what?' I'm genuinely curious now.

'You know. Downstairs insidies,' she mumbles.

I know this is a serious conversation, but I can't help bursting out laughing.

'Dear God, Lily. Please never use that term again! You sound like someone from the Second World War!'

'What would you call it, then?'

'Heavy petting if you must, or third base if you're American. Foreplay is the correct term.'

'OK. Yes, we've been doing a lot of foreplay.'

'That's great. Look, people – especially men – tend to see sex purely in terms of penetration. You can see why; it's the best bit for most of them. But focusing on penetration at the expense of foreplay is like having a snack instead of a decent meal. Do you mind if I ask whether you find the foreplay satisfying?'

She's fully beetroot now, but she nods and smiles shyly.

'So think of it like this.' I tell her. 'You've built an excellent foundation for a fulfilling sex life. The important thing is to think of the penetrative act as an add-on to what you already have, and don't let Dan get lazy and make it a replacement. Yes, there will be some times when you just don't have time for the three-course meal and need a snack just to keep you going, but don't let it become all snacks, OK?'

'Thank you,' she murmurs. 'It's been on my mind a lot, and I knew you'd be able to help.'

'No problem. But Lily?'

'Yes?'

'If I ever hear you say "downstairs insidies" again, I'm signing you up for a convent, OK?'

We both laugh, and I'm relieved to see her relaxing again.

'I've been thinking about your surf instructor,' she continues, a few minutes later.

'What about him?'

'Well, he can't come to the reception because it would totally mess up the seating plan and we've told the hotel how many people and everything, but you could invite him to the evening do, if you wanted.'

'That's a lovely idea, thank you. I'll ask him.'

I don't know whether Sam will come, but I love the idea. Apart from the fact that I won't be hanging around like a spare part trying to avoid Stuart's advances, it will be another night we can spend together before I leave. I'm so busy daydreaming about dancing with him, inhaling his aftershave and then undressing him slowly that I nearly miss the turning back into the house. On the pretext of it being easier to unload the shopping, I've helped myself to the kitchen door key again, but it's also a relief to be able to avoid whatever ongoing drama is unfolding elsewhere. Lily helps me unload the shopping and then wanders off to find the others, leaving me with the kitchen to myself. It takes me a little while to work out how to connect my phone to the Bluetooth speaker on one of the counters, but I get it sorted eventually, selecting a pop anthem playlist that I can dance along to while I cook.

I've always found cooking relaxing, and I sing along to the playlist as I peel the onions and start chopping them. The knife is blunt, as all rental property knives tend to be, and there's nothing to sharpen it with, so it takes all my concentration to chop without it slipping and injuring me. Once the onions are done and I've mopped up the tears, (a couple of them were seriously strong) I move on to the carrots, celery and mushrooms. I peel the potatoes, dice them and put them in a pot, covering them with water and plenty of salt. I remember Rose being horrified by the amount of salt I put in the water when I was cooking at home one time, and I had to explain patiently to her that most of it stayed in the water and only a little bit of it got into the vegetables. She was convinced I was trying to poison her, and I smile at the memory. Although there have been plenty of times that I would happily have poisoned her, something definitely seems to have shifted this week. She's never stood up for me to Mum before and, although it's probably nothing more than her still trying to atone for her Ceejay remark on the first night, I'd like to hope that it's something deeper than that. I'm not going to let my guard down just yet, but there's cause for optimism there.

I turn on the hotplate under the potatoes and splash some oil into another pan, adding the onions and other chopped vegetables once it's heated through. When the vegetables have softened, I add garlic, a few chilli flakes and dried herbs, enjoying the aromas wafting up at me. I'm adding the tomatoes, happily wiggling my bum in time to the music, when I become aware that I'm no longer alone.

'Can I have a word, when you have a moment?' Mum asks.

Just like that, my little balloon of happiness pops. What have I done now?

22

'I'm kind of in the middle of something right now,' I tell her. I'm livid that she's invaded my little refuge, and I'm certainly not going to drop everything just so she can tear me off a strip for whatever my latest crime happens to be. 'I'll come and find you when I've finished this, OK?'

'It's fine, I'll wait,' she replies, settling herself at the table.

I try to get back to my happy place as I add the Quorn mince and a couple of vegetable stock cubes to the pan, but I'm very conscious of my mother just sitting there. It's disconcerting and I don't like it. I'm torn. Part of me wants to keep her waiting for as long as possible to show her that I'm not intimidated by her, but the rest just wants to get whatever fight this is going to be over and done with so I can get back to my cooking and be alone again. In the end, I adopt a middle approach. Once the potatoes are soft and ready to be mashed, and the mince mixture is also cooked, I turn off the stove and face her.

'Do you want a cup of tea?' I ask. I may as well start civil, even if I'm sure she won't.

'Thank you. That would be lovely.'

She says nothing more until I've carried two mugs of tea over to the table and sat down opposite her.

'Poppy, it would appear that I've been a little harsh with you, and I wanted to say sorry,' she begins. 'I've reflected on what Rose said earlier and I agree that she might have a point. On top of that, Zoe told me that you've been, to use her words, a complete star, helping Sarah to navigate some difficult waters. She didn't go into details, but it would seem that she felt able to confide in you some things that might have been impossible for her to share with her mother. Even Rose was singing your praises, telling me that you had a very useful conversation with Olivia.'

Whatever I was expecting, it certainly wasn't this. I'm struggling to stop my mouth from dropping open in shock. I'm trying to think of something to say, but I'm so surprised that I just sit there, staring at her.

'Don't get me wrong, I still have a problem with what you do for a living, but I suppose I'm trying to say that maybe there are aspects of it that are...' she pauses to think of the word she wants, '...useful.'

It's now or never, I realise. She's opened a chink in her armour, but it's tiny and I know she'll slam it shut again as soon as this conversation is over.

'Mum,' I ask, 'what exactly is it about my job that you find so difficult?'

She sits and fidgets for ages before replying. I can see her mouth moving a few times, as if she's about to speak, but then she obviously changes her mind. I need to hear this though, so I sit and wait patiently, trying to look calm as I sip my tea.

'It's, well...' she begins, and grinds to a halt again.

'Yes?' I encourage her.

There's another long silence. She's deeply uncomfortable, and I'm trying very hard not to enjoy her disquiet.

'OK,' she says eventually. 'I just don't understand what sort of a person would want a job watching other people have sex. That sort of thing should be private, between a husband and wife. You might say I'm ridiculously old-fashioned, and maybe I am, but I can't help the way I feel. There, I've said it.'

I thank my lucky stars that I don't have a mouth full of tea, as I'm sure I would have spat it out all over the table.

'Why on earth would you think I watch other people having sex?' I reply, dumbstruck.

'That's what you do, isn't it? You watch and then give them advice on how to improve.' I don't know whether to laugh or cry. I can't believe she's been beating me up for all of these years because of an assumption that's so completely wrong, and I feel a surge of frustration and resentment. But it's also comical, in a way.

'Where on earth did you get that idea from? How the hell would that even work?' I ask her, incredulous. 'Let me get this straight. You think that people who are having difficulties with their sex lives come to see me, I get them to demonstrate what they do and then tell them what they're getting wrong, is that right?'

'Yes.' She's sounding defensive, but there's also a note of uncertainty now.

'That is the most ludicrous thing I've ever heard!' I exclaim. 'Who in their right mind is going to want to strip off and have sex in front of a stranger, especially one that's judging them? That's pretty much a guaranteed mood-wrecker right there, I would have thought.'

'Some people do,' Mum counters. 'My friend Brenda was telling me about these people who meet up in car parks and places to watch each other.'

'That's dogging, Mum, and it's a seriously niche activity carried out by a tiny number of people. I have a full book of clients, five days a week. Most of them would be completely unable to perform with someone watching. I'm a professional therapist, not a bloody voyeur! For God's sake, why didn't you ever bother to ask me what I actually did, rather than making up complete fantasies and then blaming me because you didn't approve of the absurd vision you'd come up with?'

She does at least have the grace to look a little shamefaced.

'So what do you do, then?' she asks, after an uncomfortable pause.

'I ask questions; I listen to the answers; I help my clients get to the root of whatever the problem is so they can resolve it. Sex is a wonderful thing when it's a celebration of intimacy, but all too often it becomes a bargaining chip, or someone will punish their partner by denying it. Sometimes it's used as the glue to hold a relationship together when everything else is falling apart. Sex is like dynamite; it's incredibly powerful and massively destructive if you misuse it. Quite often, the problem is not actually to do with the sex itself; it's just manifesting through sex. So it might be resentment, frustration, lack of communication, whatever. I work just like any other therapist by helping my patients tease out what is really going on, so they can fix it. It's just talking, Mum. Everyone keeps their clothes on.'

'Oh,' she says, evidently surprised. 'I was a bit confused when Anita didn't seem shocked when you told her what you did, especially with her being religious and everything. It makes more sense now.'

'I can't believe you thought that about me for all those years. No wonder you didn't like my job!'

'Well, you did have an unhealthy interest from an early age. All that stuff we found under your bed...'

'That was research, Mum! It wasn't porn or pictures of naked men. It was just articles I'd found online.'

'Oh, come on!' she replies, recovering some of her composure. 'Your father read part of one of them to me, and it was all about, well, things girls shouldn't be doing to themselves. We were mortified.'

'Are you talking about masturbation?'

'There's no need to be crude, Poppy.'

'I'm not being crude. That's the technical term for it. If I were being crude I'd have said "wanking".' She flinches at the word, but I'm unrepentant. I've got years of unjustified criticism to offload. I wouldn't mind flinging a few other sex-related slang terms at her, but I manage to bite my tongue. We're having the most honest conversation we've had in years, and I don't want to depth charge it.

'Whatever you call it, it's not natural, and it's certainly not the sort of thing fourteen-year-old girls should be reading or doing.'

'I couldn't disagree with you more. Contrary to what you were brought up to believe, masturbation is completely healthy and normal in both sexes. It's pretty much the safest way of releasing sexual tension. Also, refusing to engage with teenage sexuality is inviting trouble. Look at Sarah. Her body is changing and developing at a tremendous rate, as is Freddie's. If they don't have the right information to help them understand the way they're feeling, or they don't think that there are people they can talk to about it, the potential for catastrophe is enormous. For example, how would you feel if Sarah got pregnant because some boy told her she'd be safe if they did it standing up and she'd had nobody she could turn to to burst that myth?'

'She shouldn't be having sex at her age.'

'But people that age *do*, Mum. That's the reality. And if we refuse to engage with them and talk openly with them about it, where are they going to turn to get the information they need to make the right choices?'

'They teach it in schools these days, don't they?'

'They don't, not really. They teach contraception, but not what to do or what's normal. Teenagers are increasingly getting their sexual education from online porn, and that's causing all sorts of body-image problems, as well as normalising some pretty brutal sexual practices. It's terrifying, and I'm already seeing the results of it in my consulting room. We need to be talking to young people about this stuff, teaching them what makes a healthy sexual relationship, and what a normal body looks like. Do you have any idea how many young women are turning to plastic surgery to alter perfectly normal genitalia because it doesn't conform to the images they see on screen? Would you want that for Sarah? There's a poisonous torrent of misinformation out there and, if we don't speak up, who will?'

I'm aware of my heart thumping in my chest. Part of it is because I do genuinely feel passionate about this stuff, but it's also because I need Mum to understand why it's important to me. If I can just make her understand, even a little bit, it will be an enormous leap forward. I'm outraged too, if I'm being completely honest, but who could blame me?

'We never talked about it, and we were fine,' Mum replies after another pause. Her tone has softened a little, and I think we might genuinely be on the verge of breaking through the impasse that's existed between us for so long.

'You didn't have online porn in your day, though, did you?'

'No, that's true,' she agrees, after thinking for a while. 'Plus, your Nana Jean was so strict, she pretty much thought holding hands with a boy was tantamount to handing him your virtue on a plate.' She smiles at a memory.

'What are you thinking about?' I ask her.

'There was this one time, before your father and I were married, when he dropped me back home after a trip to the cinema. It was late, and we thought she would be in bed, so we risked having a little cuddle on the doorstep.'

'What happened?'

'Well, we were kissing, nothing more, and suddenly we were drenched to the skin. She had seen us, and she emptied a bucket of cold water over us from her bedroom window. I wasn't allowed out for weeks after that. You girls had it easy compared to me, I tell you.'

'I'm not sure I'd describe it as easy. Different, certainly. Nana Jean may have been a bit of a psycho, but there weren't the same pressures, were there? In your day, it was normal to wait until you were married before having sex.'

'Now you're the one talking nonsense,' she admonishes me, but there's none of the usual harshness in her tone. 'It was the sixties and seventies. Free love and all of that. Everyone was at it.'

'I hadn't thought about that. I can't see you as a hippy, I have to admit.'

'Oh, I wasn't. Nana Jean would have had a fit, can you imagine? No, I was a good girl who dressed modestly, did what she was told, and married a respectable man at the age of twenty.'

'It's extraordinary, isn't it?' I muse. 'Lily's practically a child bride by today's standards, and she's three years older than you were.'

'I don't regret it. There weren't the career options available that you have now, so it was either marry or go to secretarial college. I think I made the right choice.'

Our extraordinary conversation is interrupted when noises from the hallway indicate that Dan and his parents have arrived. Mum gets up to go and greet them, but pauses when I touch her arm.

'Mum, thanks for this conversation,' I say to her.

'Thank you, Poppy, and I really am sorry, both for being over harsh with you and also for making assumptions about your job rather than asking you. You've given me a lot to think about. Now, come and give your old mum a hug before I go and say hello to Anita and Richard.'

It's a long time since we've shown each other any form of physical affection, and both of us are a bit awkward, but it's still nice. I really hope we've truly turned a corner and this isn't a temporary thaw before hostilities resume; this has to be the longest conversation we've had in years that hasn't ended with one of us storming off.

'Are you planning to stay over with your surfing friend again tonight?' she asks as she releases me, and I feel myself tensing up again.

'I am,' I reply tightly, ready for the inevitable onslaught.

'OK. I know you're an adult and you know much more about all this stuff than I do, but I wouldn't be a very good mother if I didn't tell you to be careful, would I?'

'I know. I am being careful, Mum, I promise.'

'Good. Have a nice time,' she says, leaving me open-mouthed as she breezes out into the hallway.

23

'How did your dinner go?' Sam asks, once he's poured us each a glass of wine and settled on the sofa next to me.

'Good, I think. Everyone was very complimentary about the food, and they ate it all, so I'll chalk that up as a success.'

I'm not going to bore Sam with my family dynamics, but it was a slightly surreal dinner. My mother wasn't scowling at me like she normally does, and I managed to have a whole conversation with Dan's brother Stuart without him hitting on me, although I suspect that was mainly because he's still got the hots for Jessie. He certainly seemed a little upset when I told him she'd gone home. Even Rose and Steve seemed in reasonable spirits, so we were almost the normal family that my mother has been so desperate to portray.

'My sister, the one who's getting married, asked if I'd like to bring you to the evening do after the wedding. Would you like to come?' I ask him.

'I'm not sure,' he replies, after considering for a few moments. 'I wouldn't want to intrude.'

'You won't be intruding!' I exclaim. 'You'll be saving me from the advances of my soon-to-be brother-in-law's creepy brother, dancing with me and generally having a good time. You'll also, I hope, be keeping me company overnight.' I stroke his thigh as I say this, in case he's in any doubt what I mean.

He grins widely. 'Well, when you put it like that, how could I refuse? I have to warn you that I'm not much of a dancer, though.'

'I don't think it matters. As long as you get up and wiggle a bit, you can say you danced.'

'I can manage a wiggle,' he laughs.

'There you go, then. And we already know you can manage the other stuff, so it will be fine.'

'I don't know about that,' he replies, before leaning forwards to brush my lips with his. 'It's been a long time, so I could probably use some practice.'

'You're doing just fine,' I tell him as I move round to straddle his lap, taking his face in my hands and kissing him deeply. 'But I agree,' I tell him when we briefly come up for air. 'You can never practise too much.'

* * *

I'm just about to get to the good bit in a surprisingly rude dream when Sam gently shakes me awake the next morning.

'What time is it?' I ask, as he places a steaming mug of coffee on the bedside table.

'Six o'clock,' he replies. 'The storm has gone and it's a corker of a day out there. I reckon we'll get you standing up today.'

It takes me a minute to work out that he's talking about surfing. My dream and the fact that he's only wearing a figure-hugging pair of underpants have kind of focused my mind elsewhere.

'We could do that,' I murmur, grabbing his hand and pulling

him down towards me, 'or we could stay here and do something else.'

'Or,' he replies, smiling and gently pulling away, 'we could go surfing and then come back here to wash the sand and salt off. It really does get everywhere, you know. I'll probably have to help you, to make sure we get all of it.'

'Will you now?' I grin. 'In that case, you're on. Let me drink this delicious-smelling coffee, get my swimsuit on, and then I'll be all yours.'

* * *

As we step out into the early-morning light, carrying our surfboards, I feel like I want to pause time somehow and preserve this perfect moment. Even though it's the hen party later, which means I'm going to have to spend much longer than I want to in Amy's company, I feel completely happy in this instant, with the warm sun on my face, Sam beside me, and the anticipation of his hands on my body to come. I'm trying not to con myself into thinking that this will last beyond the holiday – I know I'm going to feel shit when I have to say goodbye to him on Sunday morning – but none of that matters right now. I want to record how I'm feeling so I can play it back next week, when I'm at home living my normal life again.

I'm relieved to see that the waves are back to a manageable size, and Sam is attentive and patient, showing me how to make sure I'm lined up along the centre of the board and where to place my feet. There are a few falls, but I'm getting better at remembering to close my mouth and breathe out through my nose as I go down, so I don't swallow any sea water. Towards the end of the session, I actually manage to stand up a few times and, although I don't think I will ever get into surfing in the way that

Sam has, I do feel an enormous sense of exhilaration and accomplishment.

'Enough for today. Time for a shower and some breakfast,' he declares after checking his watch, and I feel a different tingle in my stomach. After years on a sexual starvation diet, my body is obviously keen to make up for as much lost time as possible. This, combined with my excitement at having finally managed to stand and ride a wave in, means that we're barely out of our wetsuits and through the door of Sam's house before my mouth is on his.

'You're very salty,' he laughs.

'You're not so bad yourself,' I reply.

'No, you're actually salty. You taste of salt. Come on, let's get you in the shower.'

I don't need to be told twice and, after a long, lingering shower together, we retreat to the bedroom for the main event.

'I'm not normally like this,' Sam tells me afterwards. 'For some reason, I just can't seem to get enough of you.'

'It's not exactly normal for me either,' I reply. 'But I know what you mean.' As I look at him, I feel a little pang of sadness. I know it's unrealistic to expect what we have now to translate into the real world, but wouldn't it be good if it did? The logical part of my brain is telling me firmly to leave that fantasy alone, that long-distance relationships don't work and commuting between Kent and Swindon, or wherever in the West Country he decides to move, isn't really practical. Unfortunately, the rest of my brain is already working out timetables of how and when we could continue to see each other.

The problem is that I think I'm falling for him, and that was never supposed to be part of the equation. Shit. Freud's granny in the attic is loving my discomfort, stomping around saying that she told me this would happen and I should have listened to her to begin with. The gorilla in the basement is having none of it, though.

She just wants as much of Sam as she can get for as long as she can get it.

'Would you like some breakfast before I start work?' Sam asks, breaking me out of my reverie.

'I'd love some, yes please,' I reply, giving him a gentle kiss before reluctantly climbing out of bed and starting to get dressed. I check my watch to discover that it's nearly ten o'clock. I'd love to know how Sam justifies his seemingly erratic working hours to his company. I'm used to a very clearly defined work day.

'What time are you supposed to start work?' I ask him, when I join him in the kitchen.

'It's flexible, really. If I'm prepared to work later into the evening, I can start later in the morning. Similarly, if I start early then I can finish early. Why?'

'I'm just curious. I think I've worked from nine until six every day since I qualified, so the idea of starting work this late is alien to me.'

'As long as I get the job done and I show up to the meetings I'm supposed to, I'm not really sure my bosses care very much what specific hours I work. Here you go,' he says, handing me a fresh coffee and a piece of toast with some ham and a couple of poached eggs on it.

'Thank you. I think I'm going to need this today. It's the hen do, which means I'm trapped for the entire afternoon and evening with Lily's friend Amy. We're having lunch in the spa at the hotel where the wedding is, so it'll probably be a couple of lettuce leaves and a glass of kale juice.'

'Mm. Sounds enticing,' Sam remarks as we start eating. 'Are you coming over afterwards?'

'I'm not sure how late it finishes.'

'Whenever. I'll be up.'

We're interrupted by Sam's phone starting to ring.

'That'll be your boss, wanting to know why you're not at your desk,' I smile.

'Unlikely,' he replies. 'It's my personal phone, not my work one.' He picks it up and looks at the caller display. 'It's Louise, Jessie's Mum. I'd better take it.'

He swipes to answer the call, and straight away I can tell that something is horribly wrong. I can just hear Louise's voice and, even though I don't know her and I can't work out the exact words, I can tell she's extremely agitated.

'Slow down,' Sam is saying soothingly into the phone. 'Tell me exactly what they said.'

There's another burst of agitated babbling, and I see the colour drain from his face.

'Where have they taken her?' he asks, and I note that the soothing tone has gone, and been replaced with a note of panic.

'OK,' he continues. 'I'm on my way. I'll meet you there.'

'What is it? What's happened?' I ask him, as he sets the phone down.

He looks at me in surprise, as if he'd forgotten I was there. The sparkle in his eyes has vanished, and his beautiful mouth is turned down.

'It's Jessie,' he says. 'She's been in a car accident and has been taken to hospital. I've got to go.'

'Oh, God. I'm so sorry, Sam. Is she OK?'

'I don't know. Louise had a visit from the police. It sounds serious.' He's trying to conceal it, but I'm suddenly aware that he's desperate for me to leave so he can get on the road.

'I'll get out of your hair and let you pack,' I tell him, standing up.

'Thank you,' he replies, but the warmth has gone from his voice and I can tell that I'm not even registering on his radar any more. I gather my things as quickly as I can and then wrap my arms around him to give him a quick hug. There's nothing sexual in it; this is all about comfort and reassurance.

'I really hope she's all right. Give her my love when you see her,' I say as I disengage.

'I will,' he replies. 'Hopefully it's not as bad as it sounds and I'll be back before you know it. Look, about the wedding—'

'Don't worry about it. Jessie needs you. Nothing else matters right now.'

'I'd still like to come.'

'Let's see, eh? Go and do what you have to do. Don't worry about me.'

With that, I disengage from him, grab my bundle of stuff and walk out of the door. My thoughts are a maelstrom as I make my way back to our house. Foremost in my mind is how Sam must be feeling. I have no experience of being a parent, obviously, but I really liked Jessie and the idea of anything happening to her makes me shudder in horror. How much worse must that be for her parents, who have known and loved her from birth? As virtuous as I'm trying to be, I'm also sad for me. If Jessie's condition really is as serious as it sounds, there's no way Sam will be back for the wedding. I'm nearly home when the full implications of that hit me.

If Sam doesn't make it back for the wedding, I will probably never see him again.

24

My grim mood drops even further as I let myself into the house. Amy is in the kitchen, talking to my mother. That's all I need.

'Hello, Poppy. Did you have a nice evening?' Mum asks.

'Yes, thank you,' I reply. 'But Sam had some bad news this morning and has had to rush home.'

'Oh no,' she sympathises and, to my amazement, she sounds sincere. 'What happened?'

'His daughter Jessie's been involved in a car accident. She's been taken to hospital.'

'Was she the rather jolly girl that Dan's brother took such a shine to?'

'That's the one.'

'This all sounds like a *fascinating* story,' Amy interrupts, in her annoying sing-song voice. 'Who is Jessie and, more importantly, who is Sam?'

I'm just about to tell Amy that a lovely young woman being hospitalised is not a fascinating story, and the rest of it is none of her damned business, when Mum thankfully intervenes.

'Sam is a young man who has been teaching Poppy to surf, and with whom she has established something of a connection. Jessie is his daughter,' she tells her.

I can almost hear Amy's mind whirring. She locks onto anything that she considers might be even slightly salacious or gossip worthy with the accuracy of a heat-seeking missile, and she won't rest until she has every detail. She really is an unpleasant creature, and I'm in no mood to be her next target.

'I'm going to get changed,' I tell Mum. 'What time are we leaving?'

'Twelve o'clock sharp, remember?' Amy trills. 'It's not like I haven't sent you *several* WhatsApp reminders, Poppy.' She turns to my mother and sighs. 'Sometimes I think I'm the only one who's taking this wedding seriously, besides Lily, of course.'

I want to slap her already. How on earth am I going to put up with this for the rest of the day?

Mum also takes the opportunity to escape and follows me towards the door; I'm not sure she likes Amy any more than I do. I'm just about to grab the handle, desperate to flee to the sanctuary of my room, when the door bursts open and Rose appears with a face like thunder. I notice the murderous look in her eyes as she barges past Mum and me without uttering a word; anyone who knows her well would know to steer well clear of her when she's in this kind of mood. Amy, however, does not know her well.

'Rose!' she exclaims, as if they're long-lost friends. '*So* lovely to see you. Are you excited about today?'

'No.' Rose replies, abruptly, as she grabs the kettle and starts filling it with water.

Amy falters, but stupidly doesn't spot the warning signs and presses on.

'You nearly got me there! I was just about to get upset and say how much work I've put into this, before I realised you were joking.'

Rose thumps the kettle down on its stand before flicking the switch and turning slowly to face Amy. Mum has disappeared, but I'm rooted to the spot. It's like I'm watching one of those nature documentaries, where Amy is a gazelle that hasn't noticed the lion creeping through the grass.

'Listen,' Rose says menacingly. 'I know there isn't any room in your vacuous little head for anything other than this wedding, but the rest of us have real lives to contend with. My life is shit at the moment, for reasons that I have no intention of sharing with you, and I could really do without whatever bollocks you've cooked up for the day, all right? So no, I'm not looking forward to it, and I'm going to make myself a cup of coffee and try to enjoy a few moments of peace before I have to pretend I give a rat's arse about macramé, or whatever the hell it is we're doing.'

'You know what we're doing!' Amy whines, her voice sounding petulant now. 'I sent you a full timetable in the WhatsApp group.'

'Didn't read it. Didn't read most of what you sent. Now, do me a favour and fuck off out of my face, would you?'

This proves to be the straw that breaks the camel's back, as Amy bursts into tears and starts sobbing about how hard she's worked, and how she doesn't deserve to be spoken to like that. Rose completely ignores her, however, and stalks out into the garden as soon as she's made her coffee.

'Try not to be upset,' I tell Amy. I'm not sure why I'm trying to comfort her when she brought it on herself by poking the bear, but she looks genuinely shocked and today is going to be difficult enough if Rose's mood doesn't improve; I don't need Amy crying all over the place as well.

'She... she was *horrible* to me!' Amy sobs. 'Of course I'm focused on the wedding. I'm the chief bridesmaid, and I'm just trying to be a good friend to Lily and give her a lovely hen do. What's wrong with that?'

'Nothing at all. Rose is going through a tough time at the

moment. Cut her a bit of slack,' I reply, putting my arm around Amy. She folds into me and rests her head on my shoulder, giving me a lungful of her perfume as she does. It's strong, floral and sickly, and a lump forms in my throat as I think how lovely Sam smells in comparison. As soon as I think I can get away with it without causing offence, I detach myself and head for the door. I'm halfway through it when she calls after me.

'I haven't forgotten about Jessie and Sam! I want to know *everything*.'

* * *

As I climb the stairs to my room, I realise that I'm starting to feel a bit like Rose, albeit for different reasons. I'm not looking forward to today either. My mood isn't improved when, having double-checked that I have everything I need for the day, I come back down to find an enormous pink stretch limo parked outside, instead of the more practical minibus that I thought we'd managed to persuade Amy to book.

'What the bloody hell is that?' Rose thunders at Amy as soon as she catches sight of it. 'Where's the minibus?'

'I upgraded it,' Amy sings, apparently fully recovered from her previous encounter with Rose, but seemingly without having learned anything from it. 'Minibuses are for old people. We've got champagne on ice, surround sound with karaoke machine and configurable mood lighting. Much more suitable for a hen party, don't you think?'

'It looks ridiculous. I'm not getting in that. What if someone I know sees me getting into it or out of it? What on earth did it cost?' Rose isn't pacified at all.

'It was a *teensy* bit more than the minibus, I'll admit,' Amy coos. 'But when you break it down into cost per person, it's really not that much. If you're worried about your share, you can just have a smaller lunch.'

'Oh, I'm not worried about my share, sweetie,' Rose mimics Amy's tone, 'because I'm not contributing a single penny to this monstrosity. *We* agreed on a minibus. *You* booked this without consulting us, so *you* can pay for it, understand?'

Thankfully, Lily chooses this moment to make her appearance, and her face lights up when she sees the pink limo. She and Amy wrap their arms around each other and do a little dance, squealing with delight as they spin. We drew lots earlier in the week to decide who was going to stay behind to babysit; Andrew and Zoe lost, but I think Mum's on the brink of offering herself instead, if the set of her face is anything to go by. Before she has the opportunity to say anything, however, Amy hustles us all into the back of the limo and we set off.

'Dan's mum, Anita, is meeting us at the venue,' Amy informs us as she wrestles unsuccessfully with the champagne bottle.

'We know,' Rose replies sullenly. 'You told us three times on the group chat. Oh, for heaven's sake, give that thing to me!'

She grabs the bottle off Amy and somehow manages to open it without spilling any, which is quite a feat given the way that the car is bouncing and lurching along the road. Either the surface is very poor or the suspension is up the spout. Thank goodness it's not that far to the hotel, otherwise we might be needing sick bags in here.

'There you go,' Rose continues, handing the bottle back.

'Thank you,' Amy simpers. 'Of course, I usually rely on Liam to do things like open champagne. It's such a shame he couldn't come along to the stag party, but I know he's really looking forward to the wedding.' She grasps Lily's arm and leans close to her ear. 'I'm hoping it will give him a few ideas!' she trills, loud enough that we can all hear her clearly.

Liam is Amy's boyfriend. I've never met him, but I have a pretty good mental image of what Amy would look for in a man. She tried hard to inveigle him onto the stag do, from what I heard, but Dan stood firm, saying he didn't really know Liam and it would be better if he just came to the wedding. Dan went up considerably in my estimation when I heard that. Amy is not an easy person to say 'no' to, as we've discovered.

Amy pours out six thimblefuls of champagne and hands them round. I'm not sure what it is, but it's not very cold and has a nasty acidic tang to it. Dom Pérignon it certainly isn't. As I sip my ration, I look around the car. Lily and Amy are having the time of their lives and are now fiddling with the sound system to see what they can get it to play. Sarah looks overwhelmed and is sitting quietly in her corner, Rose just looks miserable, and Mum is doing the same as me, looking around and taking it all in.

'Are you OK, Mum?' I ask her.

'Yes. I think it must be a generational thing,' she replies, under her breath. 'I'm pleased that Lily likes it, but I find this all a bit tasteless. Do you know what I mean?'

'I do,' I agree.

By the time we arrive at the hotel in Newquay, some fifteen minutes later, Sarah is definitely green around the gills. Cornish roads and stretch limos are not a good combination, and we've been rocked and shaken for most of the journey. The partition between us and the driver means we couldn't even see ahead and predict which way we were going to go, so the whole effect was rather like being on a ship in a storm, or at least what I think that would feel like. Lily and Amy have whispered and giggled most of the way here, but I managed to tune them out pretty successfully. I've been trying to work out where Sam might be on his emergency journey home, and worrying about what he might find when he gets there.

Once we've met up with Anita, Amy wastes no time herding us inside to the spa, where we change into dressing gowns and slippers before making our way through to the dining room, where most of the other tables are already occupied by people dressed identically to us. I know it's supposed to be a luxury thing, but it all looks weirdly institutional to me. I'm very pleased that I was able to eat most of my breakfast before Sam got his news, as the menu is everything I feared it would be.

'We're going to start healthy and then get progressively more unhealthy as the day goes on,' Amy explains, even though she's told us this countless times before. I study the menu, which basically informs me that my lunch will consist of one of a selection of deeply unappetising sounding 'power salads', served with a fresh juice of my choosing, and then fruit. There's not a piece of meat or a decent carbohydrate to be seen anywhere. Mum, who has always been a traditional kind of cook, looks completely baffled, but thankfully Rose has pulled herself together enough to try to help her navigate her way to the least unpleasant sounding options.

I have to admit that, when the food arrives, it actually looks more appetising than the menu descriptions led me to believe. There really isn't very much of it, though, and Mum looks nearly as miserable as Rose.

'So, after lunch we divide into pairs for the mani/pedi and the massages,' Amy announces when the food has been cleared away and we're drinking a flavourless concoction that purports to be some kind of health-giving tea.

'I'm not a mani/pedi person, Amy,' Rose tells her. 'I think I'll go straight for the massage and then lie around while I wait for the rest of you to catch up.'

Amy looks like Rose has just announced she's going out to shoot kittens in the face. 'You *can't* have a massage straight after eating!' she exclaims. 'All your bodily energy is focused on digestion and you won't get the benefit. That's why I put the mani/pedi in first.

Please don't mess with the schedule, Rose. I've put a lot of work into getting it just right.'

For a moment, I wonder if Rose is going to explode again, but thankfully she manages to bite her tongue. Amy begins to pair us off: Mum is paired with Anita, and Amy pairs herself with Lily, which comes as a surprise to nobody. Sarah and I are put together, leaving Rose on her own. I wonder if Amy has changed the pairings in her head this morning to punish Rose for making her cry. I wouldn't put it past her but, if that was her intention, it's backfired spectacularly.

For the first time today, Rose looks pleased about something.

25

I haven't spent much time with Sarah since her meltdown, and I'm relieved to see that she appears to be back to her old bubbly self. She tells me that she had a grovelling text message from Harry, which she's saved just in case he decides to try to re-invent the truth when they get back to school. We don't have a lot of conversation about it, though, as we're both aware of the manicurists listening in. I feel much the same as Rose; I can take or leave the mani/pedi, but I'm a sucker for a massage. There are several moments where I groan from the mixture of pain and pleasure as the masseuse works on a couple of knotty spots, and Sarah giggles at me each time.

'I should have recorded you,' she laughs as we make our way back to join the others afterwards. 'I'm sure there are specialist websites I could sell the soundtrack to, not that I know, obviously.'

We're still laughing when we join the others, who are all lying on day beds sipping from bottles of water.

'What's so funny?' Amy is determined not to miss out.

'Oh, nothing,' I reply. I don't think my mother would get or approve of our conversation, and I don't want to shatter the truce we seem to have reached.

'Was it something about Sam and Jessie?' Amy persists.

'No.'

'Are you sure? Lily told me that you and Sam were *very* close, and he's coming along to the evening do on Saturday. I can't wait to meet him.'

'Yeah, well you might be disappointed. In case you've forgotten, he's currently on his way home to visit his eighteen-year-old daughter in hospital after a serious accident.'

Amy doesn't reply, and I hope she's realised that teasing me about Sam right now is not going to end well for her. I'm quickly proved wrong a few moments later, sadly.

'Wow, he must be seriously *old*, if his daughter is eighteen already. I didn't know you went for silver foxes, Poppy.'

'Yeah. When you're single at my age, Amy, it's pretty much the only option,' I reply sarcastically. 'I'm so desperate these days that I mainly target the ones on Zimmer frames because they can't get away.'

I can see Sarah desperately stifling a laugh, but thankfully Rose intervenes before Amy can make any more crass observations.

'I'm starving,' she states. 'When's tea?'

It's almost telepathic, because moments later the waiters are bringing in tiered platters with sandwiches, little cakes and scones for everyone. I take the lid off the teapot and sniff suspiciously, but it appears that this is ordinary breakfast tea, and I sigh with relief.

'Normally, the spa doesn't allow cream teas in, because they go against the wellness ethos that they're trying to promote. But I managed to persuade them,' Amy tells us smugly. I can't help feeling sorry for the poor sap on the other end of the phone during that conversation; arguing with Amy is probably like arguing with a rock. By the looks of things, Rose wasn't the only one that was starving, as we all fall on the platters, and soon there's nothing left but crumbs.

Amy switches the pairs around after tea, and I'm matched with Rose for the facial and body wrap that are allegedly going to leave our skin feeling as soft as a newborn baby's. We're both pretty sceptical, but, whether they work or not, the feeling of the compounds they put on us is lovely. We can't speak once they've applied the mask to our faces, so we lie there in silence, listening to the soft mood music playing in the background. Sam must be in Swindon or nearly there by now, I reckon. I imagine him running down hospital corridors in search of Jessie. I really hope she's OK.

Once our faces have been rinsed and moisturised, more compounds are applied to our bodies, and we're wrapped in cotton while they work their supposed magic. I have to say that the skin on my face does feel rejuvenated, but I've done these things before, and I know the effect is temporary at best. Still, there are worse ways to spend the afternoon.

'I'm sorry to hear about Sam. Do you know how Jessie is?' Rose asks me, now that we're allowed to talk again.

'No. All I know is that she was in a car accident and she's in hospital. Her mum sounded pretty agitated from what I could hear, so I imagine it's serious.'

'Why don't you text him to say you're thinking of him and ask how she is?'

'You're not going to believe this, but I don't have his number.'

'What?'

'I know. It sounds stupid, but we never got around to swapping numbers. We didn't need to, because we were together most of the time, and then it didn't seem appropriate to ask for his number when he was in the middle of dealing with an emergency.'

'You know his name though, don't you? He's bound to be on social media; you can find him that way.'

I sigh. 'Do you know, I only know he's called Sam? I don't even know his surname, I've just realised. That's going to make finding him next to impossible, even if he wants to be found. Neither of us made any promises about this being more than a holiday fling, so I'm trying not to read more into it than that. He did say he'd still try to make the wedding, but he's just as likely to forget all about me once he's back in Swindon.'

'I don't think you believe that, do you?'

'I think it could have been more,' I reply. 'I would have liked it to be more. But long-distance relationships aren't a great idea, and he told me he was thinking of moving further west than he already is from me. Maybe, in a funny way, it's for the best.'

'You never know, he might make it back for the wedding. I can see it now, like that scene at the end of *Dirty Dancing*. You're sitting all sad in the corner, and he comes over like Patrick Swayze, grabs you by the hand and says, "Nobody puts Poppy in a corner".'

'We can but hope,' I laugh. 'Anyway, enough about my stuff. How are you?'

'Pretty shit, as you've probably gathered. I tried to get Steve to talk to me this morning, and I got as far as getting him to admit that there was a problem, but when I tried to get him to tell me what it was, he just clammed up and said he'd tell me when he was ready. We ended up having a big row about it. So then, when Amy started...'

'You were a little hard on her,' I observe.

'She deserved it. God, she's annoying, isn't she? Have you met her boyfriend, the mysterious Liam?'

'No.'

'I feel sorry for him, don't you?'

'Maybe he likes being ordered around. Some men do.'

'I could do with one of those at the moment. I could order Steve to tell me what the hell is going on!'

* * *

Once we've been unwrapped, hosed down and thoroughly moisturised, we're finally allowed to leave the fluffy dressing gowns behind and get back into our normal clothes. We congregate back in the main lobby of the hotel.

'OK. Everyone back in the car!' Amy calls, pointing at the hideous pink limo. 'I've booked a table at an Indian restaurant that has really good reviews.'

Out of the corner of my eye, I notice my mum stiffen. She has a massive aversion to spicy food.

'Umm, Amy?' I begin. 'Did you check everyone's dietary requirements before booking an Indian restaurant?'

'What do you mean?'

'Not everyone likes Indian food,' I explain.

I can see from her face that she never considered that for a moment, and I can almost hear the cogs whirring as she tries to extricate herself from this predicament without losing face.

'It's fine,' she scoffs a few seconds later. 'They do vegetarian stuff for Sarah, and I expect they do a selection of English dishes for people who don't like curry. Personally, I like my curries like my men: the hotter the better!'

Rose and I hang back with Mum as the others clamber into the limo. 'Don't worry,' Rose tells her. 'We'll find something you can eat.'

In the end, we manage to persuade her to try a chicken tikka and, for someone who allegedly hates spicy food, she makes short work of it. The two large glasses of wine she washes it down with obviously help, and I notice Rose piling her plate with rice to try to stop her from getting plastered. Amy, true to her word, orders a chicken Madras, and then eats barely a mouthful before declaring that 'it's much hotter than at my local' and demanding something else instead. She's all talk, that one. I tried a bit of her Madras out of curiosity and, although it was fairly fiery, it wasn't inedibly hot.

'I've been reflecting on our conversation yesterday,' Mum says to me as we lurch homewards in the ridiculous limo. Lily, Sarah and Amy are singing gustily along to 'There Are Worse Things I Could Do' from *Grease* on the karaoke machine, the irony of it clearly lost on them. I don't know about Amy (and I don't want to) but the other two have certainly not been anywhere near 'a boy or two'. Rose is just sitting glumly, obviously apprehensive about facing Steve again.

'Oh?' I reply. In the end, she downed three large glasses of wine, so I suspect she's more than a little tipsy. To be fair, I'm not entirely sober myself, so neither of us are probably in the best place to have a serious conversation.

'Yes,' she continues. 'You see, I've got this friend who confided in me that things weren't as they should be between her and her husband in, you know, the *bedroom* department, and I wondered whether you might be able to give me some advice to pass on.'

I may not be sober, but I'm still alert enough to spot the glaring inconsistencies in what she's just said. There's absolutely no way any sane person would choose the most sexually repressed woman in the Western hemisphere to confide in about their love life. She's talking about herself, and this puts me in a difficult situation. I can't challenge her about this 'friend', because whatever she's about to say is probably a big deal for her and something she can only get through with a lot of wine inside her. Also, even though I deal with this stuff professionally every day, talking to your mum about her sex life is still weird, so actually pretending we're talking about someone else might help me too.

'What seems to be the problem?' I ask, after steeling myself mentally.

'Well, like me she's got four children. The last one was very large and was born very fast, which made a bit of a mess of her,' she points discreetly at her lap, 'down there.'

'It's not uncommon for women to tear or need an episiotomy during childbirth,' I remark. 'Normally, the midwife or doctor will repair the damage with stitches after the delivery.'

'Yes, but in her case, it seems the medics didn't do it quite right, and things with her husband, umm, let's just say they weren't the same afterwards. She says she tried, but it was uncomfortable, and he could see it was hurting her, so eventually they just stopped. She still feels guilty, though, because it was important to him, and she wants to make him happy. The other issue is that she's obviously been through the menopause now, and she isn't sure that she's able to, well...' At this point, even the wine isn't enough to help her and she dries up.

'Has she consulted her GP?'

'No, why?'

'There's nothing unusual about her condition, and it's often easily fixed with a small operation. She should go and see her GP and get a referral. In the meantime, she ought to experiment with some lube, to see if that helps with the menopause side of things. In fact...'

An idea has come to my slightly addled brain and, because all ideas are the best ever when you're slightly inebriated, I fight my way past the karaoke singers and press the button to lower the partition and speak to the chauffeur.

'Do you know what time the supermarket shuts?' I yell at him, over the din from the karaoke machine.

'I'm not sure. I think it stays open late,' he replies.

'Can we divert?'

'Sure.'

'Thanks. I just need to run in and grab something.'

The others have no idea what's going on until the limo pulls up outside the supermarket, which is just as well as I'm sure Amy would have vetoed it if she'd known. I leap out, ignoring the sudden cries of consternation, and rush inside. It doesn't take me long to find what I need and there are no queues at the checkouts at this time of night, so I'm probably only gone for a few minutes.

'What on earth have you been doing?' Amy exclaims crossly as the limo pulls away. 'This is supposed to be a hen party, not a bloody weekly shop!'

'I needed some tampons,' I lie. 'You know what it's like when you're caught without.'

This seems to pacify her, and the three of them resume their singing until we pull up outside the house.

'Time to get the party started!' Amy sings, as we make our way indoors. 'Where's the wine?'

'Haven't you got to get back to the hotel?' I ask her.

'I'm bunking with Lily tonight,' she tells me smugly. 'I didn't want to miss out on the beach day tomorrow.'

Oh, great. We're stuck with her for the whole of tomorrow as well. Maybe Sam will come back and give me an excuse to escape. I can only hope. I volunteer to help Lily open a couple of bottles so I can get her on her own. As soon as we're alone, I slip one of the bottles of lube I bought in the supermarket into her hand.

'For the wedding night,' I explain. 'Just in case.'

* * *

Even though we've already had a fair amount to drink, it doesn't take us long to empty the bottles. Andrew and Zoe come and join us, and somewhere along the line, more wine appears. Mum's quite flushed in the face and talking animatedly to Zoe about something, Amy and Lily are giggling like schoolgirls, and Rose is just making steady progress down her glass, occasionally muttering something to Andrew or me.

We're just about to call it a night when the boys return from their stag. From Dad's description, it sounds like Stuart in particular is going to have a sore head tomorrow. Just as he and Mum are heading for the staircase, I call her back and give her the other bottle of lube.

'For your friend,' I tell her, with a wink.

26

I'm relieved to wake the next morning with a clear head. The water I drank before going to bed obviously did the trick, although I quickly realise I'm bursting for a wee and dash into my en-suite bathroom to relieve the pressure. Once I'm more comfortable, I check the clock and discover that, despite promising myself a lie-in, it's only six thirty. I consider climbing back into bed and trying to go back to sleep, but it's another beautiful day outside and, although the rational part of me knows it's too soon, I decide to get dressed and wander down the road to see if Sam's back.

I run a hairbrush through my hair and brush my teeth, just in case, before throwing on a pair of shorts and a T-shirt. As I make my way downstairs through the silent house, I'm reminded of my first morning here. It's incredible to think that this is only the beginning of my sixth day in Cornwall; so much has happened that it feels much, much longer than that. I let myself out through the kitchen door as normal and step out onto the road. There are already surfers on the water, and I stop for a moment to watch them. It's much more interesting now that I have some understanding of what's involved, and a part of me longs to wriggle into a wetsuit and join them. Perhaps, if Sam is back, I will.

This thought spurs me on again and I quicken my pace towards his house. I know it's almost impossible that he would have driven from here to Swindon and back in a day, but I'm not thinking entirely rationally. When I get there and see that the driveway is empty and the house is deserted, I'm not at all surprised, but I feel a sharp pang of disappointment nonetheless. I peer through the window next to the front door, but can't see if any of Sam's possessions are still in the house so I'm none the wiser about whether he's actually planning to come back or not.

'Please come back, Sam,' I say out loud as I rest my hand on the front door. 'I'm not ready to let you go just yet.'

It takes a monumental amount of willpower to turn away from the door and start the trudge back to our house. Every time I hear a car, my heart quickens and I check the driver, hoping it's him. I can't remember anything about his car; I never really noticed it. I try to picture how the driveway looked while he was still around, but nothing comes. I have a vague idea that it might be blue, but it could equally be silver; I'm easily able to picture either colour. I consider calling the hospital to see how Jessie is, before I realise that I have no idea which hospital she's in and they wouldn't tell me anything anyway.

'Get a grip, Poppy,' I tell myself firmly, as I reach our house. It's just after seven now, and I'm relieved to see that the kitchen is still deserted. I let myself in quietly and make myself a cup of coffee to take outside. I've decided to sit on the sun deck and enjoy the early-morning air before the rest of my family, and bloody Amy, appear.

As I sip, I reflect on the extraordinary change that seems to have come over my mother. I'm still a bit cross that she laboured under such a ridiculous misapprehension for so many years, and never bothered either to ask me or look up what sex therapists do for herself. To be fair, I can't imagine her typing the word 'sex' into a search engine. There was a terrific hoo-ha some years ago when she wanted to know the origin of the phrase 'not enough room to swing a cat', but entered 'throw your cat' by mistake and got all sorts of suggestive results. Even so, she could have just asked. I try to conjure up a mental image of a couple getting it on while I watch and give them suggestions, but it just makes me laugh. At least it's a distraction from thinking about Sam. I can't believe I never got his phone number. There genuinely never seemed to be a need, though. I suppose I might have given him my number after the wedding, before we went our separate ways, but only if I'd felt that he might actually want to stay in touch. Nobody wants to come across as desperate.

The Freudian battle within me has definitely taken a turn. The granny in the attic is positively crowing that she knew something like this was going to happen, and that I should have listened to her all along, while the gorilla in the basement is sulking. I think the bank manager in the middle is secretly hoping the granny is wrong, but she's keeping her counsel and not saying anything. I wonder if Sam is missing me at all; obviously he's going to be mainly worrying about his daughter, but maybe there are moments when I creep into his mind. I certainly hope so.

'Penny for them?' Andrew's voice seems to have come from nowhere and I start.

'Don't do that!' I exclaim. 'I nearly spilled my coffee!'

'Sorry. I thought you heard me coming. You really were miles away, weren't you?'

'Yeah, I suppose I was.'

'Sam?' he asks.

'Maybe.'

'You know what you need, don't you?'

'What's that?'

'A distraction. Something to take your mind off things. Something like table tennis, for example.'

I can't help smiling, in spite of myself. A distraction is just what I need.

'OK, you're on. We'll have to keep the noise down though, otherwise we'll be seriously unpopular.'

'I don't think we'll be seeing anyone else for a while yet. In fact, I'm rather surprised you're awake. What time did you go to bed?'

'I don't know. It was after midnight, but I was still wide awake at six thirty.'

'Come on then, best of five.'

I follow him indoors, popping my empty mug in the dishwasher on the way, and we take up our places at the table tennis table. To begin with, my mind isn't fully engaged, and I lose the first two games to him. This is enough to make me focus, and a quiet, intense ferocity settles on us as we slog through the third game. The points are falling slowly now, and it feels like a battle of attrition as we fight for each one. Eventually, we're equal on ten points each, and the battle for the final point begins. I'm intensely aware that the match hangs on this point. If I lose it, it's all over, and Andrew will spend the whole day lording it over me. I desperately need this and, after what feels like an age, I catch him out and the point is mine.

As we settle into the fourth game, I'm dimly aware of the door to the games room opening and closing a couple of times, but I'm so completely in the zone that I neither know nor care who else is in the room. It looks like Andrew is starting to run out of steam, as I'm outwitting him more often now, and the game falls fairly easily to me. We're equal on two games each, so the match now hangs on the final game. I can see Andrew gritting his teeth with determination, but my mind is completely clear except for the ball, my racquet and the table. I don't know whether it's my total focus or whether Andrew is making mistakes as he gets more desperate, but I win the first seven points without conceding anything. He gets one point off me on the next serve, but that just spurs me on, and I win the game decisively without conceding another point. As I lay down my racquet, I become aware of applause, and turn to see Zoe and Rose clapping.

'Bloody hell, Poppy,' Andrew gasps as we shake hands. 'That was brutal. I take back everything I said about you having lost your killer instinct.'

'As you said, it was probably just the distraction I needed.'

'Remind me never to suggest that again,' he smiles.

'You were both pretty scary,' Zoe remarks. 'I've never seen such an intense match. Normally, you take verbal pot-shots at each other all the way through, but neither of you said a word during that.'

'I was going to suggest a "best of three" match later to decide the overall winner,' Andrew continues. 'But I'm not sure I want to now.'

'Let's see how we feel later, shall we?' I offer. 'Now, I don't know about anyone else, but all that concentration has given me an appetite. Who's for breakfast? I'll do eggs and bacon for anyone that wants it.'

* * *

The idea of eggs and bacon proves popular, and there's a good atmosphere in the kitchen as I hand round the plates and we tuck in. Zoe is pouring out orange juice and Rose has made teas and coffees. Andrew has even offered to wash up as his penalty for losing the match. The way he says it makes me laugh. You'd think he was offering to paint the Forth Bridge rather than just wash up a frying pan and a spatula. The banter is flowing easily as we eat, and even Rose seems lighter than usual. I'm reminded of how it was when I was growing up, before things got awkward. I'm really enjoying the company of my siblings, and I'm just about to say so when the mood suddenly changes. Rose's face tenses up and I'm pretty sure I know why. Sure enough, when I turn around, Steve is in the kitchen, moodily making himself a coffee. As soon as he's done, he walks right past us without even a 'hello' and lets himself out of the door into the garden. I look at Rose, and I can see the pain in her eyes.

'Enough,' I tell her, and follow Steve out into the garden.

I find him sitting on one of the sun loungers, staring morosely into the swimming pool. Without saying a word, I settle myself on the lounger next to him. We sit there without speaking for what seems like for ever, but is probably no more than five to ten minutes. I can feel the anguish coming off him in waves and eventually I can't bear it any more.

'Steve,' I say, 'what's going on?'

'I told you,' he replies. 'I just have some stuff I'm working through.'

'Here's the problem,' I tell him. 'You've been "working" on whatever this problem is since we've arrived, and probably before as well, and you're not getting anywhere from what I can see. It's like you and Rose have been carrying your own miniature weather system around with you for the last few days. You're not quite Eeyore, but you're definitely not happy. And Rose is tearing herself apart with worry. So, it seems to me that you're not going to solve this one on your own. If you can't talk to Rose about it, then maybe I can help?'

'You sound like a therapist,' he grumbles.

'Duh! Why do you think that is?' I laugh, nudging his arm. 'Come on. Maybe sharing it will help.'

'I very much doubt it.'

'From where I'm sitting, you have two choices. You can either continue to wrestle with this on your own, which doesn't appear to be doing you, or anyone around you, any good, or you can take a risk, talk to me, and maybe break the deadlock.'

'If I tell you, will you keep it confidential?'

'Do you know how many times I've heard that this week? As you're an adult, provided it's nothing illegal and you haven't killed anyone, I promise I'll keep it confidential.'

'I haven't done anything illegal or killed anyone, I promise.'

'Well then. It can't be that bad, can it?'

'It's bad. Why do you think I'm struggling so hard? If it was something simple, don't you think I would have managed to solve it by now?'

'Are you having an affair?'

'No!'

'Gambling?'

'Apart from a weekly lottery ticket, no.'

'So what is it then? Rose is a bit of a blunt instrument, I admit, but she's also open-minded. If you're not having an affair and you haven't gambled away the house, I reckon she'd be able to cope.'

'You think?' He smiles grimly. 'The truth is...'

'Yes?' I encourage him.

'The truth is that I've just found out I'm adopted.'

27

My first thought is a surprisingly angry, *Is that all?* but thankfully I manage to swallow that before it escapes my lips. Whatever my views on the matter, this is clearly a big deal for him. Very carefully, I arrange my expression into one of concern.

'When did you find out?' I ask him.

'About a month ago.'

'And you didn't have any inkling before then?'

'No! Why would I?'

I try to remember Steve's mum and dad from the tree-planting party that Rose and Steve held to celebrate Evie's birth, which would have been the last time I saw them, but nothing concrete comes to mind.

'Often,' I say as tactfully as I can, 'there is a physical resemblance between parents and children that is missing in adopted children, because they don't share any common genes.'

'Yeah, well, that's the irony right there, isn't it,' he says bitterly.

I'm a bit confused by his response, so I decide to change tack.

'I can see this has been a huge shock to you,' I say.

'That's putting it mildly.'

'What I'm struggling with is why you've kept it a secret from Rose. Don't you think she'd understand?'

'How can she? I don't understand it myself. Don't you see? Everything I am, everything I thought I was, is a lie. I am a lie. Who even am I? How can I be a husband to her and a father to the girls when I don't have the first bloody idea who I am?' He puts his head in his hands and his shoulders shake as he sobs.

'Have you ever met my Aunty Kath?' he asks, when the sobbing has subsided and he's noticed that I'm still sitting with him.

'I don't think so.'

'You would know if you had. She's pretty unforgettable. She's best described as "rarely sober", so she makes quite an impression wherever she goes. She's my mother's, or rather my adoptive mother's, sister. I've never liked her; she always seemed weirdly obsessed with me and I found it uncomfortable. Mum would tell her off sometimes, but she just wouldn't leave me alone. She'd always buy me the most enormous, and usually inappropriate, gifts for birthdays and Christmases. One year, she bought me a teddy bear so large it barely fitted in my bedroom.'

'What's wrong with a teddy bear?' I ask.

'I was fifteen.'

'Ah.'

'Exactly. Mum always used to tell me to humour her, that she was sad because she didn't have any children of her own and spoiling me was her way of dealing with it. That and being permanently plastered, I guess. Thankfully the gift-giving thing seemed to calm down when I reached adulthood, but when the girls were born, it all started again with them. Anyway, I happened to stop by Mum and Dad's on the way home from work a month or so ago because Dad, or the man who's been calling himself my dad, was having a problem with his computer and had asked me to look at it. When I let myself in, I could hear raised voices from the kitchen, and one of them was Aunty Kath. I didn't know she was going to be there; I'd probably have chosen another day to call in if I had. I wish I had.'

'What happened?'

'Mum was saying, "You have to let this go, Kath. It's not helping you, Stephen or the girls. You're risking doing far more harm than good," and Kath shouted back "Why shouldn't I buy nice things for *my* son and *my* grandchildren?"' He stops, waiting for me to catch up with him.

'Oh,' is all I can think of to say.

'Exactly. I felt like I'd been punched in the gut. I just stood there in the hallway, listening to everything I thought I knew being blown to smithereens. All I could think was that maybe I'd misheard somehow, that I'd got it wrong, but then Kath stormed out of the kitchen and saw me.'

'What did she say?'

'She asked how long I'd been standing there, and I told her long enough. Mum obviously heard my voice because she came rushing out and her face was white as a sheet. She started trying to tell me that Kath didn't mean it, that she just thought of me *like* a son, but it was clear from both their faces that she was lying. I still didn't know what to believe, but then Dad, hearing the commotion, came down from the spare room that he uses as an office. I think he worked out straight away what was going on, because he just said, "I think it's time you and I had a chat, Stephen." And then, very calmly and kindly, he took me upstairs and blew my life apart.'

Steve pauses and stares into the pool, and I can sense that he's suddenly miles away. I want to hear the rest of the story, but I can see how much it's taken for him to share what he has.

'Would you like a break?' I ask him gently. 'At least I can set Rose's mind at rest that you're not having an affair.'

'Is that what she thinks?'

'You have been acting strangely. It's not an unreasonable conclusion.'

'Now that I've started, I'd quite like to tell you everything. Do you mind? It's surprisingly helpful, saying it out loud.'

'Of course I don't mind!' I reassure him. 'Tell me what your father said.'

'He's not my father.'

'Tell me what your adoptive father said, then.'

'The first thing he did was confirm what I'd heard, that Kath was my birth mother. According to him, she was a wild child from an early age. My grandparents were very religious, part of this ultra conservative church, and she rebelled and kicked against it like crazy, refusing to attend the church, or wearing totally inappropriate clothing if they managed to force her to go. The more my grandparents tried to bring her into line, the harder she fought them. She smoked, she drank and she hung around with boys, all of which were considered terrible sins. Things came to a head when she fell pregnant. You can imagine that my grandparents were absolutely horrified. A termination was out of the question, of course, but so was the shame of their daughter not only giving birth to a child outside marriage, but not even having the first idea who the father was because she was sleeping with several different boys at the time. So that's when they hatched their plan.'

'What plan?'

'Kath's older sister, my mother, was respectable. She was already married, so nobody would bat an eyelid if she had a child. My grandparents hid Kath away, pretending she was ill, and spent a small fortune on fake pregnancy bellies for my mother – the woman who pretended to be my mother – to wear. When I was born, Kath was forced to sign the papers giving me up, and my so-called parents adopted me. Scandal averted, carry on as you were. Kath was heartbroken and turned back to the bottle, but that was nothing new, so it actually made the story more believable, in a funny way. And I would never have known anything about it, if I hadn't overheard that argument.'

A piece of the jigsaw falls into place. 'So, when I asked about physical resemblance...'

'Exactly. There is a family resemblance, but it's because of Kath.'

'How did you feel when you learned all this?'

'I couldn't handle it. I still can't. I stormed out. Mum and Kath were still in the hallway, obviously waiting to hear what I had to say, and I just shouted that they'd all lied to me and I never wanted to see any of them again. They've all tried to ring me since, but I don't have anything to say to any of them. I'm lost, Poppy. I can't begin to explain how it feels to find that I am literally not who I thought I was. My real mother is a drunk who I don't even like, I have no idea who my father is, and the people who I thought were my parents are actually my aunt and uncle. Can you see why I might be a little preoccupied right now?'

'Can I ask you a question?' I say, when I'm sure he's finished. 'This is a massive shock, and I can't begin to understand how it feels but, from where I'm sitting, it doesn't actually change who you are to the people who matter most to you, to the people that need you. You're still Olivia and Evie's father; that hasn't changed. Do you love them any less because of this?'

'Of course not!'

'Exactly. You're also still Rose's husband, you poor bastard, and she needs you too. Do you love her any less?'

'No.' For the first time since this conversation started, a hint of a smile plays across his lips.

'What?' I ask him.

'You don't know what I see in her, do you?'

'I don't need to. As long as you're both happy, that's all I care about.'

'You were doing so well, but you're talking nonsense now.'

He's obviously said all he wants to about his situation and wants a change of subject, so I decide to humour him. 'Go on,' I say. 'Enlighten me.'

'I know you and Rose don't really get on, so it may seem odd to you, but I was blown away by her the first time I saw her. I'd never met anyone so... I'm trying to think of the word.'

'Bossy?' I offer, with a smile.

'Forthright, that's the word I want. There's no side to her, you know? You're never in any doubt how she feels about something or what she thinks. If she has an opinion, which she usually does, she makes no bones about sharing it. She was beautiful, too – still is. I fell head over heels in love with her before she even noticed me. I used to just stare at her; I think I was awestruck. I didn't have the courage to ask her out; I barely even spoke to her.'

'So how did you end up together?'

'She caught me staring one day, came up to me and said, "Are you just going to sit there mooning over me all the time, or are you actually going to ask me on a date at any point?"' He smiles at the memory.

'That sounds like Rose!' I laugh.

'Yeah. So, anyway, I stammered out an invitation to a local pizza restaurant and the rest is history.'

He smiles again, obviously reliving the memories. After a while, it becomes clear that this conversation has also gone as far as it's going to, so I slowly get to my feet.

'Thank you for listening, Poppy,' Steve says.

'It's not a problem, really. I know it seems a lot, but I think you will find your way through this and, hopefully, forgive all of them. Can I ask one thing, though?'

'What?'

'Talk to Rose. She needs to know what's going on.'

'What is going on?' Our heads snap round at the sound of Rose's voice. We've been so focused on our conversation that neither of us have noticed her come around the corner of the house, and she's now standing behind us, her face absolutely ashen.

For a while, nobody speaks, but the atmosphere is so highly charged I can almost hear it fizzing and crackling.

'What do you need to tell me, Steve? What have you done?'

'He hasn't done anything,' I reassure her. 'He's going through some stuff, but he'll be OK. I think you both will. You two have a lot to talk about,' I continue. 'I'm going to leave you to it, but if you need me at any point, just come and get me.'

I get up and walk towards the house as Rose takes my place on the sun lounger. When I get indoors, I'm surprised to find my mother in the kitchen, making tea in her pyjamas. I don't think I've ever seen her downstairs without being fully dressed and made up before. She's waiting for the kettle to boil, and humming quietly to herself.

'Hi, Mum,' I say to her. 'Is everything OK?'

'Yes,' she replies. 'Why, shouldn't it be?'

'I don't know. I don't think I've ever seen you downstairs in your pyjamas before.'

'Your father and I decided to have a lie-in,' she says with a smile, and I notice her eyes are twinkling. 'He's just in the shower, so I thought I'd make us both a cup of tea while I'm waiting for him to come out.'

You don't have to be a mind reader to work out what has been going on here. Although I'm happy that it looks like they've rekindled their love life, it's also a little bit icky. Thankfully, Lily and Amy come into the kitchen before she can say any more. Lily takes one look at Mum and her jaw drops open.

'Mum!' she exclaims. 'What on earth are you doing?'

'I'm making tea for your father and me,' Mum replies, a note of irritation creeping into her voice.

'But you're not dressed!' Lily continues, aghast.

'So? I'm perfectly decent, aren't I? I don't understand why you girls are making such a fuss. First Poppy and now you. Lots of people make tea in their pyjamas. It's not a crime, you know.' She pours water into the two mugs and reaches into the fridge for the milk.

'I think your pyjamas are lovely,' Amy pipes up. 'Where did you get them?'

'Thank you, Amy,' Mum replies archly. 'I got them in M&S in the sales last year.'

Lily and I exchange glances. She obviously hasn't twigged what's happened, and she's looking at Mum as if she's lost her mind and needs to be carted off to the nearest psychiatric ward. Meanwhile, Mum is pouring milk into the mugs of tea as if there was nothing odd going on at all. Lily is obviously struggling to decide whether to continue this conversation or not, and I'm relieved when it seems that she's decided to leave it. Mum carefully puts the teabags into the bin and wanders out towards the staircase.

'What's got into her?' Lily asks me.

'Maybe she's just relaxed. Or she's decided to take it slow today because tomorrow is going to be full-on with the wedding. I don't think it's anything to worry about.'

'I guess so,' she concedes. 'It's still odd, though. I hope she's not going to make a habit of it.'

'Why would you care?' Amy retorts. 'You're moving out to live with Dan, dummy! Your mum could wander around in the nude and you'd be none the wiser.'

'You're right,' Lily giggles. 'Sometimes I forget. I hope she and Dad aren't planning to start a nudist colony at home now they're unsupervised. That would be too weird to contemplate.'

'Right, I'm going to make us both a cup of tea to take out and enjoy on the sun deck,' Amy tells her. 'This is your last day in this amazing house and we need to make the most of it.'

'You might want to avoid the sun deck,' I tell her, vaguely aware of my phone vibrating in my pocket. 'Rose and Steve are out there.'

'So? There's room for everyone.'

'Yes, but they're having a bit of a heart-to-heart, and I think they would appreciate some privacy.'

'They can't hog the whole sun deck! That's totally unfair. If they want privacy they should go to their bedroom. I'm going out there, and if they don't like it they'll have to move.'

Considering she's not even supposed to be here, I'm briefly amazed at her attitude, before remembering that this is Amy. She takes the word 'entitlement' to a whole new level.

'OK, fine. I'll go and tell them you're coming outside, so they have an opportunity to move.' The last thing they need is Amy eavesdropping and sticking her nose into their business, so if she's not prepared to take the hint, the least I can do is warn Rose and Steve. I let myself back into the garden and walk around the side of the house.

It turns out I needn't have bothered, as Rose and Steve are nowhere to be seen. The sun deck is completely deserted. I pull out my phone to discover a WhatsApp message from Rose.

Steve and I need to talk, so have gone for a walk. Don't know how long we will be. Would you mind getting the girls up and feeding them etc. until we get back? Rx

28

'What time are Mummy and Daddy coming back?' Evie asks me, a little sulkily. Thankfully, everyone apart from Lily and Amy has pitched in to help out, so I haven't been babysitting by myself. I think Lily would have helped as well, had Amy not completely monopolised her since breakfast. Olivia and Evie are charming girls, but I am beginning to find entertaining them a struggle, and they're now making no bones about the fact that they want their parents back. It's mid-afternoon and we're all on the beach, trying to make the most of our last day here.

'I don't know. They've got lots of things to talk about, so it could be a while yet.'

'What sort of things?' There's a definite whine in her voice now.

'Grown-up things.'

'I hate it when people say that,' Olivia suddenly rages.

'What?'

'*Grown-up*,' she mimics my voice. 'It's patriotic.'

I can't help laughing, which patently irritates her even more. She's every inch her mother's daughter, that's for sure.

'What's so funny?' she's definitely annoyed now.

'I think you mean patronising, not patriotic,' I explain. 'Patriotic is when you love your country. Patronising is when someone talks down to you.'

'Yeah, well. Whatever.' She turns back to the intricate pattern she's constructing out of sea shells.

'Do you need a break? I can take over for a bit,' Mum offers. She's still in an uncharacteristically good mood, and I'm kind of pleased for her and mildly nauseous all at the same time. She and Dad obviously think they're being subtle but, from the way he keeps touching her and looking at her, and the way she smiles knowingly at him, they might as well put a sign saying 'We had sex this morning' over their heads.

'Would you?' I reply. 'That would be great. I tell you what, why don't I go up to the shop and get us all ice lollies?' My motives aren't totally pure; as well as needing a bit of time away from Olivia and Evie, I'd also like to make a quick check on Sam's house, to see if he's back. I suspect part of the girls' frustration with me this afternoon is that I have been rather distracted. I've been scanning the beach constantly in the hope of seeing him. Every surfer has been subjected to intense scrutiny but, so far, there has been no sign of him.

At the mention of ice lollies, both girls perk up immediately, even offering to come and help carry them. I gently deflect them onto Mum and start to saunter up the beach. I'll get a load of orange ones and then nobody can complain that someone else has a bigger or better one than them.

'Poppy, could you get me one of those ones with the sprinkles at the top please?' Amy calls after me.

'I was just going to get a box all the same,' I reply. 'Otherwise the girls will think it's unfair that you've got a better lolly than them.'

'Oh, they won't mind,' she answers dismissively. 'My need is greater than theirs. After all, they're only children, and they need to understand that adults are more important sometimes.'

'I'll have a look. They might not have any.' And even if they do, there's no bloody way I'm buying you one, I think to myself.

'Thanks.' Now she's placed her order, I'm clearly no longer of any interest to Amy; she leans back in her chair and tilts her face to the sun, closing her eyes. For a tiny moment, I find myself hoping that she gets agonising sunburn, before I pull myself together and remind myself for the umpteenth time today not to sink to her level.

There's still no sign of life at Sam's house, which is both disappointing and unsurprising, and I'm wandering morosely in the direction of the shop when I spot Rose and Steve making their way onto the beach. I try to see if I can pick up any clues, but they're too far away for me to see their faces clearly. I hurry into the shop and buy a selection of plain lollies for everyone, adding four of the ones Amy asked for as an afterthought. When I get back to our spot on the beach, Steve and Rose are talking to the girls in those over-bright voices that people use when they're desperately trying to convince you that nothing is going on. I can see Mum's radar is on full alert, but she's wisely steering clear for the time being.

'Here we are. I got you all extra special ones,' I say, handing the posh lollies to Steve, Rose and the girls. Amy wrinkles her face in disgust as I hand her a plain orange one.

'This isn't what I asked for,' she complains. 'I asked for one like they've got.'

'I know, but the shop only had four,' I lie, 'and I figured their need was greater than yours.' I have to turn away so she can't see my smile. It's unbelievably petty, I know, but sometimes you have to take your victories where you can find them. Everyone else is delighted with their lollies, but every time I glance over at Amy, she looks cross. I'm unrepentant; she could have offered to buy the lollies herself and then she could have had whatever she wanted.

I take advantage of being released from childcare duties to get back into my latest book. So much has happened this week that I'm amazed that I've found any time to read at all, but I have polished off two books so far, and I'm nearly halfway through this one. Just when I feel I've remembered the story and got back into it, I sense Rose slumping down next to me.

'Are you OK?' I ask her quietly.

'Can I borrow you for a bit, away from the others?'

'Of course.' I set down my book and follow her across to the other side of the beach, well away from any eavesdroppers.

'I guess I need to say thank you, first of all. Even though it's been one of the worst months of my life, at least I know what's going on now, and that's down to you. Sorry for dumping the children on you too, but I'm sure you can understand that we needed time alone to talk this all through.'

'It's not a problem, they're charming girls, really. Tell me about you.'

'Are you going to therapise me?'

'Would you like me to?'

'Not really. I'm not sure what there is to say. My husband has just found out that he's adopted. He's very angry and is having a massive identity crisis. That's it.'

There's a long silence and I wait patiently for her. She wouldn't have dragged me here just to tell me what I already know.

'I get it,' she continues after several seconds have gone by. 'Or, at least, I'm trying to get it. Part of me can't help thinking it's all a massive storm in a teacup, and I'm trying extremely hard not to be royally pissed off with him for putting me through all this turmoil for something so simple.'

'It's not simple for him. I think that's the important point.'

'I know. But he's still Steve, isn't he? It doesn't matter who his parents are.'

'I'll admit that this is outside my direct area of expertise, but I can see why he's struggling. All his life, he's been brought up to believe that his parents are, well...'

'His parents,' Rose prompts.

'Exactly. How would you feel if you discovered that Mum and Dad were actually not biologically related to you at all?'

'After this week, part of me feels like I might be pleased!' she laughs.

'You know you don't mean that.'

'No, you're right. If any of us has a reason to wish they weren't related to Mum, it's probably you.'

'She's OK. After you shouted at her and Zoe had a word, it seems as if she's had a bit of an epiphany. It's early days, but the signs are good. We're getting off topic, though. What are you going to do about Steve?'

'Nothing. I've reassured him that I still love him, no matter who his parents are, but he's still got a long way to go. I suggested gently that he might like to return some of their calls, and it was obvious he's not ready to go there yet. All I can do is be there for him when he needs me. I can't tell you how relieved I am that he isn't having an affair.'

'Me too. He's going to need you more than ever, I suspect.'

'I know he will,' she sighs. 'And it's going to be a hell of a shit-storm until he calms down enough to talk to his family. Come on, we'd better get back. I can see Amy staring at us from here, the nosy little bitch.'

As we cross back to the others, I confess my petty behaviour with the ice lollies to Rose, and she laughs uproariously. I know it's not kind, but a good laugh at Amy's expense is probably just what she needs right now, so I'm glad to be able to give it to her.

'What's for dinner tonight?' Amy demands, as we make our way back to the house at the end of the afternoon.

'I think we're having a takeaway after the wedding rehearsal, but you'll be eating at the hotel, won't you?' I ask. Please spare me another night of bloody Amy, I think to myself.

'No. It's Lily's last night as a single woman and she needs her bestie with her,' she replies, wrapping her arm tightly around Lily's shoulder.

'But haven't you paid for the room? It seems odd to pay for a hotel room and then not use it.'

'It's OK. Liam's there so it's not going to waste.'

'Isn't he missing you?'

'Of course he is,' she simpers. 'But he also understands that I've got to be here for Lily at this important point in her life. I've promised him I'll have breakfast with him tomorrow, before we start to get ready.'

Poor Liam, I think to myself. I bet he doesn't 'understand' half as happily as Amy is portraying. If I'd been dragged across the country and abandoned on my own in a hotel where I knew nobody while my partner swanned about with her best friend and family, I'd have plenty to say about it, and it wouldn't be understanding at all. What on earth does he see in her?

29

I know I should be excited on my sister's wedding day, but I feel thoroughly depressed as I force down a piece of toast for breakfast. My morning pilgrimage to Sam's house was fruitless and I'm pretty much resigned to the fact that he's not coming back. I won't completely lose hope until I get into my car to drive home tomorrow, but the window of opportunity is closing fast. I let out a big sigh as I put my empty coffee cup, plate and knife into the dishwasher.

'Not in there,' Mum commands, as she breezes into the kitchen. 'We have to wash everything up and put it away before we leave, remember?'

'Sorry. I was on autopilot,' I tell her, as I remove the offending items and carry them over to the sink to wash.

'Are you OK? You don't seem quite yourself this morning.'

'Yeah, I'm just missing Sam, that's all.'

'I'm sure he'd be here if he could,' she tells me, in a tone that's meant to be reassuring but just comes across as condescending. I'm not going to bite though; she means well, even if her manner is a little unfortunate at times. As I wash and dry my breakfast things, I reflect on the extraordinary change in our relationship this week. From being openly hostile, she's softened to the point where she not only allowed me to challenge her (frankly idiotic) preconceptions, but also, in a very roundabout way, approached me for help. I don't know if this is a new start for us, but I hope so. It's nice not having to deal with her constant disapproval.

'Can I help with anything?' Dad asks, as he wanders in and settles himself at the table. It's a rhetorical question; I can't remember the last time he did anything to help in the kitchen. It's always been my mother's domain, and she's guarded it fiercely.

'Have you loaded our cases into the car?' Mum asks him.

'All done. I've even left a space for leftovers.'

'I don't think there will be any of those. There's a little bit of food, but it won't keep, and your alcoholic children have made sure there's no wine left.'

It's a fair cop. After Mum and Dad went to bed last night, we all stayed up chatting and drinking for ages. Rose hasn't said anything to the others about Steve, but she seemed more at peace than she has for most of the week. Amy was typically irritating, but we largely managed to ignore her. Thankfully, her car was gone from the drive when I got up this morning, so she's obviously taken pity on poor Liam and gone to meet him for breakfast.

'Morning everyone,' Lily murmurs, as she joins us in the kitchen. 'Is there any coffee?'

For someone who's getting married in a few hours, she doesn't look particularly radiant. Her hair is messy and her face is completely bare of make-up. She's wearing a plain white T-shirt over black leggings, with trainers underneath. It would be hard to imagine anyone looking less bridal.

'Sit down at the table and I'll make you one. Are you excited about today?' Mum asks.

'I don't know about excited. Nervous and feeling slightly sick would cover it better.'

'Oh, Lily, you haven't got a hangover on your wedding day, have you?' Mum gives her the exact look she used to reserve for me, and I can't help smiling a little to see it used on someone else.

'No! It's just a really big deal. Weren't you nervous?'

'It's so long ago that I don't remember.'

'You don't have to go through with it if you're not sure, Lily,' Dad pipes up. 'I can call the vicar and cancel.'

'Don't be ridiculous, Bill!' Mum rounds on him. 'Of course she hasn't changed her mind, have you?' She addresses the last part of her remark to Lily and looks suddenly alarmed.

'No, I haven't changed my mind, don't worry. I'm just aware that this is a really big thing, promising to love someone for the rest of my life.'

'Tell me about it,' Rose remarks wearily as she comes in and slumps into a chair next to Lily. 'I'll have a coffee if there's one going, Mum.'

'You'll be fine,' Mum reassures her. 'Dan's a good man. He'll take care of you, I'm sure.'

'Why does she need a man to take care of her?' Rose has her 'spoiling for a fight' tone on. This kind of remark has always triggered her. 'I'm sure she's quite capable of looking after herself, as we all are.'

'Rose,' Mum says soothingly. 'It's Lily's wedding day, OK? I really don't want to argue with you today. I wasn't making any political statement. They will look after each other; is that better?'

'I suppose.'

'Right,' I announce. 'I'm all ready so, unless you need me for anything, I'm going to head off.'

'That's fine,' Mum tells me.

'Actually, can I hitch a ride with you?' Lily asks. 'I know Mum and Dad were down to take me, but I probably ought to get there as early as I can.'

'Of course you can,' I tell her. 'But I'm not taking any responsibility for your dress. I'm not even prepared to touch it. You load it into the car and you take it out, OK?'

'OK,' she grins. 'Have I got time to finish my coffee? I think I need all the caffeine I can get.'

* * *

Unusually for her, Lily is largely silent on the drive to the hotel, but that suits me just fine. I expect she's contemplating the huge step forward she's about to take in her relationship with Dan, and I'm reflecting on the premature end of my all-too-brief relationship with Sam. It's possible that he's on his way to join me as he said he would, but something tells me it's unlikely. I knew this would happen, and of course part of me regrets getting involved with him; it would have been a lot easier to keep my distance and protect myself. But there's just something about him and, although I'm incredibly sad, I'm also happy that I got to meet him and spend the short time we had together. Maybe I ought to look at starting to date again when I get home. Being with Sam reminded me how nice it was to have someone else in my life.

The hotel has been really accommodating and accepted our request for early check-in, so I help Lily cart her luggage to the bridal suite, which is predictably huge. As she hangs her wedding dress reverently in the wardrobe, I take the opportunity to explore. Besides the enormous bed, there's a sitting area, a minibar, a balcony with two chairs and a table, and a dressing table with an oval mirror.

'You might be safe tonight,' I remark jokingly to Lily as I indicate the bed. 'Dan will never be able to find you in there.'

'Don't,' she replies. 'I'm still anxious about it.'

'You'll be fine. Remember what I told you. A couple of glasses of wine to relax you, and you also have the lube if you need it.'

'Yeah, I know. It'll be better after the first time.'

'What are you doing for contraception?'

'I started taking the pill a month or so ago.'

'Great. Sometimes people have a mild allergic reaction to condoms. It's not common, but it's one less thing for you to worry about. Don't feel pressured to do it tonight, OK? You'd be surprised how many marriages aren't consummated on the wedding night. It's a big day and you might be exhausted. There's always the morning after and the honeymoon.'

'I know, and I'm not going to pressure him. I just think I'll sleep better knowing I've jumped that particular hurdle.'

'Well, see what happens. Play it by ear.'

'Maybe we'll have a bath together first, to get in the mood. I wonder if the bath is big enough,' she muses, as she pushes open the door to the bathroom. I follow her in and have to suppress a giggle. The bath is definitely big enough, but it's surrounded on two sides with mirrors.

'Dear God,' I remark. 'If anything's going to kill the mood, seeing yourself naked in all those mirrors is pretty much a slam dunk!'

'Mm,' she agrees. 'Plus, think how many people have probably had sex in that bath. I think I'll stick to the shower instead. It looks like it's also big enough for two.'

'Lily, I don't want to traumatise you, but people have probably had sex in the shower as well.'

'Ugh, you're right. Still, at least the shower washes all that stuff away. It seems more hygienic than the bath, somehow.'

'I'll leave you to figure it out. What time do you need me back?'

'The hair stylist and make-up artist are coming at ten thirty. They're going to do the bridesmaids first, so can you be here then?'

I promise her that I will be, and set off in search of my room. Mum and Dad booked and paid for all our rooms but, as soon as they confirmed the bookings, I rang the hotel and upgraded myself to a superior deluxe room. My reasoning at the time was that I would be exhausted after a week with my family, so this would be my little treat to myself for making it through. When I push open the door, I'm delighted with what I see. It's smaller than the bridal suite, obviously, but not by much. The bed feels super comfortable when I lie on it, and the duvet is thick and luxurious, as are the pillows. It's the sort of bed that Sam and I could have got up to a lot of very enjoyable mischief in. I'm relieved to see that the bath is surrounded by ordinary tiles, rather than the hideous mirrors in the bridal suite. Poor Lily, I wonder if she's even going to be able to face the shower after our conversation. The bath is obviously a no-no.

* * *

When I get back to her room at half past ten, Rose, Amy and Sarah are already there with the make-up artist and hairstylist. The photographer has also arrived, and is taking pictures of the dress, Lily's shoes and various other things. Olivia and Evie will be riding in the car with us to the church, but Zoe thought it was probably a good idea to keep them with her until the last moment. There is a bottle of champagne in an ice bucket, with glasses laid out alongside. I fully expect Amy to demand to go first as chief bridesmaid, but she surprises me by suggesting I go first. I'm just starting to question if she's having some kind of change of heart when she gives her reason.

'I want to be the last bridesmaid to be done. That way I can see what they do to you and pick the bits I like the best. Also, it means my make-up will be fresh for the ceremony.'

OK, she's still awful. Rose hands me a cold glass of champagne as the hair stylist gets to work, and I try to clear my head and think happy thoughts. It doesn't completely work, but I'm in as good a place as I can be, I reckon. The stylist takes her time, working patiently to make sure my hair stays away from my face but still falls over my shoulders in perfect soft waves before I change seats and the make-up artist sets about me, carefully applying eyeshadow, mascara and various blushers. When I'm finally released, I'm actually quite pleased with the result. I was worried that it would be over the top but, although a lot of make-up has gone on, the effect is surprisingly subtle. Sarah is next on the conveyor belt, with Rose behind her. Once we're all done, Lily shoos us out before they start on her.

'I want to do a big reveal,' she explains.

'But you need someone to help you on with your dress!' Amy whines.

'Mum is going to come and help me with that. I'll see you later,' Lily tells her firmly.

Amy's trying to conceal her annoyance, but not doing a very good job of it.

'Fine,' she says sulkily. 'Call me when you're ready.'

It's a little over an hour later when we get the call to assemble back in Lily's room. Mum and Dad are already there, and Zoe has arrived with Olivia and Evie, who look angelic in their mini-me dresses. Lily herself is totally transformed. The washed-out look of this morning is gone, and she looks every inch the stunning bride. If

Dan's eyes don't pop out of his head when he sees her, I'll be very surprised.

After the photographer has taken a barrage of pictures of us all, he leaves to go and set up at the church, and there's a slightly awkward silence while we wait to be told the cars have arrived. When the phone rings, we all jump slightly, but Dad gets there first.

'Right,' he announces once he's hung up. 'The cars are here. Let's go and get you married, Lily.'

30

The church looks stunning when we get there. When we came for the rehearsal yesterday evening, it looked exactly the same as it did last Sunday, but now there's an archway of flowers over the door, flowers at the end of every other pew, and two huge displays near the altar. The florists must have been working flat out all morning to achieve such an amazing transformation. The organist is thundering out 'The Arrival of the Queen of Sheba' as I follow Lily and my father down the aisle, and for a moment, I wonder if Amy thinks he's playing it for her. Where Lily has her eyes focused firmly ahead, Amy is smiling and waving to people as she goes. Dan doesn't let me down, shedding a couple of tears when he catches sight of his bride for the first time. Stuart, standing next to him, is looking his usual cocky self. I hope his best man's speech isn't going to be a car crash. He strikes me as the type who wouldn't be able to tell where funny ends and offensive begins.

Most of the service washes over me. Lily and Dan nervously mumble their vows, there's a brief moment of comedy when she struggles to push the wedding ring onto his finger, and then Dan's mum and Amy read a couple of Bible passages. The vicar's sermon is pretty standard God squad stuff and, before I know it, we're being hustled into a side room for the signing of the registers. I feel weirdly detached from it all, as if I'm a neutral observer. I like weddings, but I've never met anyone yet that made me think I'd take this leap of faith myself. I wonder whether I'd have felt that about Sam at any point, had we had more time.

'Smile, Poppy,' Mum hisses, as the photographer organises us for the shots he wants. 'It's a wedding, not a funeral.'

'Sorry. Miles away,' I whisper back as I plaster a smile on my face.

'At least Rose seems like she's pleased to be here. She's looking chirpier than I've seen her all week,' Mum continues under her breath, as the photographer fusses over the shot, nudging various people left and right. I glance across at Rose and discover that Mum is right. Her broad smile doesn't look as if she's had to force it at all.

After the signing of the registers, we all follow Lily and Dan out of the church. All the guests have their phones and cameras out, and the whole experience is probably as close to being on the red carpet as I'm ever going to get. The photographer pauses us at various points so he can take photos, as the organist fumbles his way through Widor's Toccata.

Once we're outside, there's a comical battle between Amy and Stuart as they try to corral the various family groups together for the photos. Technically, Stuart is in charge of the pictures, and he's grasping the list of shots that Amy and Dan have said they particularly want. Amy is determined not to be outdone, however, and is issuing contradictory instructions, slowing everything down and generally getting up Stuart's nose.

Now that the ceremony is over, Lily looks much more relaxed and happy, I'm glad to see. She's beaming at the photographer, at

Dan, and anyone else who catches her eye. Dan looks like he can't quite believe his luck, and keeps glancing across at Lily as if he's checking she's still there and not a figment of his imagination. After what feels like an age, all the photos are done and we pile back into the cars for the short journey back to the hotel, where there will be yet more photos before the reception. It's a beautiful summer's day, and I'm vaguely cursing Lily for insisting on dark tights, as I'm quietly boiling to death in them. I glance across to Rose.

'Are you as hot as I am in these bloody tights?' I ask her.

'Oh yes. As soon as the photos are done, they're coming off,' she replies.

'You can't do that!' Amy exclaims in horror. 'It will completely ruin the look that Lily wanted.'

'Listen, honey,' Rose snarls at her. 'You can do whatever you like, but as soon as nobody is pointing a camera in my face, these are coming off. If I don't get some ventilation down there soon, I'll be able to start my own bakery with the yeast from the infection I'm going to develop.'

Amy looks horrified and vaguely disgusted, but I have no sympathy for her. You'd have thought she would have learned not to provoke Rose by now, but it seems she's a glutton for punishment. Sarah is holding her nose, desperately trying to contain her fit of the giggles. Thankfully, Rose's remark seems to have gone right over the heads of Olivia and Evie, although I'd really enjoy listening to her explain yeast infections to them.

Somewhat disappointingly, we arrive at the hotel before the conversation can go any further. The photographer has obviously got all the shots he wants with us, as he disappears into the garden with Lily and Dan. With our bridesmaid duties seemingly done, in terms of photos anyway, Rose and I head to the ladies where we rip off the tights, sighing with relief as we do. Amy seems determined to keep hers on, despite the fact that she must be roasting and, in a moment of mischief, Rose and I make a small bet on how long she'll last.

'How are you faring?' I ask Rose, as we head outside in search of a glass of champagne.

'Good, I think. Now that the problem is out in the open, it's like we're tackling it as a team. We're no closer to working out what he's going to do, but I feel we're on the same side again, if that makes sense?'

'I'm really pleased for you.'

'I'm lucky. Steve and I have always been good at communicating, which is why the alarm bells started ringing as soon as I felt he was keeping something from me. I know some people think I'm overly confrontational, but...'

'Some people?' I laugh.

'Piss off, nobody asked you!' she retorts good-naturedly. 'The point is that, although he seems mild-mannered, Steve is actually very good at standing his ground. My natural inclination has always been to go in all guns blazing, but what he does is let me do that and then say, "I wonder if you've thought of this?" or, "I hear what you're saying, but..." Where I'm fiery, he's usually very calm and measured. He's a good foil for me. So, we'll continue talking and talking, and hopefully we'll find a way through this.'

'Do you know what? I think you will.'

'I think so too. There's a long way to go, and I know I've got to bite my lip and prevent myself from trying to rush him, which is going to be seriously difficult for me. It's funny, really; even though this is a massive deal for him and his relationship with his family is teetering on the brink, we're closer as a couple than ever in many ways. Anyway, enough about me. How are you?'

'I think I'll live. Although Sam could pull it out of the hat and appear this evening, I think it's unlikely.'

'Why?'

'The way I look at it is this: if Jessie's injuries had been minor, he'd have gone home, seen she was OK and come straight back. The fact that he hasn't done that indicates that she's seriously hurt. For all I know, she's in a coma or worse. God, I hope she's not in a coma.'

'I'm sure she isn't,' Rose tries to reassure me, although neither of us is convinced.

'The point is that he's obviously going to stay with her if she's seriously hurt, I completely get that. I'd be mad to try to compete with his daughter, particularly when we've only known each other for a few days. I'm just sad for me, because I was starting to think there could have been more with him. But I'm going to try to look on the bright side, for Lily's sake. Who knows, maybe Stuart is still keen.'

'You wouldn't!'

'Of course not. I was joking! Apart from the fact that he's basically a child and I'm totally not attracted to him, what do you take me for?'

'Just checking. No need to be touchy about it.'

'Says one of the touchiest people I know. Come on, I think I can see a waiter over there.'

By the time we file in for the wedding breakfast, another hour has passed and Rose and I have had a couple of glasses of champagne each. I don't know whether it's the bubbles, but I'm aware of feeling slightly tipsy as we make our way to our table, and I make a mental note to slow down. We're both highly amused when we spot that Amy, who was so forceful about it in the car, has lost her tights somewhere along the line. Given that she's sitting on the top table with Lily, it's a brave move, but I think Lily is too ecstatic right now to notice a dress code breach, so she'll probably get away with it. Our table mainly consists of those family members not important enough to make it onto the top table, with one exception. As I approach, I spot a young man already sitting down, staring somewhat vacantly into space.

'Hello,' I greet him as I sit down next to him and glance across at the place setting to try and work out who he is. 'I'm Poppy, one of the bride's sisters.'

'Liam,' he replies sullenly. 'Chief bridesmaid's boyfriend.'

'Nice to meet you, Liam,' I smile. I'm aware that he doesn't know anyone else on the table so, when we're all seated, I take care to introduce him to everyone and try to make him feel at home. It doesn't take long for me to work out that he'd pretty much rather be anywhere else but here. I ask him a few questions about himself but, after receiving monosyllabic answers to each one, I give up. He doesn't seem to mind; he appears intent on his wineglass. By the time the starters are being cleared away, he's already two glasses down.

The food is best described as unexceptional. Lily and Dan have opted for a roast, even though it's the middle of summer and something lighter might have been preferable. It's what I would call 'generic' with unidentifiable reformed meat slices that the menu advertises as turkey, overcooked vegetables, watery gravy and soggy roast potatoes. I can't help thinking that planning their wedding in the middle of winter might have led them astray, a thought confirmed when the apple crumble and custard comes out. By the time we get to the speeches, Liam is definitely the worse for wear, and I'm anxious for the formalities to end so I can get away from him and leave Amy to sort him out.

Dad's speech gets the balance just right. He tells a couple of stories from when Lily was young and welcomes Dan warmly to the family. Dan also does well, and the round of applause when he says the words 'my wife' is enthusiastically punctuated with a few high-pitched whistles. Even Stuart doesn't do too badly in the end, although I, and I suspect the majority of the other guests, sigh with relief when he sits down.

After the cutting of the cake, the hotel staff swoop in to clear away the tables and move the chairs to the side of the room in preparation for the evening disco. I'm amused to see Amy laying into an almost comatose Liam; he's way too far gone to take in anything she says.

'Dance with me?' I look up to see Stuart hovering.

'I don't think so. Thanks anyway.' The last thing I need is him coming on to me tonight.

'Come on. You know you want to.'

'I really don't, Stuart. In fact, I'm pretty exhausted. I'm going to head to bed shortly.' As I say it, I realise that I am actually pretty tired. It's been a full-on week and I haven't had that much time to myself to process it.

'Would you like me to see you up to your room? You could show me some more of your artwork.' He smiles suggestively, leaving me in no doubt what he thinks should happen when we get there.

'No, thank you. I'm a big girl and I reckon I can find my way on my own.'

I glance around the room to see if anyone will notice if I slip away. There's no sign of Sam, as I kind of knew there wouldn't be, and I've done my official duties here. Surely I've earned a bit of me time? Some of the guests have taken the hiatus as an opportunity to spill out into the garden, while others have congregated at the bar. I head for reception, where I ask them to send a bottle of cold Sauvignon Blanc up to my bedroom. As soon as I get inside and shut the door behind me, the most extraordinary thing happens. I burst into floods of tears.

I'm not a hundred per cent sure what has unleashed this torrent. Obviously, it's the missed opportunity with Sam, but it's also worry about Jessie (who I've decided is definitely in a coma if she's even still alive), outrage at having been so completely misunderstood by my mother for all these years, plus a host of other things that I can't quite put my finger on. The guy who delivers my bottle of wine takes one look at me and flees as soon as he's handed it over.

It's been a long time since I've been so desperately unhappy.

31

Thankfully, by the time I wake the next morning, I've recovered some of my equilibrium. I glance at the clock; we're going to have a big family breakfast at nine o'clock, and then we're waving Lily and Dan off on their honeymoon before heading our separate ways. I've got two hours before I need to be ready, so I stretch out and stare at the ceiling, processing my thoughts. The bed is every bit as comfortable as I'd hoped it would be and, in the end, I hardly touched the wine, so my head is clear and hangover free. I wonder how Liam is feeling this morning; it wouldn't surprise me if Amy had locked him out of their room last night, she was so furious with him. I feel quite sorry for him, but maybe he sees a different side of her. Who knows?

My attention moves on to Rose. Yes, she is incredibly prickly and hot-headed, but I feel we've grown a lot closer this week. I have no idea how Steve's relationship with his family is going to pan out, but at least they're talking to each other about it and there aren't any secrets between them any more. It's not long before my thoughts turn, inevitably, to Sam. Freud's granny in the attic is still berating me, but her tone is softer now. The reality is that, while it hurts just as much as I knew it would when we started, I don't regret any of it. I really hope Jessie will recover; she's incredibly confident and mature for her age, and she's one of those people you just know has a glittering future ahead of them. Sam and Louise obviously did a good job, despite being so young when she was born.

I've given a lot of thought to ways I could potentially find Sam, but knowing no more about him than him being Sam the data scientist from Swindon means I'd definitely be searching for a needle in a haystack. I also don't know if this particular needle wants to be found, or if he even lives in Swindon; he could live in a village close by, for all I know. Imagine how humiliating it would be to spend months stalking social media and actually being lucky enough to find him, only to discover he wants nothing more to do with me. I think I'm going to have to train myself to look back on him fondly as 'Sam the data scientist from Swindon who I had a fabulous fling with.'

By the time I make it downstairs, I'm feeling more peaceful. I still find myself scanning reception and the dining room of the hotel, just in case he's made it after all, and there is a fresh pang of sadness when I realise that no, of course he hasn't, but it's not over-whelming; I can cope with it. Despite being bang on time, I'm the last to arrive as the whole of the rest of my family are already seated. Actually, that's not quite true, I realise. There are two empty chairs at the table, presumably Amy and Liam's. This is confirmed when my mother turns to Lily.

'Are we going to wait for Amy and Liam, or shall we crack on now that Poppy has deigned to join us?'

'Excuse me, I was on time,' I protest. 'I can't help it if the rest of you were early.'

'Relax, Poppy. I was attempting to be humorous,' Mum chides me with a smile. We've made tremendous progress this week, I

realise, but we still have a long way to go before we'll be completely
at ease with each other.

'I think we can crack on,' Lily declares. 'I don't even know if
Amy and Liam are going to make it. He was pretty drunk last night,
so he might still be sleeping it off.'

'You disappeared very early,' Zoe remarks to me as we get up
and make our way to the buffet. 'Where did you go?'

'I was exhausted, so I went to bed. Sorry,' I reply.

'Don't be, but you missed all the fun. Liam seriously overdid it
and ended up throwing up in one of the plant pots. Amy looked like
she wanted the floor to swallow her up as she dragged him out of
the function room to put him to bed. When she came back down,
she spent an unhealthy amount of time dancing and flirting with
Stuart, which I'm sure you can imagine he was lapping up. I
wouldn't be a hundred per cent certain that they didn't hook up,
you know.'

'That boy is unbelievable,' I remark. 'Is there a woman he won't
come on to? Just as well Dad was around, otherwise he might have
tried it on with Mum!'

The buffet has a selection of cereals, fresh fruit and pastries, as
well as the traditional cooked breakfast bits and pieces. As I've got a
long journey ahead of me, I decide to go for the cooked breakfast
and end up standing next to Lily in the line.

'How are you?' I ask her quietly.

'Good. Really good,' she whispers back. 'I didn't even need the
lube. I stuck to a couple of glasses of wine like you suggested, and
when it came to it, I was like, "Yeah, I can do this".'

'I'm really pleased. Just remember, don't let him get lazy, OK? I
don't want to see you in my treatment room in a few years.'

'Oh, I won't,' she smiles. 'We've got our whole honeymoon to
work on our technique.'

I help myself to eggs, bacon, sausages and a couple of hash browns. At the last minute, I add a few mushrooms and a grilled tomato in a vain attempt to make it look slightly healthier. As I make my way back to the table, a waiter is circulating with jugs of tea and coffee. I order coffee and regret it pretty much as soon as I take my first sip. There's an underlying acrid flavour to it that only comes when it's been sitting on a hotplate for hours. I recognise it instantly. When Rachel and I first set up our practice, we had one of those coffee percolator machines and it was exactly the same. The first couple of mugs were lovely, but if you left the coffee to keep warm on the hotplate, it became undrinkable very quickly. We soon ditched it in favour of one of those machines that you put pods into. Thankfully, besides the congealed fried eggs that have also suffered from sitting for too long under the warming lights, the rest of the breakfast is delicious.

'I thought you might be interested to hear that I spoke to my friend, the one with the problem that I told you about,' Mum murmurs into my ear. She's got up from her place and is currently leaning over me from behind. 'I passed on your suggestions and she phoned this morning to say how grateful she is. Apparently, the lube has helped enormously, her husband is delighted, and she's going to make an appointment with her GP next week. I just thought you'd like to know.'

'I'm glad I was able to help,' I reply. I really didn't want to know, but this is obviously a big deal for Mum, and she's holding it out as a kind of weird olive branch.

'She was very appreciative and said I was lucky to have a daughter who knew about these things. I told her how proud I was of you.'

I'm trying very hard not to fall off my chair in amazement. Did my mother just say she was proud of me?

'That means a lot, thanks Mum,' I turn and say to her. She

draws closer and squeezes me tight for a moment before returning to her seat.

We're just finishing up when Amy appears with Stuart. They come over to the table and take their places in the two vacant seats. Everyone is trying not to stare at them, and you can tell the same question is in all our minds.

'How's Liam this morning?' Zoe asks, eventually.

'I wouldn't have the first idea,' Amy replies archly. 'We broke up last night.'

'I'm very sorry to hear that,' says Rose, not sounding sorry at all. 'It must have made the sleeping arrangements awkward.'

'It would have done, had Stuart not been a complete gentleman and come to my aid. He booked the one remaining room for me.'

'Gosh, what a generous gesture, Stuart. That must have put quite a hole in your student finances,' Rose continues. Poor Amy, you'd think she would know better by now, but it's clear she has no idea that Rose's carefully and gently phrased questions are just her laying the foundations of another trap.

'What can I say?' Stuart puts his arm proprietorially around Amy, who simpers back at him in return. 'Liam doesn't deserve such a priceless treasure.'

I'm starting to feel slightly nauseous, but Rose's eyes are bright and sparkling. She's absolutely in her element.

'There's just one thing I'm curious about,' she continues. 'If you blew your budget on the last available room, where did you sleep? I'm sure a gentleman such as yourself wouldn't take advantage of a lady in distress, would you?'

As the trap snaps shut, both Stuart and Amy look mildly uncomfortable. There's a certain amount of fidgeting before Amy decides to answer the question, and the rest of us are left in no doubt that they hooked up. Stuart must be pleased as punch that he managed to fulfil his wedding cliché of sleeping with a bridesmaid after all.

'Stuart offered to sleep in Liam's room, didn't you?'

Stuart nods enthusiastically.

'And did you?' Rose presses.

Amy has the decency to blush slightly. 'No. He spent the night with me. We've discovered that we have a lot in common, and we're going to see more of each other.'

I bet you do, I think to myself. You two fully deserve each other.

'Has anyone actually checked on Liam?' Zoe asks, a note of worry in her voice. 'When people are that drunk, there's a risk of them choking on their own vomit.'

'Relax, he's alive. I banged on his door this morning and the groans from the other side confirmed it. I don't think he'll be joining us for breakfast, though,' Stuart smiles.

* * *

After we've waved Lily and Dan off, we check out of our respective rooms and load our bags into the cars for the return journey. We seem to be stuck in the car park for ages, as everyone hugs everyone else. I get particularly fervent hugs from Sarah, Rose and my mum and nobody appears to want to be the first to leave. Eventually Dad decides he's had enough. 'Drive safely, all of you,' he says, 'Come on, Hazel, I don't want to get caught up in the Sunday afternoon traffic.'

In fact, the traffic is fairly light and I make good time on the journey home. My heart starts banging in my chest when I see the turnoff for Swindon, but I resist the temptation to divert. Apart from the fact that it would be fruitless, I need to get to the cattery before they shut for the night. 'Some things just aren't meant to be,' I mutter to my reflection in the rear-view mirror.

Amazingly, the cat makes the journey home without feeling the need to relieve herself in the boot, but I still moved my luggage onto the back seat just in case. After I've unloaded her from the cat box and fed her, she makes a point of ignoring me, even moving away when I start stroking her at one point. At times like this, I seriously wonder why I didn't get a dog, but I know she'll get over it soon enough. As I unpack and put a load of washing on, I start to feel surprisingly lonely. I've never felt lonely at home before, and it catches me off guard. I'm startled by the sound of the telephone ringing, and my heart quickens, hoping for a ridiculous moment that it might be Sam on the other end, even though I know it can't possibly be him.

'Hello?' I say tentatively into the mouthpiece.

'Poppy, it's your mother. I was just ringing to check you got home safely.'

'I did, thank you. How was your journey?'

'Fine. Listen, there's something I need to tell you.'

'What?'

'It's about my friend. I wasn't being entirely truthful; I was thinking about it on the way home, and I thought I should trust you and come clean.'

'It's OK, Mum. I worked it out. Let me know how you get on with the GP, OK?'

'I will. Poppy?'

'Yes?'

'Thank you, darling. For everything.'

'So, how have things been?' It's Friday, and my last appointment of the day is ChrisTina. I'm trying to remain professional and focused, but I can't wait to fill Rachel in on the holiday during our Friday pub debrief. I've given her the highlights, but we agreed to wait until after work today to dig into the detail, as some things are best done over a drink.

'Really, really good,' Tina beams.

I'm somewhat taken aback, but pleased. 'Go on,' I say to her.

'It was massively awkward to begin with,' she says, placing her hand gently on her husband's thigh. 'I've never been comfortable talking about sex, so I found the whole thing deeply embarrassing, especially when we were just sitting at the kitchen table, fully clothed. It felt out of place, incongruous. Does that make sense?'

'I think so,' I tell her. 'To you, sex is something that belongs in the bedroom when you're naked, not in the kitchen.'

'Exactly,' she replies. 'I knew you'd set us the exercises for a reason, so I gritted my teeth and tried to engage with it, but it just gave me the ick. Chris was much better at it than I was, weren't you, babe?'

'To begin with, but tell her what happened next,' Chris encourages her.

'Well, we did the second one naked. I hated that one as well to begin with, because I'm not used to being naked around Chris unless we're, you know...'

'Making love?' I prompt.

'Yes. And I normally insist on having the lights off, so I felt very vulnerable and exposed. But then, Chris started stroking me, just very lightly, on the stomach. He told me he loved my stomach, which came as a surprise to me. I've always tried to hide it.'

'Why?' She is a curvaceous woman, but in no way overweight.

'I've got a few stretch marks. They just look really ugly to me and I hate them.'

'I love them,' Chris interjects, 'because they're part of her.'

'Anyway, he was stroking my stomach and telling me how much he loved it, and I found myself feeling less self-conscious about it. I even let him kiss it, which I've never done before. And I realised something.'

'What did you realise?'

'I like being touched. He was being really gentle, but it just felt like there were little sparks wherever his hand was. So I told him I liked it.'

'Well done. That's quite a breakthrough.'

'It was the turning point for me. I realised that I'd never given poor Chris the first idea about how I like to be touched. How on earth was he supposed to know if I didn't tell him? The problem was that I didn't really know either. It was only when he started touching me and stroking my stomach that I discovered that I liked it. So we started to experiment. We'd take a part of my body and he would touch it or kiss it, and I'd try to guide him by telling him what felt good and what didn't.'

'And how did that make you feel, Chris?'

'I loved it. It was like Tina was opening up to me on a whole new level. I felt close to her, and intimate in a way that I've never felt before. I wanted to know everything about how to please her.'

'And did you reciprocate? Did you tell Tina what you like?'

'My needs are pretty simple,' he smiles, 'but yes, we did explore a few things. The biggest turn-on was pleasing her, though. We got quite adventurous, didn't we?'

'Don't laugh, but we bought another vibrator,' Tina tells me. 'It's only little, but Chris found this website where they have videos that explain the different types and how to use them. We looked at it together, and the way they talked about them was so matter-of-fact that they made them sound like a completely normal thing to have. I still wasn't completely sure about it, but we agreed that it wasn't a big expense and, if I didn't like it, we wouldn't use it.'

'This is a big concession from you, Tina. You were very against them in our last session.'

'That's because Chris was trying to force that hideous thing on me. This time, we chose together, and Chris wasn't pressuring me at all. I had the information from the videos, and we picked one that I thought I might enjoy.'

'And how are you getting on with it?'

'I had an orgasm the first time we used it,' she replies, blushing deeply. 'I don't think I've had an orgasm before. I thought I had, but it was nothing like that.'

'You sound like you've made amazing progress. I'm really pleased.'

'I'm certainly a lot better at communicating what I like now, and I think we've both learned a lot about each other, haven't we, babe? There's just one thing.'

'What?'

'Please can we have sex?'

'Of course you can!' I laugh. 'Are you telling me that you managed to hold off, even with all the stuff you've been doing?'

Tina blushes scarlet. 'Well, we have satisfied each other in different ways, but we took the sex ban seriously.'

'I wouldn't have minded if it had all got too much for you and you'd caved in. The purpose of the exercise was to get you communicating about sex and learning to be open. From what you've told me, you've accomplished that in spades. I couldn't be happier for you.'

'So how many more sessions do you think we need?' Chris asks.

'How many more sessions do you think you need?' I reply.

'I reckon we're pretty much there, don't you?' he asks Tina, who nods happily.

'Great. I'd like to see you once more, just to check that all is well after you've restarted full sexual intercourse but, assuming all is still going well, I think I'm happy to sign you off after that. Does that make sense?'

They both nod.

'Excellent. Let's make an appointment for one month's time, just as a check-in. If there are any problems and you need to see me sooner, let me know, but I'm reasonably confident you'll be OK.'

We fix a date in the diary and I see them out. I automatically glance in the direction of Rachel's room to check that she's also finished for the day, so I don't spot the man sitting in our waiting room straight away. When I do, I feel dizzy.

Sam is here. In my surgery.

It takes all my effort to keep a professional tone as ChrisTina leave, because my heart is pounding and the butterflies in my stomach are performing some kind of aerobatic display.

'Hello,' he says simply when ChrisTina have gone.

I seem to have temporarily lost the power of speech, and it's a few seconds before I manage to croak out a reply.

'How's Jessie?' I rasp, frantically searching his face for any clues.

'She's fine,' he replies, with a smile. 'She looks much worse than she is. She's got a couple of cracking black eyes, three fractured ribs and a nasty sprain in her ankle. She's also currently sporting a neck brace to help with the whiplash, and she's incredibly stiff everywhere. She was really lucky, actually.'

'What happened?'

'A young lad with a souped-up hatchback lost control while trying to impress his girlfriend. There was nothing that Jessie could have done; he ploughed straight into her.'

'Bloody hell.'

'Yes. Unfortunately, they didn't come out of it as well as Jessie. They had to be cut out of their car, and the girlfriend in particular was pretty bashed up. It sounds a terrible thing to say, but I'm so glad we spent the money on getting Jessie a decent car. It's a total write-off, of course, but it did its job in protecting her. We went to get her stuff out of it, and I thought I was going to be sick when I saw it. I'm sorry I didn't make the wedding. We were all pretty shaken up; we still are.'

'Don't worry about that. I'm just glad she's OK. I can't believe you're here! How did you find me?'

'It wasn't hard,' he says with a smile. God, I love his smile. 'Do you know how many sex therapists there are in Kent? Not very many, as it turns out. I put "sex therapist Kent" into my search engine, and your practice website was second on the list. It had your name and your photo, as well as the practice address. You'd already told me that you worked from nine until six, so I thought I'd turn up just before you closed in the hope of catching you.'

Rachel chooses this moment to come out of her office. 'Are we ready?' she says, before she notices Sam. When she does, her mouth forms a perfect O.

'Sam, this is Rachel, my friend and colleague. Rachel, this is Sam, the guy I met in Cornwall.'

'I see,' she grins. 'I'm guessing you might want to take a rain check on our Friday-night drinks at the pub?'

'Would you mind?'

'Of course not! You and Sam probably have a lot to talk about. I'll leave you to it. Don't forget to lock up.' With that, she pops her keys in her bag and strides out of the door. I know I'll get a grilling next week, but right now I'm extremely grateful to her.

'Do you want to come in?' I ask him, indicating my treatment room.

'You've probably had enough of that room for the week, haven't you? Why don't we go to the pub your friend mentioned?'

It takes me a bit longer than usual to lock up because my hands are shaking so much with nerves. Obviously I'm delighted that Sam is here, but he hasn't told me why he's come, and I'm trying desperately not to read the wrong intention into it.

I don't get any clues on our walk to the pub either. Sam gives me a few more details about Jessie's accident and projected recovery; it sounds like she'll be pretty much back to normal by the time she starts university, which they're all very relieved about, and they're going to see about getting her another car as soon as the insurance company has paid out. He goes to the bar to get drinks, and I watch him in semi-disbelief. It seems so strange, seeing him in the context of my normal life.

'So, what made you track me down?' I ask him, after I've taken a sip of wine.

'Two things,' he replies. 'The first one is that I wanted to see you. Although I've been fully occupied with Jessie, I still missed you like crazy. I know we never talked about anything long-term, but we never ruled it out either, did we? I think we have the potential for something really special, and I wanted to see if you felt the same.'

'And the second reason?' The first is frankly all I needed to hear and I'm beaming at him, but if there's more, I'll have that too.

'Jessie told me to.' He has the decency to look a little embarrassed.

'She's a menace, that girl!' I laugh. 'She totally fixed us up in Cornwall, and she's still matchmaking from her sick bed.'

'That's Jessie,' Sam smiles. 'So, what do you think? Have we got something?'

I want to throw myself into his arms and kiss him nonstop until my lips are bruised and swollen, but there's one thing holding me back.

'God, yes!' I tell him. 'I've missed you like crazy too, and I can't tell you how happy I am to see you. But, annoyingly, we have to be practical and grown-up as well. How would it work with me here and you in Swindon, or the West Country or wherever you decide to move to when Jessie flies the nest?'

'I've thought about that a lot,' he replies. 'I'm really lucky in lots of ways. As I told you before, I can live anywhere as long as there is decent broadband so I can work. I've always thought I would move to the West Country, because it's somewhere I know and I like it there. But I've never been to Kent. I've been through it a couple of times on my way to France, but I've never explored it. From the little I've seen of it, it looks nice. I reckon I could be happy here, if we got to that stage.'

'So you're saying you'd move here? For me? That seems a big commitment to someone you've only known for a few days!'

'Poppy,' he looks at me intently. 'I know we haven't known each other long, but I feel something with you that I don't think I've ever felt before. I'm not going to call it love yet, but I've fallen for you, that's for sure. I'd love to spend more time with you and see where this goes, if you'll have me?'

'Have you driven all the way from Swindon just to ask me out?'

I ask.

'Yes.'

'Are you going back there after this?'

'I rather hoped I could buy you dinner first, but yes, that's the plan. It's actually not as far as I thought it might be.'

I can't bear it any longer. The hope and uncertainty in his face, plus the fact that Freud's gorilla is going to completely smash the place up if I don't act soon, drives me to lean forward and place a long, lingering kiss on his lips.

'I feel just the same as you.' I tell him. 'I've fallen for you too. I can't tell you how much I missed you. I was checking your house several times a day after you left, in case you'd come back, that's how pathetic I've been. Tell me, is there something specific you need to get back to Swindon for tonight?'

'I don't think so. Jessie's at her mum's, why?'

'How are you with cats?'

'Fine, I think. I'm not allergic or anything. That's a pretty random question, Poppy. What brought that on?'

'I'm working on a plan.'

'Are you going to share it?'

'It's not very complicated. I think we should get the hell out of here and you should come and spend the weekend with me. What do you think?'

'I think that's a brilliant plan,' he says, as we leave our drinks unfinished and walk out into the warm evening air. 'I just have one question.'

'What is it?'

'You do have broadband in Kent, don't you?'

'We do,' I tell him as I take his hand in mine, 'but it's very unreliable, particularly at weekends.'

'You're making that up!' he laughs.

'I might be, but who's to know, eh?'

ACKNOWLEDGMENTS

Thank you so much for reading this book. A lot of the inspiration for the sex therapy elements of the story comes from years of avidly reading Suzi Godson's column in *The Times* each week, so a huge thank you to you, Suzi, and all the other sex therapists out there doing amazing work.

As always, I want to say a massive thank you to my editor, Tara, and all the Boldwood team. We have had some very interesting discussions during the editing of this story, most of them unprintable, but I really appreciate the unstinting support and wise advice through every stage of the editing process and beyond.

Mandy and Robyn, once again you have done great work as my alpha and beta readers, and I want to say a big thank you to both of you for that. To my family, who are so supportive and make space for me to write, thank you to you too. And, of course, to our dog Bertie, who forces me to make space in the day to walk and plot.

MORE FROM PHOEBE MACLEOD

We hope you enjoyed reading *An (Un) Romantic Comedy*. If you did, please leave a review.

If you'd like to gift a copy, this book is also available as an ebook, hardback, large print, digital audio download and audiobook CD.

Sign up to Phoebe MacLeod's mailing list for news, competitions and updates on future books.

https://bit.ly/PhoebeMacLeodNews

Explore more heartwarming romantic comedies from Phoebe MacLeod.

ABOUT THE AUTHOR

Phoebe MacLeod is the author of several popular romantic comedies. She lives in Kent with her partner, grown up children and disobedient dog. Her love for her home county is apparent in her books, which have either been set in Kent or have a Kentish connection. She currently works as an IT consultant and writes in her spare time. She has always had a passion for learning new skills, including cookery courses, learning to drive an HGV and, most recently, qualifying to instruct on a Boeing 737 flight simulator.

Follow Phoebe on social media:

 twitter.com/macleod_phoebe

 facebook.com/PhoebeMacleodAuthor

instagram.com/phoebemacleod21

Boldwood

Boldwood Books is an award-winning fiction publishing company seeking out the best stories from around the world.

Find out more at www.boldwoodbooks.com

Join our reader community for brilliant books, competitions and offers!

Follow us
@BoldwoodBooks
@BookandTonic

Sign up to our weekly deals newsletter

https://bit.ly/BoldwoodBNewsletter